SHATTERED FATE

T. L. ANDERSON

This is a work of fiction. Names, characters, places, and incidents either are the products of the author's imagination or are used fictitiously. Any resemblance to actual persons, living or dead, business, companies, events, or locales is entirely coincidental.

SHATTERED FATE
By T. L. Anderson
Copyright© 2018 by T. L. Anderson
All rights reserved.
Except as permitted under the U.S. Copyright Act of 1976, no part of this publication may be reproduced, distributed or transmitted in any form or by any means (electronic, mechanical, photocopying, recording or otherwise), or stored in a database or retrieval system, without the prior written permission of the author.

This eBook is licensed for your personal enjoyment only. This eBook may not be re-sold or given away to other people. If you would like to share this book with another person, please purchase an additional copy for each person. If you are reading this book and did not purchase it, or it was not purchased for your use only, then please return it and purchase your own copy. The scanning, uploading, and distribution of this book via the Internet or any other means without the written permission of the author is illegal and punishable by law.

Cover design by Cover by Combs
www.coversbycombs.com
Edited by: Katrina Crane
http://katrinacrane.wixsite.com/kcauthorandeditor
Formatted by: Keyminor Publishing Services
www.keyminorpublishing.com

*For all the souls who feel lost and defeated.
Remember you are strong and brave,
never let anyone make you feel like less.*

PROLOGUE

JUNE 2008

THE BELL RINGS LOUDLY THROUGHOUT THE SPEAKER system as the class rushes to pack up their books, everyone ready to be out of school for the summer. I grab my notebook and toss it into the trashcan by the door as I slide my backpack over my shoulder. The halls are packed and vibrating with laughter. Someone yells out from down the hall and a few catcalls are whistled as the senior girls sway their hips past the junior football team. I roll my eyes as I navigate through the hormone infested walkways. My body is brimming with excitement for the last day of high school. I can't believe I'm officially an adult. Ready to walk out into the world and make my mark.

I shove past a few freshman who are throwing a football around in the courtyard. The cool breeze whips my hair across my face as I inhale a deep breath and I almost choke on my own hair. With a gag, I wipe the strands out of my mouth.

"That's attractive," a cheerleader mutters as a group of them pass by me.

I shrug at the comment and continue walking toward the parking lot. Ignoring the sideways glances I'm receiving, I grab my curly, reddish-brown hair and tie it up into a cute ponytail to prevent anymore wind-blown mishaps.

A heavy arm lands on my shoulders and I take a deep breath, inhaling his cologne. "Why did you put your hair up? You look gorgeous either way, it just makes it more interesting when we make out and I can grab a handful." Colton's deep voice reverberates through my skin. I shiver.

I keep watching my feet as I try not to think about the insinuation of his words. "To prevent further episodes of asphyxiation," I state dryly.

His arm tightens as he pulls me into his chest and places a kiss on my forehead. "Asphyxiation, huh? Well, that would be a good reason to put it up then." He chuckles as we continue walking toward the cars.

Butterflies battle it out in my stomach as his thumb rubs against my arm, sending heat to my core. "Yeah, it would be good to stay alive and live another day. I wouldn't want my last words to be muffled by me gagging on my own hair." I wrap my fingers through Colton's as we start walking towards his car. This is something I'll miss this summer since I decided to take on two jobs. I mean I need to save money for my first college semester, but is it worth missing out on time with Colton?

"Don't worry, Ash, I'd save you. I wouldn't let anything happen to you." He stops as we reach his car. He slowly backs me against the door and settles me between his legs. His arms rest against the top of the car as he looks down at me with his blue eyes. "I'm helplessly in love with you."

My heart skips a beat and I rest my hands against his chest. I knew he loved me, he tells me daily, but this confession seems like so much more. "And I am with you," I whisper. His eyes heat as his gaze pulls toward my lips. I inhale sharply as I imagine his lips on mine.

"I got you something to remember your senior year with." He smirks.

As he slides a small box into my hands, my pulse races wildly out of my chest. I gently flip open the lid and peer at the silver charm bracelet resting against the white fabric. "It's gorgeous, Colton." Along the silver chain rests three charms, a graduation cap, a small fish, and a blueberry muffin. My fingers outline the small charms as tears well in my eyes. Three small charms that mean the world to me.

He lowers his mouth only millimeters from mine and with each word his breath caresses my skin. "Be mine, Ashley. Be mine forever." The world shifts from under my feet as I try to steady my weak knees. I nod as I grip his shirt in my fist. He closes the distance and his warm lips embrace mine, slowly and gently at first. Each soft stroke builds a fire under my skin. I pull him tightly against me as he picks up speed, both of us fighting for air with each drowning kiss.

We pull apart panting, but neither of us move more than an inch. Our hearts race in tune to each other. "Holy shit," I breathe out.

He smirks and rests his forehead against mine. "You can say that again."

I chuckle at the whole situation, "We should probably get going before someone kicks us off school property for PDA."

His finger tucks a loose strand behind my ear as he places a gentle kiss against my lips. "You're probably right." I see the struggle in his eyes as he pulls away from me finally. "I'll meet you later tonight after your shift. We can grab some dinner."

I nod my head as I hold my hands against my chest to try and steady my beating heart. "See you around nine."

I watch as he climbs in his car and sends one last glance over his shoulder toward me before he pulls out of the lot. *That boy has my heart in his hand*, I think as he drives out of sight. I glance at my watch and see I have ten minutes to get across town to work. Shit. I take off toward my car and hope to make it in time.

I PACE THE SIDEWALK OUTSIDE OF THE THEATER AND glance at my watch for the third time in two minutes. It's already quarter past ten and no Colton. A gust of wind blows and sends a chill down my bare arms. I wrap my arms around my waist and try to generate some body heat. Where the hell is he? I walk to the end of the building and peer down the road looking for his car. Nothing but the sound of the wind greets my ears. I hope he's okay, I hope he wasn't in an accident. I continue pacing, but as the clock ticks on I know I need to leave soon. Maybe if I head home there will be a voicemail from him. With one last glance, I pull my keys out of my purse and head toward my car. My shoes crunching against the gravel of the parking lot echoes off of the empty cars around me. What if someone's hiding behind one of the vehicles watching, waiting for me? I pick up my pace to a steady jog.

As the door clicks shut behind me and I slam my

finger onto the car lock, I let out the breath I've been holding. I need to stop letting my imagination get a hold of me every time I'm alone. I shove my key into the ignition, turning it over and bringing my car to life. *He better have a damn good excuse for ditching me*, I think as I head home.

Climbing out of my car, I head toward the front of my house as car lights cast a shadow over me. I stop and turn to see who is here this late at night. Colton's car sits at the end of my driveway, but he doesn't get out of the car. Thank God, he's alive. I release the tension I didn't know I was holding and head down the driveway toward him.

"Hey," I call out as I approach his driver's side door. He looks at me, but his eyes are blank. Emotionless. "Are you okay?"

He stares without blinking, then with a slight shake of his head he pulls his gaze from mine. His hands tighten on the wheel and his jaw clenches. I wait for him to break the silence but with each passing second my heart falls a little deeper into my stomach.

"What's wrong, Colton?" I shift closer to his window.

He closes his eyes and exhales. "I can't anymore."

My pulse races and I wipe my sweaty palms against my pants. "You can't what, Colton?" I swallow past the lump forming in my throat. "You're starting to scare me."

"It's over, Ashley. I can't do this anymore." He refuses to make eye contact with me as he sits there like a statue.

Vomit weighs in my throat with each syllable that passes his lips. "What?" My voice cracks, giving away my broken heart.

"We're done," he barks.

With those two words, my heart shatters in two. I back away from his car door, tears stinging my eyes. Screw him, screw him and his cruel words. I refuse to listen any longer. I take off up my driveway, putting as much distance between myself and him as I can. I barely hear his car door opening over my beating heart.

"Ash, wait." His voice breaks as he calls out to me. The pain reaches my ears and I slow in my tracks. I know I shouldn't turn around, but my traitorous heart has me hoping this is all a nightmare. "I…" he stops, his body right behind mine now.

"Why?" I sob, and the tears break free.

His silence feels like a knife in my chest, breaking apart another piece of my heart.

I start walking again, but his warm palm encircles my wrist, stopping me. "Ash…" He turns me toward him, his blue eyes rimmed with tears. I don't understand.

"Tell me it's a joke, Colton. Tell me you're just kidding," I plead. I wipe the snot and tears onto my arm.

He backs away and places his hands behind his head

as he silently watches the stars. Eternity seems to pass as I wait for him to say something. Anything.

"Whatever it is, we can fix it. Colton..." A sob wracks my body. "Don't give up on us. I love you."

His eyes close and a silent tear falls down his cheek. When he finally opens his eyes, there's a wall placed over his features. It's not my Colton looking back at me. "I'm sorry, Ash. You deserve better than me."

I shatter at his words, my legs giving out under me as I fall to the ground. He turns his back, leaving me in a crumpled mess on the floor as sobs tear through my chest. I try to beg and plead, but he keeps walking and never looks back.

CHAPTER 1

TEN YEARS LATER

A glass dinner plate sails through the air and shatters against the wall, almost drowning out the shouts directed my way. I silently watch as my once happy home crumbles around me again. "You bitch!" Greg circles the kitchen table, his eyes glazed. "Who the fuck do you think you are telling me what to do?"

He lunges toward me but cracks his knee off the edge of the coffee table. As I press my back harder into the wall, I can't help but wish that the wallpaper would swallow me whole, leaving this moment only as a distant memory. Greg's curses drown out my hopes of this ending anytime soon. "Son of a bitch! Why the hell did you move the coffee table, Ashley?" He wobbles on his feet as he glances around the room.

I snort quietly in disgust at him, but mostly at myself for allowing these nights to keep happening. The table has been in the same spot since we moved here years ago, but I don't dare correct him now considering the whiskey coursing through his veins. No, that would lead down a path I'm not sure I want to tread tonight.

Instead, I grab my prepaid cell phone that he's clueless about out of my pocket while he collapses onto the recliner, rubbing his knee. There is only one number programmed into it. Looking at the contact list, I pull up the number and wonder if it is even still the same. Has it changed all these years later? With a deep sigh, I snap the phone shut and hide it in my bra. Honestly, it doesn't matter if it is the same because I'll never call it. I don't deserve that privilege. With a quick glance at the clock on the stove I see it's ten minutes past midnight already. Hopefully he passes out, and soon.

I turn and place my hand on the counter to steady my shaky legs and a sharp burning sensation slices through the palm of my hand. I glance down at the blood-soaked shard of glass stuck in my palm. Shit, that hurts. Tears blur my vision as I feel around for a towel to stop the bleeding. This isn't how life is supposed to be; I'm not supposed to be pulling glass from my hand at midnight. Sucking in a deep breath, I hold still as the cool air pierces my skin. With clenched teeth I wrap the towel tightly against my palm.

"Who knew asking you why you're late from work would cause World War 3?" I whisper.

"Don't psychoanalyze me, bitch. You lost that job remember?" Greg taunts from the other room. "You should thank me...I gave you..." -hiccup- "...you a better life than your ex ever could." He rubs his head and I wait for him to start the fight again, but no more spiteful words spill from his lips.

I unwrap the kitchen towel from my throbbing hand and stare at the gash in my palm. The blood is slowly clotting in the wound, tender but no longer weeping. Just like my heart. I snort at the irony in that thought. Tossing the blood-soaked towel in the garbage, I turn off the lights in the kitchen. I sneak a glance into the living room and notice he's already passed out in the chair, his brown hair swept to the side. As I watch him sleep, the fact that he looks so peaceful and content isn't missed by me. Funny how one moment he can be the monster of my nightmares and the next he resembles the man I once married. The mask he used to wear is firmly back in place, hiding his true self from the world.

The day I met him seems so long ago. I was just starting out at college and was running late for the Psych class. I remember running into the room just moments before it was supposed to start. I decided I wasn't going to let anything get in the way of my dreams, not after Colton left me. It took me months to let the wounds heal and I still wasn't fully on my feet yet, but they say fake it until you make it. So that's what I did. I rushed down the stairs to the front of the hall so I could get a closer seat. Tripping over nothing, my feet slid out from under me as I watched the stairs came toward my face. I always was clumsy, so I immediately braced myself to try and prevent as much damage as possible. My books flew from my arms, but before the impending impact I stopped in midair. A strong arm wrapped around my waist and pulled me against a hard body. Both of us breathing heavily. I still remember his first words to me, "Are you okay? I tried to move my bag before you tripped, but I wasn't fast enough. I hope I didn't hurt you." When I was steady, he loosened his hold on me and I turned around to see those concerned brown eyes looking me over, trying to find anything out of place that he may have hurt. My heart stuttered at his kindness and that day I decided to sit next to him in class instead of up front.

Where did it all go wrong? I shake my head to disperse those treacherous thoughts and memories. I can't dwell on those tonight, I need my sanity. I try not to wake him as I slip down the hall toward our bedroom and close the door behind me. With a sigh of relief, I grab my pajamas and lock myself in the bathroom. My new nightly routine: clean up the mess he makes, wait until he passes out, and hide in the bathroom until I can no longer stay awake.

Most women have husbands that are their safe place, somewhere they can turn to when they are scared or hurt. Me, I have a locked bathroom and even that's not one-hundred percent safe. I shake my head at the self-pity path I'm traveling on once again. I've always told myself it's better not to dwell on the what if's; there are ugly things that lie beneath your subconscious. Once you open that Pandora's box, you can't easily close it without losing a piece of your sanity.

Shutting the medicine cabinet, my gaze catches a glimpse of my reflection. The woman looking back at me in the mirror is unrecognizable, a stranger even to me. I raise my hand to my cheek and watch as the person in the mirror imitates me. The dark circles under her eyes add ten years to her age and their once hazel color is now a dull, lifeless brown. Her red hair that at one time used to hang down her back now resides in a messy bun. My fingers run along her cheekbones that push tightly against her skin. Who is this staring back at me and when did I become so lost?

I cringe at the stranger in the mirror, and my heart aches. This is not who I want to be anymore. I open the medicine cabinet again and turn the mirror towards the wall, making the worn-out version of myself fade away.

My fingers tighten around the edge of the sink and the cool porcelain digs into my palms, keeping me grounded. "I can't do this anymore, God. I can't handle any more," I whisper as I stare at the ceiling, begging Him to strike me down right there in that spot. My chest constricts with each shallow breath and a sharp pain shoots through my heart. What is happening to me?

I suck in more air, but can't get enough oxygen into my lungs. With weak legs, I slide down to the floor while clenching my chest to try and ease the pain. The warm tears pour down my cheeks like a raging river. Gasping, I try so hard to pull oxygen into my lungs. This is it, God finally listened and he's taking away my pain. A sudden calm acceptance washes over me as I curl into a ball on the floor and squeeze my legs to my chest. The toilet in front of my eyes becomes blurry and with each breath my head starts to feel fuzzy.

With shaky hands, I find the cool metal bracelet around my wrist and absentmindedly twirl the charms through my fingers. With each inhale of breath, the dizziness dissipates and it becomes increasingly difficult to move. The weight presses down against my limbs as exhaustion washes over me. I continue to twirl the bracelet between my fingers. It's my only reminder of Colton, who gave it to me years ago on the night he left me behind.

After several minutes, my breathing returns to

normal and my vision is only blurred by the unshed tears. Moaning, I roll to my back and stare at the bathroom ceiling. A sheen of sweat coats my forehead. God didn't put me out of my misery; it was just another panic attack. That makes ten in the last two days. I wipe the tears from my eyes and sigh. Why couldn't my life have taken an easier road? I must have really fucked up in one of my past lives and this is karma seeking its revenge.

The room spins as I pull myself up on the counter. I take a steadying breath and wait for the room to right itself. Pulling my phone out of my bra, I glance at the time; it's after two in the morning already. I must have laid on the floor longer than I thought. The medicine cabinet is still open, saving me from having to glance at my true form again. It's so much easier to pretend, even if I know deep down I'm a wreck.

I open the bathroom door to peer out at the empty bed. With a deep sigh, I walk into the room. Hopefully Greg will stay in the living room all night; it will save me the stress from having to deal with his drunken ass. As I slide into my side of the bed, I pull my journal out of the nightstand where I have it hidden under some magazines. I guess it's my own form of coping with everything, a way for me to say my true feelings without others hearing the whispers of desperation cross my lips.

Tuesday October 15th

Another fight, another normal night in the

Hensley household. Nothing changes around here anymore, besides my desire to run and never look back. What started the fight tonight? Let's see I asked him why he was three hours late from work, apparently that's not a question a good wife should ask. His words, not mine.

I could smell her on him when he got close. The smell of her cheap, whorish perfume made me almost wretch on his shirt. Of course, he denies everything. But I've found the emails on his laptop before. Not only is he cheating and lying to my face about it, but he's leaving it out for me to see and still denying it. Narcissistic much? The emails were two days ago...I now have a heart made of stone. I'm planning on leaving him, but I'm biding my time until I can squander some more of the grocery money he gives me this Friday. God, the next three days can't come soon enough.

Earlier, he chucked a plate at the wall. Normally I'd jump in fear, but tonight I was mesmerized as I watched the glass pieces rain down around me. Each shard reminding me of a different memory from my life with Greg. It felt like I was that glass, finally freed from the pain and torment that molds us together.

I still had another panic attack, but the

reality that it's almost over made it a little more bearable. His words may hurt me, but I'm not letting him destroy my heart any longer. There are still pieces of me that he hasn't broken.

Tears stream down my cheeks and I can taste the salt at the creases of my lips. Who knew I had any tears left in me? I should have dried up long ago. The sound of the recliner being adjusted sends my pulse racing. Oh no. Normally, he's out all night. I shove the journal back into the drawer and flip off the light on my night stand, curling under the covers. I hold my breath to try and steady my beating heart. Maybe he'll just go to bed, forget about the fight from earlier. Heavy footsteps approach from down the hall. Pulling the covers over my head, I listen for any sign to indicate how the rest of my night is going to go. My breathing becomes irregular with each passing second. The door slams open with a crack. Shit...

"Where the fuck are youuuu?" Greg slurs as he wobbles in the doorway. He stumbles over his own feet and falls onto the edge of the bed. "I've been calling you for over thirty minutes! Wh.,.why don't you" –hiccup- "answer me when I call?" His weight shifts on the bed. The heat from his body radiates into the covers, spreading warmth up my body and vomit weighs heavily in the back of my throat. "Did you hear me?" His roaring voice shakes the bedframe and the covers pull off of my head with a flash. Greg's eyes are bloodshot and radiating hatred.

I push myself against the headboard to put as much space between us as possible. This can't be happening, he was sound asleep for hours. How is he still this angry and drunk? He leans over and places his face an inch from mine as his putrid breath fans over my skin. "I want something from you and you're going to give it to me without a complaint. You hear me? Now be a good wife and get undressed."

I shake my head no while I start to roll over off the edge of the bed. Unfortunately, his reflexes are faster than I thought in his drunken state. Ripping my arm behind me, he yanks me back onto the bed. Pain shoots through my shoulder and tears spring to my eyes as I struggle not to scream out. He likes to hear my pain and I refuse to give him that satisfaction. Shallow breaths ease the ache in my dislocated shoulder.

His grin widens into a sneer, his eyes alight with something darker than I've ever seen before. "It's okay, Ashley. I'm going to take good care of you. You know I'd do anything for you. I didn't mean to scare you. You know that right?"

Shaking my head no, I wince as he pulls my arm farther from my body. He places his left knee on my right arm and maneuvers on top of my chest. He whispers in my ear, "You think I don't know what you're up to? I know everything, Ashley. I know every thought you have and every emotion you're feeling. I can read you like an open book." Grinning, he yanks my arm sideways while trying to adjust himself and a loud pop causes a scream to reverberate out of my mouth. The sharp shooting sensation of my arm being thrust back into socket throws my dizziness into over drive. Dry heaving, I try to roll out from under Greg. But each time I squirm he presses down harder on my chest, impeding my airway. "Why are you trying to get away? I love you. Don't you love me too?" He brushes the sweat soaked hair behind my ear.

I stop struggling, fascinated by his quick change in demeanor. His eyes are softer as he wipes the tears from my cheeks. I don't know how to act right now. I've never seen this side of him before. My pulse races with each passing second. He slowly caresses my cheek and runs his hand over my collar bone. I hold my breath, waiting to see which Greg I'm going to see when he looks at me. His eyes turn up to meet my gaze, and I stiffen under him. With the slight movement calm Greg slips away. And without any warning his hand slaps across my face. A white light flashes behind my eyelids as the metallic taste of blood fills my mouth. What the hell is happening right now? My fight or flight instinct is battling its way to the surface.

"Please… Greg…" I whimper.

"Please… Greg…" he mocks. A silent tear rolls down my cheek. His eyes soften a fraction. "I only do this because you refuse to listen. If you would stop struggling none of this would have happened." He brushes another tear from below my eye and I have to hold back a cringe. "You're so beautiful."

I take a deep breath and watch as his eyes glisten with tears. He looks like the young man I fell in love with again. "Greg, please stop." My lip quivers with each word. I slowly wiggle my legs and arms, trying to find any way to escape.

A small tear trickles from his eye. "I'm so sorry, Ashley. Look what I did. I promise it won't happen again." He places gentle kisses along my cheek where it still burns from his hand. The scent of whiskey stings my nose with each inhale.

"I know, Greg. I just need some rest. Please, let's just get some sleep, baby." I choke back my nausea as I plead with the man staring down at me.

The kindness I saw in him only moments before disappears once again, this time I fear forever. "I told you to stop playing that psycho-babble bullshit with me, you stupid whore. I know you keep talking with that dumb fuck Colton. Are you still seeing him?" This time as his hand comes down I brace myself and turn my face into the pillow; the blow lands next to my ear instead. "You. Are. Mine," he seethes.

I try bucking him off of me, but his grip just tightens. Now I can't even feel my fingertips as his hands cut off circulation to my wrists. Hot tears run down my face and my body stills. I just can't anymore. Any energy I had leaves as I come to terms with my punishment. I hope he kills me and puts me out of my misery.

Feeling the tension and fight drain from me Greg coos, "Good girl, Ashley." His fingers brush my hair behind my ear as he cups my face with his palm. His eyes lose some of the malice as he rubs my busted lip with his thumb. Tears shine in his eyes. "I really don't like hurting you, Ashley. I love you. You're my wife. I don't understand why you make me do these things to you." Rubbing his forehead against mine, he breathes out a sigh. He places his lips gently on mine and kisses the edge of my lips while working his way up to my cheek.

Each kiss causes the revulsion I feel to intensify. I can tell he's on the edge of hitting me again. I can't believe he actually hit me this time. The tears rush down my face with each replay in my mind. I have to give him what he wants, then he will pass out and I can sneak out. I'm afraid if I fight and don't escape, he may actually go too far. After my breakdown earlier, I know now that I want to live.

Just hang on for another ten minutes or so, Ash. You can do this.

"Shh... sweetie. Stop crying. I'm going to make you feel better." Brushing the tears from my eyes, another glimpse of the young man I fell in love with years ago appears. "Are you going to be still for me, Ash?"

Nodding my head, I just hope this is over soon.

"Good girl." He slips his belt from his waist and grabs my wrists one at a time from my sides. He loops the belt around both wrists, binding them so tight that my skin feels like it's being cut into. With a forceful tug, he wraps the remaining length of the belt around the bedframe, completely immobilizing my arms above my head. "I'm going to move off of your chest. If you move, I'll tie your legs to the bed too. If you understand just nod. Don't speak. Do you understand?"

Nodding my head, I close my eyes and push more tears down my cheeks. I can feel him shift off of me and each breath returning to my lungs sends a burning sensation with each inhale. I try to give my hands a gentle tug, but from the weakness in my shoulder I can barely stand the pain from the odd angle of my arms. I hear him fumble with his zipper. Just a little longer then he will be done. A little longer I have to survive. The thud of his pants hitting the floor shoots fear straight to my heart. I hear the tear of the wrapper before he climbs back on the mattress. As the bed shifts, his long fingers glide over my hips. Slipping his hands in the waistband of my shorts, he slowly slides them down my thighs. I squeeze my eyes shut and I picture Colton.

The memories flood through my mind. Colton leans against my car, his shaggy brown hair rests in his eyes as he stares down at his shoes. I watch as he tucks his hands into his pants pockets and his black t-shirt pulls tighter across his chest muscles. My heart skips a beat at the thought of him. Colton waiting for me by my locker every day after lunch, his blue eyes sparkling and the same heart melting smile on his face as he carries my books to our next class. I see us at our prom; he's holding me during a slow dance and humming the words in my ear. His cologne filling my senses and calming me.

We're at the park having a picnic: the food I had prepared is left sitting untouched on the blanket all while we have a water fight in the river. I grab an empty cup from our lunch and fill it with water and while his back is turned I dump it on top of his head. Pretending to pout, Colton lifts me up and spins me in the air. Then he runs full speed into the river, soaking us both from head to toe. The giggles and happiness surround us in our own private world. His blue eyes sparkle with happiness as he brushes his brown hair back with his palm.

Sucking in a deep breath, I cringe with pain, and Greg moves into my thoughts. I push the present out of my mind as I speed up the memories of Colton and I throughout school. Holding hands in the halls, sneaking kisses under the stairs, flowers delivered on my birthday to the front office, skipping class to sneak up to his house during the day, homecoming, proms and date nights all flood my thoughts. Finally, the last words Colton spoke to me the day he left me play in my mind, *"I'm sorry, Ash. You deserve better than me."* He turns his back, leaving me in a crumpled mess on the floor as sobs tear through my chest. I try to beg and plead, but he keeps walking and never looks back.

The last of my tears dry up on my cheeks as Greg's weight shifts to his side of the bed. I feel him fumbling with the belt and after a few moments my arms fall to my sides, completely numb and lifeless. I lie still, scared to move as exhaustion overcomes me and I pass out with Colton's eyes pictured behind my eyelids.

CHAPTER 2

The sun blinds me from the window next to the bed. Groaning, I move and every freaking muscle in my body burns. My face feels like it was hit by a truck and my eyes feel puffy from the overuse of my tear ducts. Rolling to my side, I sit up and groan as a sharp pain shoots straight through my shoulder. All of this a sharp reminder of what happened the night before. I grab my journal to document everything that happened just in case I will ever need it in the future. My lengthy entry fills the final pages of my current journal. As I lay the book on my bed I notice the eerie silence of the house. Greg is at work for the day and probably won't be home until hours past his clock-out time.

Guilt weighs heavily in my stomach as I remember the fight from last night. Maybe if I had just left it alone, if I wouldn't have pressed him about why he was late, none of this would have happened. I shove a stray hair behind my ear as I squeeze my eyes shut, fighting the urge to call him at work and apologize. I know he loves me. Maybe it is me that's the problem. I shake my head to disperse the thoughts. Every time we fight, the next day my mind feels like a jumbled mess and I can never tell what is my fault and what isn't.

I slowly ease myself off the bed and head to the closet door, swallowing my guilt back down to a subconscious level. Behind boxes filled with mementos and pictures from earlier days, I shuffle through the totes of old clothes that don't fit anymore. At the bottom of one of the totes is a cardboard box. I pull it out and grunt with the heaviness in my arms. Sitting back on my heels I lay the box at my knees and pull the lid off, looking for a clean fresh journal I can use. I pull out scraps of paper from my high school newsletter and a picture of Colton falls to the floor. His lazy smile and crystal blue eyes look up at me, judging me. I slam my hand over the photo and shove it back into the box, tucking him away with the rest of my painful past.

As I sort through the items, I pull out each journal I can find, flipping through the ink-stained pages. Snippets pop out at me from the pages: concussion, broken arm, sprained ribs. I shudder as the pile at my feet stacks up higher, each book a reminder of the last seven years of marriage. My breathing becomes harder as I peer through the tears in my eyes. My hand runs along the first journal I ever started; it's dated two months after our wedding day. I open to the first page and read a few lines. *Today I noticed a change in Greg, he seems to anger more easily and becomes defensive if I ask questions. I had a picnic planned for us, it's really a beautiful day out, sunny and warm just like it should be in summer. I had everything packed and waiting for him when he came back from a jog. The second he saw the basket and the bottle of wine his eyes glazed over, then he grabbed the wine bottle and smashed it against the kitchen wall.*

With a cringe I slam the book shut, refusing to read anymore. I fall back onto my feet and look at the stacks of journals before me. I try to count them, but lose track after I hit ninety-five. Over one hundred journals lay before me and reality starts to sink in. Nothing is ever going to change, it's always going to be like this. With shaking hands, I reach into the box and pull out the picture I hid earlier. Colton's eyes stare back at me and guilt turns in my stomach. How could I have let it go this far? A silent tear streams down my cheek as I slip the photo into my pocket. I grab all the journals and shove them into the tote, afraid if I touch them too long the memories will imprint on my skin. Pushing the box to the back of the closet, I hide it underneath some old clothes again. I take a deep breath, but with the evidence once again hidden it doesn't seem to ease the pain in my chest.

I push my way out of the closet to try and find air, sucking in deep breaths between sobs. I grab the journal off my bed. The last entry has my pain scrawled across the pages and tears watermark their truth. This is it; If I want to survive, I have to leave today.

With a new resolve, I push myself up and head into the bathroom. The mirror is facing me and before I can avert my eyes, I catch my reflection staring back at me. My right eye is swollen halfway shut and a large deep purple bruise runs the length of my cheek. The corner of my lip is gashed with dried blood smeared across my chin along with a large welt adorning the left side of my face. The dullness in my eyes is the scariest; I don't see any resemblance to myself looking back at me. Slipping off my shirt, I glide the tip of my finger over the large bruises on my arms and on my chest from where Greg sat on me. Tiny bruises line my inner thighs and I don't even want to know where else.

"I can't let this happen again. I won't survive the next time." I pull my gaze from the bruises and climb in the shower. I can't help but wonder what life would have been like if Greg was a normal husband. Maybe we would have had kids and a dog. I'd probably wake up every day excited for the future instead of in fear. Pushing the thoughts aside, I fall back to reality. As the steam fills the small bathroom, the pain in my lungs eases with each inhale. The hot stream of water trickles down my sensitive skin. I try to erase his touch with each forceful swipe of the washcloth, causing my skin to turn blood red. If only it was as easy to clear the scars from inside my mind. The water swirls down the drain, disappearing from view and I wish I could send my memories with it.

Shutting off the water, I wrap myself in a warm towel and the softness comforts me. How could I not see the signs sooner, before it came to this? My body on autopilot, I scoop up my shampoo and body wash and shove it all into a small bag from under the sink. As I head back into the bedroom, I glance at the small life we built together. The few trinkets we bought in the beginning of our relationship line the top of the dresser, each one a painful reminder that my life will never be normal. I pull my gaze from the lies lined neatly on the dresser and grab a small backpack to toss some clothes in. My heart slams into my chest, and a buzzing sound becomes louder in my ears at the thought of him finding me. Doubt slips in and I stop packing. Am I doing the right thing? It could all change. Maybe it's not as bad as I think.

I slip my hands into my pockets and the corner of the picture rubs against my palm. A reminder of the hundred journals in the closet. It won't change.

Throwing on a loose pair of jeans and long-sleeved t-shirt, I sharply inhale at the pain shooting down my arm whenever I move. The tiny ache in my chest starts picking up in intensity with each breath I take.

No. Not now. I can't afford to have a panic attack now.

Squeezing my eyes shut, I twist my bracelet through my fingers and picture a safe place, anywhere that he can't reach me. I inhale a deep breath through my nose as I release all the tension. The beating of my heart slows with each inhale, leaving me more exhausted, but at least functioning. Stumbling over to the bed, I grab my journal and tuck it into my backpack amidst the clothes. With one last glance around the room, I try to steel my heart for the new journey I am about to embark on. I will never step foot into this house again; a sob tears from me as I look at the memories I could have had, should have had with Greg. I shake my head and walk out the door, leaving that world behind me. With my bag packed and memories held at bay, I pull my cell phone out of my pocket to dial a cab.

Ten minutes later the cab driver pulls up and I climb into the backseat. I lock my eyes forward, refusing to look back. With a gentle voice the driver asks, "Where to, ma'am?"

Shit. I didn't even think about where I should go. Back when I was still working, some of my patients went to a shelter. What was the name of it? I swipe my clammy palms against my jeans, stalling my jittery fingers. Deep in contemplation, I barely hear the driver gently talking to me. I just stare at him, lost in thought, fear clutching at my chest that I might not be able to make it on my own.

"Ma'am?" The driver eyes me through the mirror.

"Sacred Heart Shelter. Do you know the address?" I rasp out. Shit, my voice is so damn scratchy - probably from crying and screaming.

He nods and with a quick glimpse in the mirror he pulls his eyes away from my bruised face. "Yes, ma'am."

"Thank you." I lower my head, staring at the dirt stains on the floorboards beneath my running shoes. With a turn of the wheel, he pulls away from the curb of the house I know will haunt my dreams.

After a few twists and turns we end up in a part of town I've never been to. The outside of the brick building beside my door is nothing spectacular to look at. Honestly when the cab driver opens the car door for me pointing to the sign I think he is mistaken. I grab a few dollars out of my pocket and pay him for the ride over.

As he pulls away from the curb, I glance around at the surrounding area of the city. There are a few small bars lining the street, a Laundromat three buildings down, and some row homes lining the block. It doesn't look like the best neighborhood, which should scare the shit out of me, but honestly it comforts me knowing

Greg won't look for me here first. He would never think I would travel this far into the city. Glancing back at the building, the small faded sign on the wall just reads Sacred Heart. There is nothing to indicate that it is a women's shelter. Taking a deep breath, I close my eyes and count to ten, calming my shaking hands. I can do this. I will not allow my fear to rule my life anymore. This is the first step to a new beginning. I open my eyes and head to the locked door. As I ring the buzzer, the butterflies continue to flitter anxiously in my stomach.

"How can we help you?" The gravelly voice comes through the tired speaker, and I notice that a small camera faces the doorway on the side of the wall.

"Um, I need a place to stay," I whisper. What if they don't have room or turn me away? My pulse quickens in my ears, drowning out the traffic sounds around me.

"Are you alone? Is anyone threatening you or making you try to gain access?" The gravelly voice speaks again.

Frowning I reply, "Yes, I'm alone and no, no one is making me come here to gain access." Shaking my head, I wonder why they'd even ask that as I hear a little click on the door. I pull on the handle and the metal door swings open. With one last deep breath, I head towards my new future.

White walls surround a small reception desk and a few seats line the waiting area like a doctor's office would have. There is a young security guard sitting next to the desk. He eyes my small bag and my face. With a sad glance he turns back to reading his paper. The desk is empty and I look around to see where everyone is. Am I supposed to say something? Shuffling my feet, I contemplate what I am supposed to do.

A cheerful voice pulls me from my overthinking. "Hi there. My name is Chelsea. How can I help you?" A petite, blonde girl that looks no older than twenty comes out from a locked door behind the desk. She's wearing jeans and a black t-shirt, along with a radio on her right hip. She has keys dangling from her belt loop. Her cheery smile and young presence makes me feel even more exhausted. My body sags at the weight of everything closing in around me.

"I uh...I need a safe place to stay." I switch my bag to my other shoulder wincing with the movement.

Chelsea's eyes soften. "Alright, dear, let's get you registered and explain the rules. Then if we are a fit for what you need I'll give you a tour of the place. Does that sound alright with you?"

Nodding, I adjust my backpack on my shoulder.

"Great. Well our first rule is that we have to search any belongings before you can go behind the locked door. It's for your safety and the other's as well. Is it okay if Brad here searches your bag while we talk?" She nods her head at the young security guard. His brown eyes are watching my every movement.

"Sure...I just- do you mind if I keep my journal with me? I just...I don't want..." Stuttering to find the words, my pulse quickens again. *Seriously, Ash, get yourself together.*

Chelsea relaxes and calmly speaks, "Of course. He'll just flip the pages open upside down to make sure nothing is hidden in it then he'll hand it right back to you. You can take it with you while we fill out your paperwork."

I slide the backpack off of my shoulder and exhale with each movement. I swear this shoulder better heal and fast because the stabbing ache that shoots down my arm with any movement is almost unbearable. Brad gently takes the bag from my hands and unzips it, pulling out my journal he turns it over and shakes the pages upside down. Apparently satisfied nothing was concealed within its darkened pages, he hands it back to me. A small smile graces his face, but doesn't reach his eyes. I take my lifeline and hug it close to my chest as a reminder of why I'm here. Why I have fallen so far.

Chelsea moves from behind the desk and over to a locked door next to it. "If you would just walk through the metal detector you can follow me." As I head through the detector I glance up at it expecting it to go off screeching, *'She's a fraud, she doesn't belong here!'* but with its silence I head to the door where Chelsea stands. She pushes open the door leading to a room with a small table, a few chairs, and a filing cabinet in the corner. The white walls are depressing in such a small space. Pulling a chair out, she sits at the end of the table with a small packet of papers. I slide into a chair, resisting the urge to bolt. I can't believe I'm doing this.

"Let's start with simple things first, I see you have auburn hair and brown eyes…"

"Hazel," I whisper.

"I'm sorry, what did you say?" Chelsea asks.

"I said hazel. My eyes are hazel."

Smiling, she turns back to her paper and crosses out what she originally wrote. "Okay, hazel eyes and auburn hair." She glances up at me, looking for approval. I nod. "I need your name, sweetheart. You don't have to worry about someone tracking you down here. Everything is confidential."

"Ashley. Ashley Graves." Why I feel safe with a last name that's not even mine I don't know. But I know it feels right, it feels like hope. My eyes fill with tears.

"Okay, Ashley Graves. We will only ever call you by your first name here just to keep you safe. The next question is there someone we need to be on the lookout for?" she asks.

I know she's referring to the person who put me here. The person who did the damage to my face and my heart. I shudder at the thought of him. "Yes…his name is Greg Hensley."

"Can you give us a small description of him so we

know what he looks like?" She scribbles his name on her paperwork.

"Um...he's about six feet tall. He has brown eyes and brown hair. He tends to wear business suits and a pair of black rimmed glasses, but not always." Shrugging, I picture Greg in my head. To the outsider he looks just like a typical business man who has a family and a job he loves. He looks like anyone you would meet at a local bar and have a few rounds with. But I know the truth. I know the monster that lives inside of him.

"Alright, I'll give his description to all the security guards that work here. Does he know you left yet?" She slides the top page under another sheet. Shaking my head, I picture what he will do when he finds out tonight that I'm gone for good. I didn't leave a note, but he will know the second he walks in. I placed his computer in the kitchen sink soaking in water before I left; the anger was consuming me and I had to punish him somehow. That stupid laptop was his baby.

"We'll warn them to keep an eye out for him. The last thing we need to do is document the injuries you have. Now this is up to you, but we strongly recommend it. It will keep a record of what happened to you on file and we can do a police report too if you'd like. Is this okay with you?"

"I can't...I can't file a report." Panic floats to my chest as my eyes swim with tears. This was a bad idea.

How stupid could I be thinking this place or anyone could protect me from him? Shaking I start to stand, ready to bolt out the door.

Chelsea raises her hands and in a soothing voice pleads, "Please, Ashley. Think about this before you run. I know you're scared; the fear of him finding you probably has you gripped so tight you can barely breathe. You don't have to file a report, but you are much safer here than out there. We can protect you. These are just questions we have to ask everyone. Yes, they're scary, but what is worse, thinking about what could happen if you stay here or knowing what will happen if you go back to him?"

Somehow during her speech, she has moved to my side without me realizing it. She cautiously lays her hand on my arm, causing me to search her face for the truth. All I see is concern and determination in her eyes. "Please, will you give us a chance?"

The thought of knowing what will happen if I go back to him keeps me planted in the room with her. I can't take that chance again because I might not survive the next time. Falling back into the chair I sigh, "Okay, I'll stay, but no police report."

After we finish with the pictures of my face, ribs, and shoulder I write out my statement of the events from last night. With each word on paper it drills into my head why I left and that I made the right decision. Chelsea grabs my bag from Brad for me and I slip my journal back into it tightly along with the copy of the pictures she printed off. I can't look at them so I slide them upside down at the back of the journal.

She leads me back through the large, locked double doors. I notice a small camera pointing into the waiting area at the corner of the doorframe as we pass through. "This is our day area with a television, a small bookshelf, and some couches. During the daytime hours most shelters lock the women out, but we are more of an unconventional shelter. We allow the women to stay here all day for the first week they arrive. Then after that we encourage them to look for jobs to get back on their feet. Most of the women find part-time jobs around the area and are building a future for themselves."

"How long can we stay? I mean is there a cut off like three weeks before we get kicked out?" I glance around the small area filled with second-hand store furniture. It will do for now until I can find my own place. A few girls are sitting around the television watching the news while a couple of children play with toys in the corner. One girl looks over her shoulder and her bright green eyes catch mine. She doesn't smile or say anything. I admire her for not putting on a fake smile to welcome me. She knows none of us come here because we want to. Nodding, I show my acknowledgement. She nods back and turns back to the TV. As she turns I see she has blue highlights mingled in her blonde hair.

"Well, we encourage everyone to find a job and save money to move on. Of course, as long as you're showing effort and working on bettering yourself you can stay as long as you need." She lowers her voice, "A lot of them stay a month at the most before they run. Not because anyone found them, but out of fear. Fear of their future. So they run to the next shelter. It's really sad that they have to live their lives constantly running, but we always accept them back." Sadness creeps into Chelsea's features as she stares off into the distance.

Somehow Chelsea has been through this process personally. I can see it in her eyes. Turning, I glance around at the walls. "So um…where's the bathroom and area to sleep?"

Pulling herself together, she places the wall back over her features and points down the hall. "Right through there is the restroom and a shower area. There are a couple of showers and they all have curtains for privacy. I suggest waking early if you want to be sure to get one right away. They tend to get busy after eight a.m. Then over here through this door are the bed areas. Unfortunately, we have multiple beds but not enough rooms so our overflow area is open with cots. We will put you on the list for a bed. It won't take too long, normally less than a week. I hope that's okay with you."

"Sure." I shrug and look around the open area with about ten cots laid out. There are a few that are empty. Others have a shirt or towel lying on them to mark them as someone's personal area.

"Great. Well, this cot right here is open. Feel free to place your stuff on it, but I wouldn't leave any valuables in it. We can't guarantee it won't be taken. Most of the women here are respectful and understanding, and it is very rare we have a theft. Just to be safe though, I would keep all money on your person."

She points to the cot closest to the clouded window as she shuffles off to the side to give me room to place my backpack down. I pull out my cell phone and cash to tuck them into my bra. "Okay, well, Ashley that ends the tour. You are more than welcome to take a nap, or you can go in the day area with the other girls. You'll be assigned a social worker to help you develop a plan while you're here. One of them will be reaching out to you shortly. After you meet with them, feel free to leave and scope out the area, but be sure to be back by 11 p.m. That's the curfew time when we lock the doors. Once the doors are locked you can't get in until 7:00 a.m. the next day unfortunately."

"Thank you, Chelsea, for everything." Sitting on the cot, I pull my backpack next to me. Chelsea waves and heads out the doors we just came through. Sighing, I lay back and stare at the ceiling, counting the tiles to ease my racing mind. So, this is where I am in life: lying on a cot in a women's shelter, bruises fresh on my face, with a few hundred dollars to my name. The reality of my situation was daunting.

The shelter is quiet, but I know I can't stay here long. Quickly, I pull my money out from my bra. Shuffling through the bills, I glance around making sure no one else is watching.

Crap, I only have $200. I need to find a job and fast. Lying back, I close my eyes, fighting the storm inside of me as a silent tear escapes down my cheek. I run my hands over the cot and the scratchy material soothes my urge to run out the door. Pulling my cell out of my bra, I glance at the time and see it's already 2 p.m.

Longing for a connection to someone, I slowly dial in my mother's number and try to summon the courage to hit the call button. It's been so long; will she even want to talk to me? Before I lose my nerve, I hit the button. My pulse is racing and my palms are sweaty. By the third ring I start to give up hope of anyone answering.

"Hello?" My mother's voice floats through the phone.

I take a shaky breath and try to steady my voice. "Mom?"

Silence greets me and after a few seconds I expect to hear a dial tone. "Ashley?"

"Hey, mom. I'm sorry I haven't called in a while. I just wanted to see how things have been."

"You haven't called in years, Ashley. I would say that's a little longer than a while." She blows out a deep breath through the receiver. "If you are calling to ask for money, you can just forget it. I told you years ago that man was no good for you. Greg should be the one taking care of you, not your mother. So if that's all you wanted, you might as well hang up now."

My chest aches with her spiteful words. Tears well in my eyes and I fight the urge to lash out at her. *She's your mother*, I tell myself. *Just play nice.* "I'm not calling to ask for money, mother." She mumbles something into the phone that I can't quite make out, almost like she's covering the mouthpiece with her hands. "You could have called me, too," whispers from my lips.

She huffs into the mouth piece. "Why would I want to call you, Ashley? Every time I did you would tell me how horrible of a mother I am. I don't deserve that. It's not my fault you picked a narcissistic abuser for a husband."

Shame fills me at hearing the truth in her words. I did pick a real winner for a husband. "I'm not going back this time," I whisper more to myself than my mother.

"Hmph," she snorts. "I'll believe that when I see it. It's been seven years, Ashley. It doesn't even take an imbecile that long to learn when it's time to leave. You never were good with knowing what's best for you. You should have stayed with Colton, but you had to go and screw that up too." Her condemnation burns me to the core.

Tears well in my eyes and guilt weighs heavily on my shoulders. I know it's my fault for letting this happen again, but I don't need to hear every horrible thought my own mother has about me. "I won't bother you again, Mother. I'm sorry to be such a burden."

She sucks in a breath, probably to start another tirade. I shut the phone before I can hear any more words fly out of her mouth. Placing the phone back into my bra, I run my hands down my face. I'm starting fresh and I just have to let the painful words go. I can't force my mother to accept me for who I am, but I can't help but wonder, if she knew what I was going through would she still treat me this way? I blow out a sigh and push out all my frustrations. "Well I guess it's time to move on and start over. No more pity for the day, Ashley. You can do this." Pulling myself up, I grab my backpack and shove it under the cot against the wall out of view of the others. With a deep breath and a fake bravado, I head out into the day area.

CHAPTER 3

THE FEW GIRLS GATHERED AROUND THE TV ARE NOW watching some talk show about cheating boyfriends. Rolling my eyes, I head over to one of the chairs by the small bookshelf and tuck my legs under me. Perusing the books, I see a couple of old romance novels. Yeah, no thanks.

There are a few self-help books along with pamphlets on how to identify if you are in an abusive relationship. Well, I'm sure the bruises on my face are a pretty good indication that I am.

Leaning back in the chair, I close my eyes and try to relax. If this is going to be my option for some sort of entertainment for the next couple of weeks I'm going to go insane in here.

The clearing of a throat has my eyes popping open.

In front of me stands the girl who was watching television earlier. Her green eyes look me up and down, taking in my bruises. With her arms crossed over her skull t-shirt she looks badass, but I see the fragility she's trying to hide. I look her over too since she's assessing me. Her blonde and blue hair hangs over her shoulder. She has on dark eye shadow and eyeliner, making her eyes pop. She seems to be a little shorter than myself, but it's hard to tell from my sitting position. I must have passed her approval because she relaxes and sits in the chair across from me. "My name's Mia," she starts.

Relaxing, I reply, "Ashley."

She waits to see if I give her more. Once she realizes I'm not planning to she sits back and sighs. "I'm not going to say it's nice to meet you, Ashley, especially in these circumstances. But welcome to purgatory."

I admire her boldness. "Purgatory, huh? It doesn't seem that bad."

"It's not the place itself that's purgatory. It's the thoughts in your head that you have to deal with now." She runs her hand through her hair and twirls a piece between her fingers absentmindedly. "The memories and the terror that you have to fight. That's the purgatory. We each have our own demons to beat." She looks me dead in the eyes, a light flaming in their depths. "Not many can handle their purgatory, but the ones who do survive."

Crossing my arms under my chest, I hug myself as her words ring true. This is my purgatory and I need to claw my way out. "Well, Mia. I plan on surviving. Do you?"

She watches me intently for a second. "Yeah, I plan on surviving and I will." Shifting her feet under her, she gets comfortable. A sad smile graces her pink lips. "I like you, Ashley. I think we'll make great friends."

Nodding, I agree with her. We both sit there in comfortable silence for a while. Both of us lost in our thoughts. "So, what is there to do around here? Do you just stay in on most days?" I ask, breaking myself from my thoughts.

Mia turns toward me, shrugging. "Well, there's TV, but good luck getting the remote from those two. They love daytime drama shows. Otherwise there's a slim selection of books as you see there. Me, I usually go out and window shop. I like to pretend I'm a working-class lady who can afford the finest in life." She holds her pinky out and pretends to sip a glass of tea while rolling her eyes. "Seriously though, I work in the evenings at the bar down the street, but today's my night off. So I'm here bored out of my mind. I usually like to torment the double mint twins over there by interrupting their shows, but today it wasn't as much fun."

Glancing over at the two by the TV, I giggle at Mia's

reference to them. "I guess I better find a job fast so I'm not bored out of my mind every day."

A portly, older woman is walking toward us. Her brown hair is tied back in a bun and she's carrying a stack of papers. "Be prepared to be bored for the next few hours,"

Mia mumbles under her breath.

The woman stops beside Mia's chair and glances down at the paperwork in her hands, "Are you Ashley?" Her voice reminds me of the school teacher from Charlie Brown: gravelly and annoying.

I nod and get ready to stand. "Yes, that's me." I raise my hand out to shake hers.

"I'm your social worker, Prudence. I just have a few pamphlets to go over with you and then we can start figuring out a job that will be suitable and help you get on your feet." She let's go of my hand and shuffles the papers again. It almost seems like she's not sure where she wants to start the process. "If you want to follow me to my office, we can get started. It shouldn't take too long."

As she turns to walk away, I send Mia a grimace. I'm not in the mood to go over anything at the moment and just from the few sentences I've heard Prudence speak I'm afraid I'll fall asleep on her in our meeting. Mia was right, the woman's voice is enough to bore you to death.

"Hey Pru," Mia calls out. "I could probably get Matt

to let Ashley work at the bar with me. He's been looking for a new waitress on my shift."

Prudence, turns around with a look of annoyance. "That's nice and all Mia, but we have to find a good fit for Ashley," she tuts.

"I don't mind working at a bar, plus it will be nice to have someone from here working with me," I interject before Prudence completely shuts down the opportunity.

"Well, let's think on it during our meeting. Come on, Ashley." She heads across the room toward her office.

"Fingers crossed." Mia smirks.

I head off to my meeting with Prudence and hope it doesn't last too long.

AN HOUR LATER, I'M COMPLETELY BOGGED DOWN WITH information overload. I have a stack of pamphlets that range from job-coaching to signs of an abuser. Mia strolls over, pulling me from my thoughts and I'm extremely grateful for that.

"How did it go?" She looks at the stack of paper in my hands.

"It went okay…I think. It was a lot of information." I head towards the room with our cots and Mia follows.

"Yeah, they really try to help people get back on their feet as soon as they can, but they want everyone to have all the resources available." She shrugs, "It makes sense, no point in sending someone back out into the world without knowing how to find the help they need."

I pull my backpack out and place the pamphlets inside, promising myself I'll read them later. "True, you wouldn't want anyone to feel helpless and go back to the situation they're running from. It's just a lot to absorb currently."

She plops down on the cot across from me. "I understand that feeling…what did Prudence say about a job?"

"She caved and said I can look into a job at the bar with you. She didn't have time to call them yet to set up an interview though."

She glances at my bruises and busted lip. "We could head over there now. Matt's working today. I'm sure Pru wouldn't mind. It might take a little stress off her plate too."

My finger gently reaches up and feels the tenderness still present there. Sucking in a deep breath a fresh spurt of tears form in my eyes from the immediate pain. "Maybe when I look a little more presentable, and not like the walking dead, we can go over and I can apply?"

Mia watches me for a minute. "You know if you put a little concealer on, it won't be as noticeable. We could head over now before the dinner rush at the bar."

"I don't have any make-up. I wasn't allowed to wear

any for the longest time." Shit, did I say that out loud? I shudder at how pathetic I sound.

"No worries, I have some you can borrow. We look to be about the same skin tone. I'll help you cover up those bruises if you want." She stands up and stretches.

"Sure, I mean, if you don't mind." I stand too and bright spots burst in my eyes from the shooting pain in my ribs. Reminder to self: don't sit still for too long until I fully heal.

"I don't mind at all. I'm bored anyhow. It'll give us something to do." Mia heads to the other side of the room and grabs her pillow off of a cot along with a small bag she had hidden under it somewhere. She carries it over and places it on the cot across from mine. "There, now we can chat at night if we can't sleep." Rummaging through her bag, she pulls out the concealer and some mascara.

"How come you don't have a room yet? Is the wait list really that long?" I ask without thinking. She stops what she's doing and just stares off into space. My hands start shaking again with my obvious slip-up. "I'm sorry, it's none of my business. Just forget I said anything."

She shakes her head and finishes grabbing her makeup. "No, it's okay. I just choose to stay on a cot. It's easier for me to remember why I'm here instead of being comfortable in a room. Besides, I like that I can hear the front door from here. It gives me time to prepare if need be."

My heart aches for Mia. I can't imagine what she's been through, but I know she has some pretty deep scars she's carrying around. "That makes sense. I think I'll stick with a cot too. You can never be too safe."

Smiling for the first time since I met her, she sits down and pats the spot next to her. "Come on, I'll help you cover up those bruises. Then we can get out of here before Prudence tries to bore you to death some more."

We both laugh even though there's a shred of truth to that statement. It feels great bonding over something so trivial and ridiculous. I sit next to her and allow her to work magic on my marred face. As we chat about small stuff and crack jokes I feel safe for the first time in a long time. I know I made a friend for life with Mia and I have a feeling that's a hard feat to accomplish.

CHAPTER 4

As we head toward the bar down the street, I feel confident with Mia's makeup application skills. You can barely tell anything is wrong with my face unless you look closely. I glance around and notice the street is pretty dead for the afternoon. It must be the downtime between lunch and the end of the work day. A slight twinge of fear hits me as I think of Greg heading home. I push the thought out of my head as we walk into the bar where Mia works. A young guy, not much older than myself, stands behind the bar wiping down glasses. He has a few tattoos lining his forearms, a small piercing on his right eyebrow, and dark black hair that hangs loosely in his eyes.

"Hey, Trent." Mia walks over and hops on the bar stool, smiling while puffing out her chest. Shaking my head at her attempt to flirt, I walk over and sit next to her. Greg always hated when I went out without him. Even now, it's hard to swallow back the feeling of unease. My hands tremble and I have to clasp them on my lap to keep them from shaking.

Trent's smile lights his whole face when he sees Mia. "Hey, baby girl. What are you doing in here tonight? Aren't you off?"

Mia shifts slightly, leaning on the bar, and grabs two glasses from behind the counter. She grabs a bottle of Jack Daniels while she's at it, and fills up the two shot glasses. "Yea, I'm off. I came in to talk to Matt for a minute. Is he here?" She slides a shot glass over to me. Trent's smile falters and he pulls back a little, the hurt in his eyes evident. I'm not sure why he would care if we were here to see Matt. Shit, I hope we don't step on any toes.

"Mia, it's okay we can come back another day if he's busy," I whisper. Trent turns, noticing me for the first time since we entered the door. He seems to relax a little and his smile comes back.

"Mia, aren't you going to introduce me to your friend here?" He says as he slides the bottle of Jack Daniels back under the counter.

She shrugs and throws back the shot in one gulp. "Sorry, Trent. This is Ashley. She's looking for a job so I thought we'd come by and talk to Matt."

I can feel the heat rise in my cheeks at the mention of me needing a job. It's been so long since I've had to look for one. Trent eyes me up and down for a second. I don't usually drink, but the extra attention is too much for me right now. I put the shot glass to my mouth and say a prayer. *Please Lord, don't let me spit this out all over them and give me the strength to make it through today.* With the final mini prayer, I toss the contents back. The warm liquid slides down my tongue, warming the entire way to stomach.

Trent nods and pulls out the Jack Daniels bottle. He pours three more shots and places one in front of each of us. Lifting his glass, he declares, "To new beginnings." Clinking our glasses together we all throw them back. The warmth from the second shot eases my nerves and my hands are no longer shaking.

"So is Matt in his office?" Mia jumps up with an extra pep in her step. I giggle to myself as I picture Mia being peppy. From what I've seen of her, she's the complete opposite of peppy, with good reason I presume.

"Yeah, he's back there. Just knock before you go in. You know he hates it when you barge in, Mia." Trent clears the bar and starts wiping down the counter.

I follow her to the back of the long hallway near the bathrooms. There's another door tucked into the side with no markings on it. She grins at me as she pushes open the door without knocking. My heart speeds up; didn't Trent just tell us to knock first? What is she doing?

"What the hell!" A man behind a large desk stands abruptly causing his chair to fly back against the file cabinet.

The loud crash causes me to jump back to last night: the screaming and plate crashing against the wall. My breathing increases as the room spins. "Shit! Matt look what you did acting like a huge asshole." Mia gently lays her hand on my arm, tugging me over to a chair. "It's okay, Ash. Take a deep breath. You're safe here," she whispers in my ear. The spinning slows as I take deep breaths.

I'm okay. I'm safe. It's not Greg.

After a few minutes I get my breathing under control. "Sorry about that," I say. Now that the panic has subsided embarrassment seems to be on the menu. Well, aren't I a big ball of fun today.

"I'm sorry for scaring you. I wasn't expecting anyone to come in and it caught me off guard. Are you alright?" Matt's concerned voice floats to my ears.

Glancing up from under my lashes, I look at the man for the first time. He has sandy blonde hair that's receding a bit in the front with brown eyes that are looking at me with pity. Damn, again with the pity. He looks to be about mid-forties, but in pretty good shape for his age. He could definitely handle himself if someone really was breaking into his office. "It's not your fault. Don't mind me at all. I'm sorry we caused you trouble." Standing, I hold my hand out to him. "My name's Ashley."

He breathes out and his shoulders relax. "I'm Matthew Preston, but you can call me Matt." Shaking my hand, he sits back down at his desk and gestures for me and Mia to sit too. "So, what can I do for you both?"

Mia plops into the chair nearest his desk and props her feet up on the edge. I get the feeling she likes pushing boundaries with Matt. "Well, Matt. My friend here needs a job, off the books, like me." She nods my way and a moment of silent communication passes between the two.

Clearing my throat, I interrupt, "Um…It doesn't have to be off the books. I can work any hours you have available if you need me to. I just um…I just really need something and Mia talked highly about you all." I slide my hands under my thighs to steady them. Damn it, not again.

Rolling her eyes, Mia kicks her feet off the desk edge. "Come on, Matt. You know why she needs to be off the books for the time being. We don't need to get into it here, but she needs a place to lay low and make money fast. So, can you do us a favor and give her something? Besides, it's not like you're running a really legit business in the basement on Friday nights." She winks as Matt's eyes widen.

What non-legit business is she talking about? There is no way I'll be involved with drug dealers or anything like that. I need a fresh start, but not that bad. I tuck that bit of info away to ask Mia later when Matt's not around.

He steeples his fingers under his nose as he sits back, eyeing both of us up. His brown eyes scrutinize the situation. "Have you ever worked in a bar or restaurant before, Ashley? What kind of experience do you have?"

I clench my hands under my thighs and lean forward. "Well, I've never worked in a bar or restaurant before, but I'm a fast learner. I won't lie. I haven't worked in over six years almost. My last job I was working for a Mental Health facility as a psychologist. My license is expired though and I can't renew it currently, even if I wanted to. I promise I'll work hard and whenever you need me to without a complaint." Shit, I'm rambling again. Just shut up, Ashley.

Mia looks at me with wide eyes as she realizes my previous profession. She's probably wondering how I ended up where I am with that background. I guess abuse doesn't discriminate and anyone can be affected by it. "See, Matt, she's perfect. With her background she can deal with the drunks and you can tell she's willing to give it her all."

Matt runs his hand through his hair as he exhales. "Fine, I'll give you a chance to learn the ropes. Under the table pay only. I don't want to take any chances." His eyes flick to Mia and back to me. With a gentler tone he proceeds, "If you're in a situation that we need to be aware of or keep an eye out for anyone in particular, just give us a description. We'll be discreet, but I'll let all the bouncers know who to look out for and Trent too. This way we can protect you while you're here. Will that work for you?"

Why does everyone keep asking if it works for me? They're going out of their way to help me, but they want to make sure I'm okay first? "Yes, that will be fine. Thank you so much, Mr. Preston."

Smiling he grabs a paper out of his desk. "Just call me Matt. I have a feeling you'll become a friend soon enough. Especially if Mia trusts you. That's saying something." Mia scoffs at his remark and folds her arms over her chest. Chuckling, Matt slides the paper to me across the desk. "Fill that out with the name and description of the person you want us to keep an eye out for. You can even put what kind of car he drives on there too if you want. This will be confidential like I said, but I'm going to let the bouncers know."

Nodding my head, I scribble out my description of Greg. I shiver at the thought of him showing up here.

Handing the paper back to him, I stand and shake his hand. "Thank you for this. I truly appreciate it."

He takes the form and places it facedown on the desk. "You're welcome. I would suggest not letting anyone know your full name either. Just in case."

Mia hops up from her chair clapping her hands together with a smirk on her face. "So, can she start tomorrow night with me and I can show her the ropes?"

Shaking his head, he smiles. "Fine, but Mia you better work. No goofing off and being all girly and shit now that you have a friend. This is still a place of business, if you want a paycheck you work for it. Got it?" Out of the corner of his eye he winks at me with the smile still on his face. "Ashley, you can just work whenever Mia is scheduled for now until we get you fully trained in. Will that work for you?"

"Yes, sir, and I promise we won't goof off. I'll show you I can do this job well."

Chuckling, he sits back down busying himself with the stacks of invoices on the desk. "Good luck with that if you're working with Mia. Don't worry about it. You'll do great. I only pretend to be a hard ass."

"Come on, Ash, let's go get you a copy of my schedule," Mia says as she heads out to the bar. As we leave I hear Matt still laughing to himself in his office. A smile graces my lips, I finally feel confident I can make good things happen for me.

Mia grabs a copy of her schedule and gives me a quick tour of the bar. "This is the main bar area with a few dining tables. We get pretty busy during the dinner rush, but it'll die down most nights around nine." Pointing to a small window in the wall behind the counter, she pulls my attention away from the tables. "This is where the orders will come up when they're ready. And over here just to the left of the hallway are the restrooms. I would suggest not going in there unless it's an absolute emergency. The men tend to use the women's when theirs is overcrowded. It can get pretty hazardous in there."

Trent guffaws at Mia's accusations. "Are you saying men are dirtier than women?"

Narrowing her eyes, she crosses her arms and replies, "Well for some reason drunken idiots can't seem to hit the actual toilet bowl when they go. The piss ends up on the floors and walls more than in the actual toilet. So, yes, I say you all are a bunch of disgusting assholes when you're drunk."

A large smile breaks through Trent's hardened face as a deep, hearty laugh bursts from his lips. "Yeah, you're right. I won't even use the restrooms here either. They're hazardous. Unless you're wearing a hazmat suit, it's best to avoid them at all costs, Ashley." Winking, he heads over to the end of the bar where a few customers just walked in.

"Just ignore Trent. He likes to joke around and agitate me every chance he gets." Rolling her eyes, Mia slides a copy of the schedule into her pocket and hands me one. "Let's get out of here before the dinner rush. I don't really want to be suckered into working tonight." I shrug at the prospect. Anything would be better than lying awake, thinking, or Greg.

CHAPTER 5

As we head back to the shelter I tuck the schedule into my jean's pocket for safekeeping. It looks like we work the rest of this week from 2:00 p.m. until 10:45 p.m.

"Matt made special hours for me when I first started so I would have plenty of time to get back to the shelter before lockdown. You'll work the same shift as me for a while." Mia falters in her steps.

I stop myself before I run straight into her back and turn to see what has captured her attention. A man stands a few feet from the shelter's doors and his hands are wrapped around a woman's arms pinning her in place.

"I told you, you couldn't run from me. We're leaving

here now," he demands, attempting to pull the woman toward a waiting car.

Her eyes look up and reach mine, and they are wide from fear. My heart slams against my chest and I see spots dancing before my eyes from holding my breath too long. When I finally exhale, I barely recognize the sound of my voice. "We have to help her."

Mia snaps out of her shock and runs to the door, slamming her finger repeatedly on the buzzer.

Brad's gravelly voice floats through the speakers. "Are you alone? Is…"

"Brad get out here now!" Mia let's go of the buzzer and takes off after the couple still screaming at each other.

"Stay out of it. This doesn't concern you." The man shoves Mia out of the way as he pulls harder on the woman's arm.

Where's Brad? I can't seem to move. Vomit builds in my throat as a loud smack reverberates to my ears. The man lifts his arm again and the woman cowers in fear against the wall. With a loud crack his hand impacts her cheek. A low whimper slips past her lips.

The shelter door flies open and Brad comes running out, followed by another security guard. He glances at me and I point with a shaky finger to the scene unfolding a few feet away. They both turn and run, calling out to the frightened woman. Brad steps between her and the man as a barrier while Mia crouches beside her. Mia helps her stand and wraps an arm around her shoulders, walking her towards the shelter.

"Hey, Ash, can you ring the buzzer for us?" Mia watches me with her brows pulled in concern.

I nod and urge my feet towards the door. My entire body is shaking and as the seconds tick by they become more violent.

Chelsea's voice rings out over the speaker, but her words don't reach my ears.

"Can you let us in? Brad has everything under control," Mia speaks up for me.

With a click the door unlocks and I pull it open out of habit. My body is making the necessary motions, but my brain has shut down. As we all usher through the door I hear sirens in the distance getting closer. A chill runs down my arms as I cut off the sound with the locked door slamming shut.

"Bring her in here, Mia." Chelsea rushes behind the desk to the locked door where I met with her earlier. Mia follows, helping the sobbing woman to the room.

As Mia walks out of the room she disappeared into a few moments before, her eyes are distant and lost. "Well, that was interesting," she dryly states, trying to break the tension and fear we both feel.

"Does that happen frequently?" I move towards the day room doors, needing to put space between myself and the outside world. Mia walks with me and as the seconds pass I wonder if she even heard my question.

"Honestly, no. That was a rare occurrence." She opens the doors to the day room and silence greets our ears. It's empty except for one girl sprawled on the couch by the television.

"I can't stop shaking. How did he find her?" With thoughts of the fight, Greg's face replaces the man's in my mind. If it happened to her, it could happen to me.

Mia shrugs. "She might have contacted him hoping to work things out or she went somewhere familiar and he saw her." Her words are not convincing me.

I can tell she's trying to comfort me to keep me from running out of fear. "I don't know if I can stay here, Mia. It's only been a few hours and someone already had a fight. What if Greg finds me? What if he's out there when I leave to go to work tomorrow? Or any other day?" My words fly out in a rush. My chest rises and falls violently with each new fear scrambling through my brain.

"Hey, calm down. Take a deep breath." She lays her hand on my arm and guides me to a chair. "That out there wasn't Greg. He was some asshole, but he wasn't Greg. If you leave now he'll have a better chance of finding you." She flops down across from me.

My eyes won't meet hers. The need to run is overwhelming me. I kick my shoes together to try and calm the urge.

"You saw how fast Brad made it out there. She's safe and that jackwagon is most likely sitting in the back of a cop car right now. You're safer here than out there." She points to the doors behind me. "Give it a chance here, Ash."

I look up and the determination lining her face breaks my resolve. "Alright. I'll give it a chance, but if he does find me I'm running." A chill spreads down my spine. "I refuse to let him touch me ever again."

Her eyes harden. "If he ever touches you again I'll personally kill him for you."

"Thanks, Mia. It's nice to have someone in my corner for once." I let out a sigh as I sit back in the chair, pushing the horrid thoughts of what might happen out of my mind.

"That's what friends are for, Ash." We both sit there in silence, running from our demons.

A savory scent reaches my nose and my stomach grumbles. "What's that smell?"

"It's almost dinner time. Let's go check on our stuff then head to the dining hall," Mia says.

"I didn't realize this place had a dining hall. That's nice they supply food for us."

"Yeah, it's only dinner for now. We used to get breakfast too, but with the supply of donations dwindling the staff had to cut it out. They keep some snacks for us in case of emergencies. The staff provides it out of their own pockets." Mia moves to her cot and looks underneath at her bag.

"I can't imagine they make much money working here to be able to afford that." I check on my bag. Nothing has been touched that I can tell.

"They all work here voluntarily. They don't get paid anything. Most of them have been victims in the past or they know someone who was abused. I don't get it completely. I don't think if I ever get on my feet I'd be able to step foot in a shelter again. Don't get me wrong, I'd donate to them, but never work inside one." She tucks a strand of blonde hair behind her ear while zoning out into the distance.

"I think I can see why they do it. I hope one day we both have enough strength after we get out of here to volunteer. I think we'd both make great mentors." I turn towards the doors with a renewed meaning to my life and a strength I was missing a few minutes ago. Mia is still in her thoughts, haunted by something. Gently, I touch her shoulder. Her green eyes snap to mine and then focus on my hand. "Come on, Mia, let's go eat." Nodding, she glances away and swipes a small tear from her cheek.

Heading toward the door, the smell of food wafts to my nose and my stomach growls as I realize I haven't eaten all day. Most days I skip meals and it wouldn't even phase me. Greg always noticed if I gained a pound and would berate me for hours, so I learned to eat only if I was extremely hungry just to avoid his punishments. But today the stress must have been too much. I'm famished.

"It smells like taco night. They're delicious, you're in for a treat." Smiling, she pushes open the doors to the dining hall. A few small round tables are placed around the room with mismatched chairs. "They get most of the furniture from donations in the community. It's all a mix of different colors and shapes."

"Hey, I wouldn't complain if I had to eat on the floor. Anything is better than…" My thought trails off as I realize Greg would be home by now. He would have realized I was missing.

"Let's not think about that. Come on, let's grab some food and sit while there are still some seats left together." Nudging me with her shoulder, she winks before her tough girl exterior comes back.

The tacos are actually pretty damn delicious. We each get two, but with the amount of toppings available it feels more like three when I'm finished. The cook made the meat with his own homemade seasonings, not one of those little packets I used to buy.

After dinner most of the girls went back to the day area to watch television. Yawning, my eyes start to drift closed as the old movie plays in the background. My body jerks awake and I rub my eyes. "Mia, I'm heading to bed. I can't keep my eyes open."

Stretching, Mia gets up too. "No worries, I am too. I can't take another minute of this drivel. Come on."

Grabbing my bag from under the cot, I pull out a sweatshirt and put it on over my t-shirt. Mia crawls on top of her cot fully clothed also and spreads out on her stomach. Her eyes drift closed once she hits the pillow. "Just a heads up, most of us sleep in our clothes, it makes it easier if...well, you know."

"I had a feeling I would want to stay prepared. I'm just throwing on a sweatshirt to warm up. It's chilly in here." Pulling the small blanket over me, I lay on my side facing Mia. I run my bracelet through my fingers and try to find a little peace. "Mia...Thank you for today. It means a lot to me."

One of her eyes cracks open and she stares at me, "You're welcome. Thank you too."

With a smile I close my eyes, feeling safe for the first time. "Goodnight, Mia."

"Goodnight," she mumbles.

CHAPTER 6

COLTON STANDS AGAINST THE WALL IN THE GYMNASIUM, HIS tux pulling against his chest perfectly. I watch him from across the room as my heart flutters with each passing second. His carefree laugh rings out and sends butterflies straight to my stomach. Grabbing a sip of my punch, I wash away the dryness in my throat from singing at the top of my lungs for the last few hours. I wasn't even planning on showing up to prom, but Colton persuaded me when he met me at my front door holding a long-stemmed lily and a corsage in his other hand. The moment my eyes traced over his tux I would have said yes to anything.

The heat from everyone dancing has sweat falling down my back and I know my makeup is smeared. I wipe my fingers under my eyes and walk towards Colton. He turns, almost like he can feel my presence, and his ice-blue eyes capture mine. I have to remind my feet to keep moving even though they feel like jello under his gaze. He pushes off the wall and glides over towards me, meeting me halfway. "May I have this dance, Miss Andrews?" His husky voice sends a chill of excitement down my spine.

"Of course, Mr. Graves." I place my hand in his. He slowly sways with me and sings the lyrics to the song in my ear. With a sigh, I pull myself closer and rest my head on his chest. Being surrounded by his touch is the only place that feels like home to me anymore. Without warning he twirls me and pulls me in again, causing a string of laughter to burst from my lips. He places a gentle kiss to my forehead and warmth rushes through me along with a deep need.

"Miss Andrews, I must say you look quite stunning tonight." I can feel the smile forming on his face as he tries to act proper. His hand slips down slowly along my dress as he squeezes my ass cheek. Ah, there's the boy I know and love. Bad boy Colton could never keep his hands to himself for long when it came to me.

"Mr. Graves, you should really remove your hand from my behind before we're kicked out of the dance." I turn my face into his chest to hide the grin that is spreading across my lips. His hand squeezes once more then moves back to my hips.

"You're beautiful tonight, Ash. I just want you to know that." Smirking, he twirls me again as the last chords to the song play. As the music transitions into an upbeat pop song he wraps his fingers through mine and pulls me along behind him. "Come on. Let's get out of here while the night's still young." With the thrill from skipping the dance coursing through us, we both burst into laughter as we run out into the parking lot from the school gymnasium. The stars above us cast a soft glow on the football field and the parking lot. As we reach his car I wrap my arms around my sides and try to catch my breath. This is the most fun I've had in ages. Colton gently pushes my back against the car and places his arms on either side of my face. His eyes fall to stare at my lips, causing me to lick them out of need. With a groan he leans his forehead against mine. "Do you have any idea what you do to me, Ashley Andrews?"

I shake my head and bite my lip, trying to hold back my smile. "What do I do to you, Colton Graves?" Sucking in my breath, I can feel his heart beating rapidly through his chest as he moves his lips centimeters from mine.

His breath fans over my lips as he speaks, "You stole my heart the moment I laid eyes on you. I knew you were going to be mine." His hand caresses my cheek. "You have the power to destroy me. Please don't destroy me, Ash."

"Never," I breathe out as his lips capture mine. His tongue slides against my lip, probing for entrance. With a sharp inhale, my lips part, allowing him in. He tastes like mint with a hint of tobacco. The taste is comforting to me. It's home. His tongue wrestles mine gently as he slides his hand through my hair and tilts my head back. Pulling my hips towards his, my core rubs against him with the shift. I moan with the contact and arch my body closer.

A low growl rumbles from his throat as he breaks the connection. "Jesus, Ash, are you trying to kill me?" His chest rises and falls rapidly with each breath. His blue eyes shine from behind the hair that's hanging in his face. I brush my fingertips through it so I *can see him better and he shivers at my touch. "I love you," he whispers.*

"I love you too, Colton." And I knew at that moment I would never love anyone as much as I loved him.

As he pulls away an eerie chill runs down my spine. I look over my shoulder to see if someone is watching us. The darkness covers anything that could be hiding in the shadows. Turning, I reach out to Colton, but he's no longer there. Spinning in circles, I search frantically for him. My heart speeds up in my chest as I try to call out his name, but nothing comes out of my mouth. A low laugh resonates next to my ear and a cool sweat washes over me with his voice. "Are you looking for me, Ashley?" Greg appears and circles me like a predator would its prey. Sneering, he grabs my arm and twists it. "How dare you leave me, bitch. I'll always find you." My heart slams into my ribcage as a guttural scream rushes past my lips; I pray someone will hear me.

"Ashley, wake up." Someone whispers next to my ear while they shake me. Bolting upright, I almost fall off my cot. Mia crouches next to my side watching me, silent questions float across her face. I'm thankful she doesn't ask whatever is on her mind.

I wipe the cool sweat from my brow with shaking fingers. "Sorry, Mia. I didn't mean to wake you." Rubbing my arms, I try to fight the feeling of Greg's touch.

"It didn't bother me. Trust me, at least a few of us

have nightmares at night. We've all done it before." Her haunted eyes watch me.

"It was definitely a nightmare." I mutter. "I'll try not to wake you again. I really am sorry." Rolling over onto my side, I breathe out and try to ease the cold grip of fear and anger that are battling it out in my heart.

Mia stays next to me, hesitating to move. "Just know if you ever need to talk, I'm here." Her cool fingers rub my arm and she crawls back into her cot facing me. We both lay there staring at each other, wondering what demons the other is running from. I try to fight the pull of sleep, but my eyes drift closed with defeat.

CHAPTER 7

I JOLT OUT OF A DREAMLESS SLEEP FEELING LIKE I'VE been hit by a truck, and my legs and arms ache with each movement. Stretching, I pull my cell phone out of my bra and turn it on to check the time. It's a little after six a.m. I blow out a sigh and grab my bag from under the cot to head into the showers.

As I reenter the day area after my shower, I notice that others are starting to congregate around the television before they leave for work. Avoiding the crowded area, I curl up in the small chair and grab a book about starting over off the shelf. I'm halfway through chapter five when Mia shows up freshly showered and wearing another skull t-shirt, but this one is hot pink. "Morning, Mia. Did you sleep well the rest of the night?" I ask. She peers around the room and glares at the girls giggling across the hall to each other. A smile tugs at my lips as she scowls at me.

"Ugh...I swear those cots are the most uncomfortable object to sleep on." Moaning, she plops down into the chair across from me. Her green eyes are a little dull this morning and I notice she hasn't done her makeup yet. She looks young and innocent without all the eye makeup. "I was going to get ready for work shortly before all the others wake up. Did you want me to do your makeup for you again?"

"If you don't mind or if you want to teach me how I can try myself too." When I looked in the mirror this morning I nearly screamed. My face was a deep purple with a hint of green at the edges. I know that means it's healing, but I was afraid she wouldn't be able to cover it as easily.

"I don't mind. I'll teach you in a couple days when the colors on your cheek start to fade. It'll be easier for you to work with. Especially if you haven't put makeup on for a while." Standing, she heads towards the cots. I start to stand, but she shoos me back. "I'll grab it and we can do it out here. That way we won't wake anyone."

As I watch her disappear through the door, I wonder who could possibly want to hurt Mia. She seems so strong and confident. I don't understand how she ended up in a place like this. I snort to myself, I also once thought I was strong and confident too, but now I'm beginning to understand I was young and naïve.

Mia saunters back in with her bag under her arm. "Scoot over." She slides next to me on the large armchair. Turning slightly toward her, I watch as she picks out the different makeup she needs to make me look presentable again. "Is it okay if I put a little eye shadow on you today? It might make it easier to blend the bruise to look like it's makeup."

"Sure. I don't care what you put on me as long as it looks better than this." I wave my hand towards my face.

She stops sorting. "Ash, you're beautiful no matter what." She sighs. "I can't imagine the pain you felt when he did that to you. If I ever met him, I could kick his ass for you." She grumbles as she grabs a different shade out of her bag inspecting it closely. "Just remember he can never take away the beauty of your spirit. I'm not trying to be all sappy and shit. It's just when I saw you come in here yesterday with your head held high and that done to your face…I knew you were going to survive this shit. You have a beautiful spirit. Don't lose that. Okay?" Unshed tears fill her eyes when she glances up and are barely held at bay. She clears her throat and grabs the concealer sponge placing some under my eye.

I swallow over the lump that has lodged itself in my throat. "I promise I won't. You promise me you won't lose that fight you have in you."

Her hand stills for only a second then returns to blending the makeup. "I promise I won't either. Now let's fix us both up and have a kick-ass day." Grinning, she starts brushing eyeshadow on my eyelids.

We leave the shelter early to head to the bar. Mia informs me that Matt lets her eat lunch there when she's scheduled to work; he just deducts it from her pay. Although he charges her a total of two dollars a week for feeding her daily and she always has extra tip money left over. As we walk through the doors, a different guy is behind the bar playing on his phone. His light blonde hair is in a buzz cut revealing some wicked tattoos of tree branches intertwined running up his neck. He's a lot larger than Trent, his one arm is the size of my thigh. Mia waves at him as we sit down at the end of the bar.

"Who's that?" I whisper to Mia. She snickers at my not so subtle ogling. While he may be easy on the eyes, I wonder why Matt needs such large guys working for him at a small town bar named 'The Groggy Inn'. The name and the décor of the bar makes me think of an old 1800's saloon with its oak furniture and an old bar with rickety stools. Matt did upgrade to new sturdy looking stools though, so they don't wobble when you sit on them. You almost feel like you've entered a different time zone.

"That's Phil. He's the daytime bartender and works as the bouncer some evenings." Mia smiles as she pours us each a glass of soda. Winking, she heads back to the kitchen, leaving me alone with Phil.

I swear he can hear my heartbeat from across the bar it's so loud. Should I sit down? Am I supposed to help working? Shit, I don't know what I'm supposed to do. Standing there, I wring my hands together in my lap and look around the room, pretending to be interested in the decorations lining the walls.

"You can sit, ya know." Phil's deep voice reverberates from across the bar. He barely looks up from his phone before typing into it again.

"Um…thanks. I was just um…" I sit down gently on the bar stool trying to think of an excuse. What the hell am I doing?

"It's okay. I'm sure you're nervous on your first day, Ashley. We've all been there before. Just relax and take a deep breath." He smiles as he fiddles with his phone some more.

"How'd you know my name?" Startled, I bite my lip without thinking and suck in a breath at the sharp pain shooting through my swollen lip.

"You're Ashley, right? I figured since you were here with Mia that's who you were. She doesn't have any other friends she hangs with." His eyes lift and I can feel his heated gaze fall over me. "Matt said she took a liking to you quickly so it should be interesting to see what you're like. It could go either way." Grinning, he shoves his phone into his jeans pocket, causing them to pull down and expose a little skin.

I can feel the heat rising in my cheeks as I turn toward the kitchen door. *Mia please come back; don't leave me alone out here*, I plead silently. "What do you mean it could go either way?" I gulp a little soda and the bubbles tickle my throat.

Phil scoots down the edge of the bar and leans against it, bringing his bright green eyes into my line of focus. His gorgeous smile is contagious as I feel the corners of my lips turning up. "Well, you could either be exactly like Mia: stubborn, bossy, a little on the cranky side, and a real pain in the ass to work with. Or you could be the opposite: sweet, kind, a little shy, and entertaining to work with." Winking, he leans back and crosses his arms over his chest, amused with me squirming in my seat. "So which one are ya, Ashley? Or are you going to make me wait to find out?"

I bite my lip again and stare down at my hands. "Um…I'm not sure. But I don't think Mia would be a pain to work with and even if she's a little cranky she's extremely strong and caring. At least she has been to me." My frustration increases with his harsh words about Mia. "I think you'll have to form your own opinion about me eventually, that is if you ever pull your head out of your phone long enough to pay attention to anything else."

He stares at me for longer than I thought possible. I'm starting to worry I offended him and I'm going to get fired on my first day. His eyes crinkle at the sides and a huge smile spreads across his face. Snorting, he claps his hands together. "I like you already, Ashley. You, girl, are going to be a treat to work with." He walks away laughing as Mia comes out of the kitchen.

She places two hot plates of food down in front of us and slides onto the stool next to me. "What's he so happy about? Normally his nose is shoved so far into his phone he doesn't say two words." She grabs one of the burgers with fries and starts chowing down on them.

"Nothing. He was just introducing himself." Her eyebrow reaches her hairline as she waits for the punchline of a joke that's not coming. "These look delicious. Did you have to make them yourself?" Taking a bite, I savor the juices from the burger. I feel like I haven't eaten in ages.

"Nah. I was back there with Gordo, the cook. We were just chatting; he's excited to meet you later."

"Gordo? Is that his full name?" I ask around bites of my burger.

"His name is Gordon, but we just call him Gordo. He seems to like it." We continue eating in silence, both of us too busy enjoying the food to think of anything else to say. Finishing off her burger, she sits back a little and rubs her stomach. "I swear his cooking is delicious, but

I'm going to gain so much weight if I keep eating here daily."

Giggling, I shove another fry in my mouth. "I agree about it being delicious. We'll just have to be careful not to eat too many burgers in a day."

Mia starts giggling too. Phil's head whips to us, his eyes wide in surprise. Mia grabs our empty plates and heads back to the kitchen with them. "You're good for her, Ashley. Keep doing whatever it is you're doing," he states. I nod my head in acknowledgement, not entirely sure what he's getting at.

Handing me an apron, Mia turns and points to the small window to the kitchen area. "So this is where we place the orders for Gordo, and when the order is up he dings a little bell. It's hard to hear over the crowd on some nights so whoever is bartending keeps an eye out for us too." Mia grabs a small order pad and places it in her apron. She hands me one too. "You look freaking hot in that shirt, Ash. It hugs you in all the right places. The tips will be awesome tonight."

I glance down at the shirt that feels like it's suction-cupped to my breasts. If I wasn't so nervous about my first night waitressing I would be having a damn panic attack about this shirt. "It's a little tight, don't you think?" Pulling on it, I try to stretch the material out.

Mia chuckles. "Leave it for tonight. I'll have Matt order you a size bigger later. They don't keep many women's size uniforms around here, that small is all we had."

"How come?" I ask.

"Matt doesn't usually hire women. He thinks it's not a great place for women to work. I think he said something like 'a bunch of drunken bastards shouldn't be who women have to work around'. He hired me only because I threatened a discrimination lawsuit." Grinning, she grabs a pitcher of beer. "Little did he know at the time that I was completely bullshitting. He learned fast though that I could handle myself so he let me stay."

"If he doesn't hire women how come he gave me a job still? I mean I can see you can handle yourself. But I don't think I'm as brave as you are, Mia. What if I'm not cut out for this job?" Fiddling with my apron, I wipe my sweaty palms.

"Ash, you're stronger than you think. He hired you because he saw in you what I see: a fighter, and that's what he wants. He wants fighters and strong people in his business. Just stick close to me tonight until you get the hang of it. You've got this and I'll back you up too." Mia hugs me gently and then heads toward the first table that has a few college kids at it.

Phil walks by me and whispers, "I told you. She's changing because of you. Welcome to our family, Ash." Winking, he heads toward the door as Trent takes over the bar. I blow out a sigh as I head over to Mia and start shadowing her routine.

The first few tables were easy, a few beers and burgers for most of the patrons. Then, I had some college kids, who thankfully were too busy paying attention to the game on the television that they didn't notice I forgot half their order the first time around. Mia rushed over with the remainder of their food and saved me from embarrassment.

The draft that keeps blowing in from the front door sends chills down my arms, causing the tray to shake in my hands every few minutes. I glance over, watching Phil check IDs at the door. Most of the customers coming in are college students. A few business men walk through; Phil eyeballs them and nods without asking for ID. I guess if you look old enough to buy a couple hundred-dollar suit you must be old enough to drink.

Most of the tables are slowly filling up with a good mixture of men. I haven't seen any women walk in yet and we've already been here a few hours; I can see why Matt keeps mostly men working for him. I can't imagine if a brawl breaks out amongst anyone that Mia and I would be able to stop them. Walking behind the bar, I place the tray down on the counter and brush my dampened hair behind my ears. My legs are shaky from the constant moving, and all I can think about is sitting down and never getting back up.

"How're you hanging in there?" Trent hands a beer over the counter to someone while nudging my shoulder. He crosses his arms and smirks at me as he turns around.

Shrugging my shoulders, I sigh. "I feel like I'm barely making it through. I don't know how you all keep up with so many orders." I place my heel on the edge of the wall and stretch my hamstrings to try and get some circulation back into my legs. "Plus, I don't think I've walked this much in a year, let alone one day."

Trent shakes his head while chuckling. "You'll get the hang of it. It's your first day. I wouldn't sweat the small stuff. As for your feet aching, that never goes away." Winking, he heads back down the bar to help a few customers.

His words stick with me as I pull my shoulders back and mentally prepare myself for the remaining hours until I can go to bed. I glance around and see a few of my tables look ready for a refill already, I swear I just dropped off beers less than five minutes ago. With a sigh, I head over to check on the customers and silently pray for the strength to not cry and quit on my first day.

Around ten thirty the crowd dies down a bit and mostly the regulars are just left, according to Mia. "You did awesome tonight! I think we found your calling." She pats me on the shoulder.

"You must not have been paying close attention, honestly I'm surprised I made it through the night." I roll my eyes at her and look away. Catching Trent's gaze, I wink at him. After my mini freak out earlier things really did get better. I felt a little more comfortable after a few more hours of waiting tables.

Mia whips off her apron and pours two shots of Jack Daniels. Handing me one, she holds hers up toward me. "Cheers. To a great first night even if you think you sucked, which you didn't. You totally made bank on your tips so you must have done something right." Clinking our glasses, we both giggle and down the shot, the warmth settling in my stomach. "We should head out if we want to be back in time for curfew." She glances at the clock, grabs her small purse, and then waves to Trent and Phil as we head out the door.

"Be safe you two. See you tomorrow night and don't forget Wednesday night is free wings until six so it tends to get crowded," Trent calls as we leave.

Phil waves back with a smirk on his face. "You two definitely made the night go fast. It's amazing how many customers stayed later tonight because of your awesome personality, Ashley. I can't wait for tomorrow night; I bet the crowds will be huge, which means even better tips." He high-fives Trent as we head out the door. It's nice knowing I made a few more friends.

The cool night air chills me on contact. Reminder to self: buy a jacket sooner rather than later. Shivering, I wrap my arms around myself and prepare for the five-minute walk to the shelter. "Mia, can we go to a store tomorrow so I can buy a new jacket? It's getting a little chilly and I didn't bring mine to the shelter."

"Sure thing. We'll get up early and head out in time to still grab lunch at the bar before work." She slides her arm through my elbow and we lean into each other trying to warm up.

When we reach the door she rings the buzzer as I peer nervously around us. After the fight yesterday, I can't fight the feeling that someone's lurking just around the corner. The gravelly voice rings out and we answer the same routine questions as before and the buzzer sounds. I rush through the door behind Mia and pull it shut tight. When I hear the click I push out a deep breath.

There's a new guard on duty who doesn't even glance up from the book he's reading. He looks a little older then Brad and a little less friendly, if that's even possible. If that's who's protecting us from the outside world, I'm glad I made sure the door shut tight. The silence of the day area washes over us as we walk through, only the sounds of our shoes on the tile echoes around us. My heart drops and a sadness washes over me, I guess this is what loneliness feels like. As we get closer to the cots, my feet start to ache even more and I can't wait to fall into bed and just be done with tonight.

Mia and I head to our cots and crawl under the

covers facing each other. "Thanks, Mia, for everything." I yawn.

"You're welcome, Ash." She yawns too.

My body settles and the pain slowly subsides. "I'm glad to finally be able to lay down. I don't know how you do that every night without being exhausted. I feel like I've been running a marathon," I whisper.

I hear her push out a deep breath. "When life becomes all about surviving the moment or day you can do anything. It'll get easier, I promise."

The raw pain in her confession kicks me in the gut. Is this what we are doing with our lives now? Merely surviving?

"Goodnight, Ash and thanks for everything," Mia whispers.

"Night," I say as I roll over and a new dread settles in my mind. I silently pray, *please let the nightmares stay away just for one night.* I struggle to keep my eyes open, but finally they close and I succumb to the darkness.

CHAPTER 8

I HEAR THE FOOTSTEPS SHUFFLING DOWN THE HALLWAY; A loud crash is followed by a curse. My heart beats so hard in my chest I feel like it's going to pop through the skin. I pull the covers tighter around me trying to form a barrier between myself and him. The door swings open and he stands there leering at me. "You bitch! How dare you run from me!" Lunging at the bed, Greg tries grabbing for my leg. I scramble off the side and fall to the floor. The sharp pain in my wrist sends me reeling back in shock. Greg flies over the bed and grabs my hair, yanking me back onto the mattress. I struggle to fight him off, clawing at his eyes. "You will pay, bitch. Do you hear me? You will pay!" Screaming, I kick out.

My foot connects with the air as Greg disappears. I'm suddenly lying in the grass staring at the stars and a warm hand encircles mine. My stomach flutters with desire as Colton leans on his elbows over me. He lets go of my hand and traces my jaw with his finger.

Brushing my cheek, he wipes the tears that are flowing freely. His eyes crease in concern. "What's wrong, baby girl? Tell me what's wrong so I can fix it for you." They continue to fall and I'm unable to speak. The tears turn to rivers the color of Colton's eyes and as the darkness consumes me, dragging me under the river, I reach out to Colton, but he's gone as well.

Jerking awake, I sit up panting and try to push the last bits of the nightmare from my memory. I wipe the sweat from my forehead and stare out the clouded window. I lie back on the cot and stare at the ceiling. This is where my life has taken me and I'm starting to think I will never heal from the memories. Wiping the tears from my face, I run my fingers through my hair.

I wonder if Greg is still out there looking for me or if he decided to give up and move on with his side-fling. I hope he moved on. I hear silent sobs from across the room as someone else wakes from a restless night. Rolling over to give whoever it is some privacy, I glance at Mia. She's sound asleep on her stomach, her head facing the opposite way, her blonde and blue hair glowing in the moonlight from the window. I close my eyes and say a prayer, "Please God let me just sleep without any dreams. Let my mind stop thinking for just a couple of hours." I yawn and within a few minutes I feel the pull of sleep tugging at my eyelids.

I awake from a dreamless rest and see the sun slowly peering through the window. I wipe the sleep from my eyes, I won't let the dream haunt me at night and during the day. I need to get myself together, it's a new day. After the warm shower I head back to the day area with my journal and see a few girls sitting in front of the television watching the local news. Honestly, my life is depressing enough I don't need to watch the news right now too. I sit in my usual chair opening my journal to the next blank page.

Wednesday

This is my third day at the shelter since I've left Greg. At first, I felt like I was making the wrong decision when I came here. I felt like maybe if I tried harder Greg would go back to the way he used to be. But now after a few days without him I realize he's the one to blame. He's always been controlling in his own way, only getting worse with each year. I truly believe he would have killed me eventually if I stayed. I pray he never finds me that he forgets about me... I don't know if my prayers will come true or not. The fear of knowing I'll always have to run from him, looking over my shoulder is paralyzing me.

I made a friend here named Mia. She's been my rock since I walked into this place lost and confused. I see the pain she tries to hide, the scars she's running from. I hope someday I can help her beat her demons too. That's all I have left in this world. Hope and praying… and fear.

"What ya doing?" Mia plops in her usual chair across from me. I glance up at her while closing my notebook. Her eyes have dark circles underneath, her cheeks are a little more sunken in than just three days ago, and she looks paler.

"Nothing much, waiting for my daily meeting with Prudence." Shoving my journal to the side, I fiddle with the pen. "Are you ok? You look a little tired today."

Mia blows out a breath. "Yeah, I'm just not sleeping well at night. Those cots are extremely uncomfortable."

Biting my lip, I wonder how far to press her for answers. "Are you sure that's all that's bothering you? I just want you to know, I'll listen if you need to talk."

She leans back and closes her eyes for a few seconds. "I'm good, Ash. Thanks for looking out for me, but I'm good."

My fingers itch to fiddle with something; trying to release the nerves shooting through me, I jump up. "Hey, let's go get ready and we can head to the shops for a jacket after my meeting. The fresh air might cheer us up." Pulling on her hand gently, I help her stand.

"Okay, okay. I'll get a shower, but first I'm grabbing a cereal bar. You want one?"

Nodding, I call out, "Yeah, grab me one please. I'll eat it on our way out." I head towards Prudence's door for my meeting. I thought I would dread these visits, but they are pretty helpful. It's nice talking with someone about the thoughts and fears floating in my head. I knock on her door and as she calls out for me to enter I silently hope it goes by fast today, I'm feeling antsy and can't wait to get outside.

WALKING A FEW BLOCKS OVER, WE HEAD TO A SMALL strip of stores. Being out in the open for the first time since I ran from Greg, I can't help but feel paranoid. I glance nervously every few seconds behind me, searching for those honey colored eyes. "Ash, calm down. I don't think he's going to be out this way during the middle of the day." Mia rests her hand on my arm, pulling my focus to her. Her green gaze searches mine. "How far away did you come from?"

Rubbing my hands on my pants leg, I search the streets once more. "Um…I'm not completely sure. I was a little shocked on the drive here and I've never been down this way before. I just can't shake the feeling he's watching me." Someone bumps into me causing me to jump back and crash into the brick wall. A young man about eighteen glances up from his cell phone and then continues walking not paying attention to others.

"Whoa, buddy! Put the damn phone away and

watch out for others!" Mia screams at the oblivious kid. "Jackass," she mumbles under her breath.

My chest feels like it's ready to explode. Leaning over, I take deep breaths. "Is this what society has become? Everyone's nose stuck in their phones?"

Mia snorts. "Well, yeah. Where have you been? It's been like this for years now." At the realization of her comment her face falls and fear creeps in. "Oh, shit! I'm sorry, Ash. I didn't mean it like that. I forgot you haven't really been around this for very long. Please forgive me…Shit."

Glancing up, I smile in between my panting. "Mia, has anyone ever told you that you swear like a sailor?"

Her face relaxes a little. "Shit, I don't swear like a sailor. I enunciate my words, so it makes me a lady."

We both burst out in a fit of laughter. A few random people stare at us while passing., but the pressure in my chest is almost gone. "Thanks, Mia, for saving me from myself again."

"Eh, we all have our issues. As long as we don't stay stuck in them forever and fight our way out we'll be okay." Turning around, she glances down the street. "Right over there is a little second-hand shop. We can find you a nice jacket there for cheap. Come on before people try to have us committed." She winks and struts down the street.

That girl is a blessing in disguise. Heading after her, I

finally relax enough to only glance over my shoulder every few minutes, not continuously.

"Hey, this is a cute jacket." I pull the light pink tweed coat off the rack and hold it up to show her.

Mia's nose scrunches up as she looks in disgust at my choice. "Sure, if you're eighty and have twenty cats." She pulls another one off the rack. "This is the one. Try it on!" She squeals with excitement.

Grabbing the all black jacket, I take it off the hook and slip it over my work t-shirt. The black wool material curves in all the right places accentuating my figure. I tie the belt around my waist and glance at my reflection in the mirror. The jacket makes my breasts look bigger than normal and my hips are recognizable with the belt on my waist. I twirl and for the first time in years I feel like a woman. My face is still sickly skinny, but the cheeks are slowly filling out. The black circles under my eyes are still showing through even with the gallons of makeup we put on this morning. Pulling my eyes away from the mirror, I turn to Mia. Her eyes are alight and a huge Cheshire grin gives me her approval.

"Girl, you look hot! I mean you're beautiful without the jacket too, but that…that right there is freaking hot. You look a little badass in it too. You need to get it." She claps her hands like it's a done deal.

"I do feel amazing in it, but do you think it will keep me warm enough? I mean I want to be practical too. I feel silly wearing such a beautiful jacket just from the shelter to work and back." Doubt slowly creeps in. What am I doing here? What am I doing with my life?

"Ashley. You're buying that jacket and I'll tell you why. First, you look freaking gorgeous in it, but most importantly you lit up when you looked at yourself in the mirror. For the first time since I met you, you looked genuinely happy when you saw yourself in that jacket. If there was ever a good reason to buy that jacket it's that. Get your happiness back. Don't let him steal that from you forever. Don't second guess yourself either. If you're happy get it."

I swallow over the lump in my throat. "I'm getting it. You're completely right I look freaking hot and I feel good in it. It's time I make myself happy and I'm starting by buying this jacket." Sliding the jacket off my arms, I search the rack for the sweater I saw earlier. "Hey, is there anything you're getting or need?"

Glancing around the store, she runs her fingers over the different shirts feeling the materials. "Nah, I don't need anything right now. I'm going to head outside while you buy that then we can head in for lunch."

Watching her leave the shop, I slip the other sweater into my arms and head towards the counter. I drop my two items for the cashier to ring me up. The older woman eyes me wearily while she adds up the total. I roll my eyes at her condescending look and I view the small cases next to the register. My eyes fall on the perfect necklace I just have to buy. Gently pulling it off I hand it to her also. "This too please." Casting my eyes downward, I slip the money out of my front jean pocket. I pay her the total and smile politely as the lady watches me leave. She probably thinks I'm going to steal something. If only she knew the life we lived maybe she wouldn't be so quick to judge. Pushing the front door open, I head over to Mia. "Hey, I'm ready if you are. Do you think my bag will be ok if I leave it behind the bar tonight?"

"Huh?" She turns her focus to me.

"You alright?" She nods in response. "I was just wondering if my bag will be okay behind the bar tonight."

"Oh…yeah Trent's working again he'll keep an eye on it for ya." Wrapping her arms around herself, she glances back up the hill we need to walk to get to work. "You ready for this hike?"

My stomach growls at the thought of food. "Yeah, I don't mind the hill as long as we can eat something when we get there." Smiling, we both head up the sidewalk.

CHAPTER 9

THE BAR IS A LITTLE BUSIER THAN I EXPECTED FOR A Wednesday afternoon. There are a few tables filled with some local suits and college kids. Sitting at the end of the bar, I watch Mia head back to the kitchen. When I went back there last night to meet Gordo I saw how tiny the space is. There's definitely not enough room for me and Mia with Gordo working. Tapping my finger against the bar top, I rest my head in my left hand and stare off into space.

"Hey there, gorgeous. Can I buy you a drink?" A deep voice states.

Turning to see who he could possibly be talking to, I see a handsome man staring right at me with an amused expression on his face. I stare uncomfortably at him waiting for the joke. His black hair is trimmed neatly, he has a chiseled jaw that gives him that refined, manly look, and he's wearing a suit that costs more than any money I will ever make. He raises his eyebrow and his grin widens. "Um…are you talking to me?" I gasp.

His full-blown smile causes two dimples to appear. "Well, I was trying to see if I could buy you a drink. You looked quite lonely over here."

Clasping my hands in my lap, I squeeze them tightly. "Oh…well thank you for the offer, but I'm about to start work and I shouldn't drink on the job."

He looks down at my chest and sees The Groggy Inn logo on my shirt. "I respect that. Perhaps next time I'll get lucky and you won't be working." He winks at me and places his palms out while shrugging. "I'll just have to make sure I come in more often. You can't work every day." He smiles while backing away to his corner table.

My heart flutters in my chest while heat rises in my cheeks. "You alright?" Trent walks over and leans on the bar next to me.

Glancing up, I swallow trying to wet my dry mouth. "Yeah, I guess so."

Trent's eyes harden as he watches the man over my shoulder. "If anyone bothers you, you just let me or Phil know. We'll take care of it for you."

It's kind he already worries about me. "Trent, I'm fine. I just wasn't expecting to be hit on by a man of his caliber. It caught me off guard."

"What do you mean 'his caliber'?" He tilts his head and watches me. "Ash, you must not realize it, but every man in this room watches you the moment you walk through that door. You need to start paying attention to your surroundings more." He stands back crossing his arms over his chest causing his biceps to bulge.

Snorting, I chuckle at his attempt to show off his testosterone to the other men. "Jesus, Trent. Put the damn guns away and go find something to do." Mia snaps as she drops our plates onto the counter with a thud.

Trent's jaw twitches. "I wasn't showing off, Mia. I was just trying to comfort Ashley. What the hell is your problem?" He turns and walks away. "You know what? Forget it, Mia."

"Why would he be trying to comfort you? What happened?" Mia shoves a fry in her mouth while angrily glaring daggers at Trent's back.

Picking up a fry, I savor the salt and grease as it touches my tongue. "Some guy was hitting on me and I became a little flustered." I shrug and pop a fry into my mouth. "Trent was just making sure I was alright, Mia. That's all. Are you okay? You seem off today."

Breathing out, she pushes her hair back into a sloppy bun. "Sorry, I'm being such a bitch today. I'm just crankier than usual. I'll be fine after a good night's rest." She swirls another fry in a heap of ketchup. "Anyways, enough about me. Which one of these assholes hit on you?" She turns in her stool whipping her viper gaze over the customers.

"I think he left. It was just some guy in a fancy suit. He wasn't bad looking, but not my type." Taking a bite of my burger, I wonder if I will ever date again. I shudder at the thought of trusting another man again. The worst part is I saw a little bit of Greg in that cocky bastard who tried picking me up. "Honestly, I don't think any guy will be my type for a while. I'm just going to work on being by myself for a bit."

"I agree on that girl. Men suck." Mia shoves a huge bite of her burger in her mouth while silently watching Trent. We both finish our lunch in silence.

The rest of the night is so busy it flies by. I'm even able to work some of my own tables since it's so crowded. Early on, I messed up one order but thankfully the older gentlemen and his wife understood. Mia and I talked twice the whole night and it was during our two fifteen minute breaks. I didn't think a small bar would be that busy on a Wednesday night.

"Dang, I can't wait to get back and take these shoes off. My feet are killing me." Sitting on the bar stool, I twirl my ankles trying to loosen up the muscles.

"You'll get used to it eventually, but some nights are harder than others. Wednesday and Friday are our two busiest days a week. On those days I try to mentally prepare myself for the pain I'll have afterwards." Mia stretches her arms above her head, cracking her shoulders. "Man, that felt great."

"We should probably head back, it's already quarter to." I stand, pulling my bag out from under the counter.

"Yeah, I really don't want to be locked out for the night." Mia heads out the door without another word.

Trent watches her while shaking his head. When he turns our eyes meet. Shrugging my shoulders, I head towards the door. "Night, Trent. Try not to worry about her. It's just been a rough day," I say over my shoulder.

"Night, Ash. Be safe and watch out for her," he calls back.

Breathing the cool air into my lungs, I relish in the calmness of the night. "It wasn't too bad of a night for tips. A couple of days like that a week and I bet we can save up money pretty quick."

Mia's hair glows in the moonlight as she skips ahead of me. "Yeah, it's not too bad of a job. I like it and I think you're catching on pretty fast. It's nice working with you too. It gives me a break from all the testosterone in there."

"I see what you mean. I think I only saw a handful of females tonight."

Nodding her head, she turns and watches me while walking backwards, her hands in her pockets. "This is most definitely a guy's bar. Wait until Friday night you'll see what I'm talking about."

"What's on Friday? I know tonight was free wing night. Do they have a special promo on Friday's too?" I will my feet to keep walking even though they are throbbing out of my shoes. I can see the door to the shelter just ahead.

"Something like that." Mia avoids the question. Since she's been in an off mood most of the night, I'll just chalk it up to that.

"I heard you mention to Matt it was illegal." I slow my pace and hope we don't make it to the shelter before she can answer me. "It's not drugs or anything like that is it? I don't think I can work there if it is." I start rambling again and fear spikes in my chest. Not only will I be on the run from Greg, but also on the run from the cops because of drugs. What did I get myself into?

Mia chuckles. "Don't get yourself all worked up. It's not drugs or anything like that. You'll see on Friday, but it's definitely not something you need to stress over."

My shoulders relax a little with her reassurances, but my mind still spins with possibilities. What in the world could Matt be up to? "Will I go to jail for it? I don't want to be running from the cops. I'm already running from something."

Mia stops and looks me over with her bright eyes. She slides her arm through mine and smiles. "I promise,

Ash. I'll help keep you safe. I can't tell you more just yet. But please don't worry about it. It'll all make sense eventually." She turns and we walk back to the shelter arm in arm. Dread settles in my stomach like a boulder with her words.

After our little spiel with the night guard we're allowed entrance. We are also informed that five minutes later and we would have been locked out. This causes Mia to tell him to 'shut the fuck up'.

Heading over to our cots, I slip my shoes off and rub my feet to try and ease the cramping. Mia just throws herself face down on her cot and spreads out with her head turned toward me. "I'm so fucking beat. I better stay asleep all freaking night." She sighs.

"I know the feeling. It'd be nice to sleep through a full night." Lying back, I pull the covers over me. It all feels like a nightmare, lying on a cot in a shelter and hiding from my husband. A shiver runs down my spine as I remember Greg knows I'm gone.

"The nightmares will stop eventually," Mia mumbles into her pillow.

I push thoughts of Greg out of my head and close my eyes. "I hope so."

CHAPTER 10

"Ouch!" I hiss as I roll over and accidentally slam my arm onto the cool cement floor. I cradle it and glance around the room to make sure I didn't wake anyone. Mia's not in her cot. Crawling out of bed, I head into the day area looking for her. It's early in the morning and most of the other girls are still asleep. I fumble for the light switch only to lose my balance. Wham! I hit the floor hard, knocking the wind out of my chest.

"Hey, you okay?" Mia leans over me, holding my eyelid open, her eyes inches from mine.

"Yeah. I'll survive." I suck in another deep breath as I slowly sit up.

"What are you doing on the floor? Was the cot not hard enough for you?" Mia giggles, trying to lighten the mood.

"Ha. Ha. Ha." Grumbling, I stand, swaying on my feet. "I slipped on something and knocked the wind out of me." Rubbing my wrist, a sharp pain shoots up my arm. "Shit."

"Hey, you should get that looked at. It looks like it's swollen already." Mia pokes my wrist, causing light to flash across my vision.

Yanking my arm away, I swat at her hand. "Don't poke it! It hurts." Slowly circling my wrist, I try to work out the kinks. "It's not broken. I probably just sprained it." I watch wearily as she eyes my wrist like it's a fun new toy to poke at.

"The front desk has a few medical supplies. Maybe they have a splint or something to help ease the pain." She heads toward the front door out into the waiting area. "Come on. Let's see if Chelsea's working."

I limp after her, cradling my wrist. Of course only I would end up hurting myself by slipping on an invisible spill. I hope this doesn't screw up my chances at work. I practice carrying a tray and a burst of pain shoots through my arm. Nope, that's not going to work. Walking through the locked door behind Mia, I notice she already has a brace in hand with Chelsea following her.

"Here, try this." Reaching for my arm, Mia attempts to slip the brace on.

Taking the brace from her grasp, I move my arm out

of the way carefully. "Thanks. I'll try to get it on myself. No need to have you poking me again." Smiling, I wink at her.

"What happened?" Chelsea hovers next to me, inspecting the injury.

"I slipped on something in the day area. Then I tried catching my fall and obviously made it ten times worse." Gently, I pull the brace over my wrist and tighten it. The pain eases significantly with the extra support. "It fits. Is it okay if I wear this for a couple days?"

"Of course, you can use it as long as you need to. And if you decide you want to see a doctor we can take you down to the walk-in clinic. They have x-ray machines there." Chelsea smiles, but the concern is etched into her face.

"I'm fine. Honestly I'd rather avoid anywhere I have to give out my information."

"I figured, but I wanted you to know it's an option if you need it."

Mia chimes in, "I don't know if you should go into work tonight with that. It looks pretty rough."

"Nah, I'll be fine. Maybe I can help out with light items or stocking. Just for tonight, of course." I really don't want to miss work. It's my only access to making money and it's a nice reprieve from my thoughts.

Mia nods, knowing my thoughts. I think she likes going to work for the same exact reasons.

"Well, just be careful and take care of that arm. You want it to heal not get re-injured," Chelsea says as she heads behind the front desk.

"Thanks, Chelsea, for the help. Have a good day." We both head back into the day area.

Mia runs her hands through her tangled hair as she speaks. "I can't sleep anymore. I'm going to head into the shower then after do you want to head into work early? We can eat some food and make out our schedule for next week. What do ya think?"

I watch Mia carefully. She looks exhausted with the dark circles under her eyes and a distant look. "Sure, that sounds like a plan. I need a shower too. Meet back here in twenty and we can get our makeup done? My bruise is lightening up so it's looking even more disgusting on my face." Touching the corner of my eye, I test the skin for pain.

"Yeah, I'll help you out. See you in twenty." She heads off to the showers without another word.

After Mia puts on the last touch of concealer, I look in the mirror. You can't even tell anymore that I have a black eye. She should look into cosmetology with her skills. "You did an awesome job. Thank you so much!" I beam at her.

Her lips turn up at the corners. "Well, you don't need much help in the beauty department. You're gorgeous to begin with. That bruise is the only blemish on your entire skin. It was easy to fix." Grabbing her makeup, she slips it all back into her bag. "You ready to head down to work? Gordo should be there and if he isn't we can just hang out in Matt's office until he gets in. At least it will be better scenery than this hell hole."

"You think they'll be open this early?" Pulling my hair up into a loose bun, I chew on my lip to stop myself from pressing her further. I really want to know why she's so down, but I know she'll get defensive if I outright ask.

"Yeah, if we take a walk around the block and window shop for thirty minutes or so they'll be open. It's not that early anymore since you decided to fall on invisible objects." She points to my brace. I scowl at her comment. "I'm just teasing you. I hope it feels better soon though. It's a bummer that's going to be on there tomorrow night. Friday is the best tip night."

Looking down, I move my wrist back and forth like I'm holding a tray. Yeah even with the brace on there's no way I'll be able to carry a tray on this wrist, but if I can learn to carry with my left arm I should be fine. "Sure. I'm ready to get out of here today too."

Walking out into the chilly air, we pull our coats around us tighter. "I'm thinking we should just head to the bar. It's a little too cold to be walking around out here." Mia shivers with each word.

"I agree. Let's get out of this weather." Pulling my

hood up, I try to block out as much of the wind as possible.

Mia opens the door to the bar and the warmth envelopes us instantly. Sighing, I pull the hood off my head, my ears tingling from the heat. Gordo walks out from the kitchen, his stained apron hanging over his paunchy stomach. He's in his late fifties, but with his receding hairline and graying ends he looks at least ten years older. He carries a large bowl of soup over to a disheveled man sitting alone at a table. "It's on the house. Try to stay warm out there and come in anytime you need a warm meal." He pats the man on the back before turning around.

"What are you two doing here so early? You scared the heck out of me sneaking in here." He shakes his head while pointing his finger at us.

"Sorry, Gordo, we couldn't stand staring at the shelter walls anymore so we came in early to work on our schedule." Mia pulls her coat off and drapes it over the barstool.

"Sorry, Gordo…we didn't mean to frighten you." I shuffle my feet, wiping my sweaty palms on my jeans.

"Ah…it's fine. I'm just giving you two a hard time." Beaming, he claps his hands together. "So what do you want for lunch? I felt like cooking up something special for this weather so I made a big pot of chili. Would you two like some?"

Mia flops down at the bar. "Yes, please! That sounds fantastic. Maybe it'll warm up my face that feels frozen off." She pokes at her cheek.

"That would be nice. Thank you, Gordo." Sitting down next to Mia, I rest my arm on the countertop, the throbbing increasing as it warms up.

"What happened there?" Gordo barks as he spies the splint on my wrist. His eyes narrow with each passing second.

My heart picks up rapidly; I move my wrist to my lap to conceal it from sight. "Um…I slipped on the floor earlier. It's just sprained."

Gordo's eyes flash with anger. "Are you sure that's all that happened? You can tell me the truth. I will kick whoever's ass needs to be kicked for hurting you," he proclaims.

His kindness is something new to me. The pounding in my chest eases. "Honestly, I only tripped on the floor. I'm sure if you want to kick the cement's ass you can, but it might be kind of pointless." I place my arm back on the counter, relaxing a little more.

"She really did fall, Gordo. Trust me the asshole wouldn't be standing if I saw him hurt her." Mia spins on the stool while fiddling with her hair.

Gordo's face relaxes as his smile slowly comes back. "Good then. Well, not good that you're hurt, but good that it wasn't some jerk who I would have to smash their face in." Heading back to the kitchen he continues mumbling under his breath.

I watch Mia out of the corner of my eye. "You okay over there?"

"Yeah, I'm fine. Let's eat." She jumps up and heads into the kitchen without another word.

Bringing back the chili, she sets down a large bowl for each of us. We eat in silence, neither of us saying what's on our mind. "We should probably fill out our schedules before it gets too busy." I say after I place our plates in the kitchen sink.

"Yeah, next week you can just follow my schedule again. Come on and I'll show you how to fill it out." Mia heads off to Matt's office.

We end up working more days than usual next week, Monday through Saturday are all filled in. Mia slips our schedules into the tray on Matt's desk. "He won't care how many hours we work. He saves money by paying us under the table." I would feel awful if Matt ever gets audited while one or both of us are at work.

By the time we're done with our schedules the bar is already bustling with the usual customers coming in from the cold. We hurry and grab our aprons while welcoming the people walking in the door. Trent is behind the counter and as he sees Mia nearby he turns his back to us, resuming his conversation with a man at the end of the bar.

Mia grumbles and slams her notepad down on the counter, causing Trent to tense, but he doesn't turn around in acknowledgement to her temper tantrum. "Asshole," she mutters as she storms off to wait on a few of the tables. I grab my notepad, wondering what the hell happened between those two before I rush off to help with the full bar. The rest of the night we spend waiting tables and stocking shelves in the back in between awkward silences with Trent.

"Holy crap, am I exhausted." Mia grabs her coat off the rack on the wall. "You ready to get out of here? I just want to crawl into bed."

"Heck yes. My feet are killing me after tonight." We call out our goodbyes and head back to the shelter.

As we climb into our cots, we both face each other just like every other night. It makes me feel comforted knowing I have someone there going through the same thing as me. "Mia, can I ask you a question?"

She eyes me wearily. "Sure, I guess."

"What's going on with you? I know something is bothering you, do you want to talk about it?" I fiddle with the stitching on my cot.

She shifts her eyes to the blanket wrapped around her hands. "I'm fine, Ash. Get some sleep." And with that she rolls over, facing the opposite way.

My heart shatters; I wish she would trust me enough

to talk to me. "Night, Mia," I whisper as I close my eyes and fight away the day's perils.

Colton's blue eyes and dimpled smile appear before me, calming the anxiety raging through my body. With each breath, I relax into his arms.

CHAPTER 11

The morning comes way to fast. Looking at the clock, I realize I slept in a lot later than I ever have since being here. Pushing myself up from the cot, I stretch out my tired muscles. Mia comes waltzing in from the shower with a small smile on her face. "You seem better today. I'm glad to see you smiling again," I mumble as I rub the sleep from my eyes.

"Thanks, Ash, for understanding me and my crazy mood swings. I think tonight will be a better night." She pulls on her shoes. "You better hurry and get ready or we're going to be late."

Pulling the small bag from under my cot, I wrap my hand around the trinket inside. "Yeah, I'll get a quick shower, but first there's something I wanted to give you."

She cocks her head. "What could you possibly have for me? We're together 24/7."

"Well, I heard Chelsea talking the other day and... well, here." Handing her the small box, my hands begin to sweat. I hope she likes it and doesn't get mad at me.

Eyeing the box cautiously, she slowly pulls the lid off. After a few moments of her staring at the contents my heart rate speeds up. Crap, she doesn't like it. What do I say? "If it's not your style we can return it. It won't hurt my feelings." Biting my lip, I watch her.

She touches the object inside and delicately pulls the necklace out of the box. "I...I love it," she whispers. The golden puzzle piece charm dangles in the light the inscription stating, 'Two pieces form one bond.'

"I bought myself the other one that fits into that one. I know it's cheesy, but I wanted you to know you're not alone. We'll always have each other." Pulling the golden chain out from my shirt, I show her mine. "You always have me, just like the puzzle pieces will always fit together so will we."

"It's beautiful, Ash. I can't believe you thought of me when you bought this." Twirling the charm in her hand, she admires it. "Thank you. Thank you for being there for me." As she looks up, unshed tears glisten in her eyes.

Biting my lip, I hold back the tears in mine. "Happy Birthday, Mia."

Her eyes grow round. "How did you know?"

"I heard Chelsea say it. But the important thing is I didn't want you to feel alone on your birthday. Plus, everyone should get a present on their birthday, silly."

"This will never leave my neck. Thank you so much." She jumps up and squeezes me in a bear hug.

Gently hugging her back, joy fills me at seeing a little of her spirit return. "I got you something else, but this one is practical. When I saw it, I knew it was meant for you."

She lets go and pulls back. "You shouldn't have gotten me anything. I can never repay you."

Shaking my head, I hand her the bag. "Shush and just say thanks. It's not wrapped all fancy, but I think you'll like it."

She pulls out the black sweater that I purchased the other day. "Oh my goodness. This is so freaking awesome!" She squeals while turning it around to look at the front. In the middle is a bright pink skull and on the arm of the sleeve it says "Badass" in pink cursive.

"I knew you would like that. I saw it and I thought of you. I'm so glad you love it."

"Hell yes I do! I'm wearing it tonight to show everyone at work! Speaking of which, you better hurry up so we can get down there." We both glance at the clock.

"Shit! Okay I'll be back in ten then we can head out." Grabbing my clothes, I run towards the showers.

"Thank you again, Ash!" Mia calls out as I make my way into the bathroom. The happiness leaking from my heart has me walking on air.

After the world's fastest shower and speed dressing I throw on my brace as we head down the sidewalk to the bar. "So how busy is it going to be tonight? I'm not sure I can carry a tray at all. My wrist is killing me."

Mia glances over. "Well, it's going to be packed, but Matt usually has extra bouncers at the door with Phil. We can pull Phil in to help us if we need to."

"Why does he need extra bouncers for this small of a bar? I don't get it." Since I started working here the most excitement I had seen was the one man hitting on me. That's it. Not even a small bar room brawl has broken out.

"I can't say, but you'll find out soon enough. And tonight is supposed to be a good night too." She pulls her fingers across her lips like she's zipping them closed. That's fine. I'm sure I'll find out soon enough.

As we walk into the bar, I'm taken aback by how many people are already there. Every single seat and stool in the bar is taken. There are even people standing against the back wall. "Holy shit," I breathe out.

"Exactly. Come on, let's get to it." She puts her arm through mine and pulls me behind the counter in my shocked stupor.

After a few hours I've completely lost track of which

table I am supposed to be helping. The entire bar is filled and there isn't even standing room anymore. I hear someone calling out something in the background, but I can't make it out over all the other's talking around me. "I'll be back, I need some fresh air," I call out to Trent as I walk out the front door.

The cool air hitting my sweat slickened skin is a relief. Closing my eyes, I allow myself to think for the first time tonight. I feel like a bad modern-day superhero, hiding out at a shelter during the night and working at a bar during the day. I snort in disgust. I really thought I would be anywhere but here with my life. No one wants to be twenty-five and running from their husband. Opening my eyes, I watch the stars and let my mind stop. I can't allow myself to dwell for longer than a few moments otherwise the despair will paralyze me. As I walk back into the bar, I notice the quietness of the area. Where did everyone go? There are only a few older couples sitting around the tables sipping on a beer or two.

"Where is everyone?" I ask Phil. Did they all disappear like in that one book I read years ago?

"What do you mean? They all went downstairs for the start of the fight." Phil looks at me like I've lost my mind. I think he's lost his damn mind.

"What fight? And there's a basement here?" I search for Mia, but she's nowhere to be found.

"Mia didn't tell you?" Phil busts out laughing. "Damn, that girl has some balls I tell you. She really wanted to throw you to the wolves tonight without any warning." Shaking his head, he stands up and grabs my hand. The warmth from his touch causes me to reflexively tighten my muscles. As I stiffen in his grip, the look of pity I've become used to crosses his face. "It's okay, Ash. I just don't want you to get lost down there. This…" he holds up our hands, "is just so I can keep you close. It's going to be crowded."

I nod as he gives my hand a gentle squeeze. We head down the hallway past Matt's office to a small set of stairs I never noticed before. The sounds from below become louder as we descend. The shouts and cheering are enough to send my heart into my throat. As we round the corner, all I see are people everywhere. The crowd looks twice the size of what it was upstairs. With each step into the area my fight or flight kicks in. Bodies are everywhere; someone stumbles into me, another brushes past as she pushes her way to the front. I try to pull my hand out of Phil's grip, but he tightens his hold. I have to get out of here. There are too many people and the sound is deafening to me. I try tugging my hand again and Phil turns back concern etched on his face.

Whatever he sees on mine causes him to pale as he pulls me into his chest. "Ash! It's okay. I won't let anything happen to you. Can you hang on a little longer so we can get to the other side out of this mass of people? I promise it's calmer over there."

I grip his hand and bite my lip to hold back the screams I want to let out. I nod. I don't think I can hold on much longer. As we struggle through the crowd of people my body is bumped and brushed by strangers. Phil has his arm around my shoulders and he holds me protectively as he shoves his way through the crowd.

"Almost there, Ash. Hang on," he shouts over the cheers of the crowd. I don't even know why they are all pumped up. I just hope it keeps them distracted long enough to get me out of the middle of the crowd. As we push through the last few people, a large bar comes into view where Trent and Mia are standing. Phil guides us behind the bar and into the safety zone away from everyone. "Are you okay?" He searches my face.

I shake my head as I glance around with wide eyes. In the middle of the room there is a large make-shift ring set up. Everyone is standing around the edges cheering and chanting. "What the hell is this?" My lips quiver.

"Ash! Are you all right? You look like you've seen a ghost!" Mia places her hands on my shoulders trying to direct my attention to her.

"Why the hell didn't you warn her, Mia?" Phil growls. "She almost passed out when she saw all of this. Didn't you think it might set her off with everything that's happened to her?" Phil clenches his hands into fists by his side. I suck in a tight breath with his movement. He sees me eyeing them out of the corner of his eye, he relaxes his hands and slides them into his jeans pockets.

"Shut up, Phil! I didn't say anything because I wasn't sure if Matt would want her to know. I was going to tell her earlier, but we were so busy I didn't have time," Mia spits out.

"Hey, hey now. Let's all calm down here." Trent steps between Mia and Phil. "Are you alright, Ash?" Trent's pity eyes are enough to almost send the tears over the edge. I can't believe how weak I've become.

"I'm fine. Just shocked that's all…What is all this?" I cross my arms over my chest and silently hug myself.

Phil sighs and turns towards the ring, completely blocking out Mia. "Matt has an underground fighting ring. Tonight his best fighter is going against some out-of-towner. They call him the Ghost. Apparently he knocks his opponents out after a few seconds then disappears from town the same night. No one knows who he is, but he's undefeated. Matt thinks his guy's going to win tonight though." Phil watches the crowd. "Anytime the word is out that the Ghost might show up the crowds come in tenfold. They all want a glimpse of him." He shrugs like it's an everyday occurrence.

"So they just fight for fun?" My voice squeaks. I can't watch this. I've seen enough fists fly in the last few months and I cannot imagine it being a sport to be admired. "I can't watch this. I need to go." I turn my head to try and decide the best way out without getting trampled.

A hand wraps around my waist, pulling me backwards. "You can't leave now, especially by yourself. You'll get hurt out there," Phil says next to my ear. He places me next to Mia, blocking the path to the exit of the bar. "They're all drunk and their common sense is not currently working. Once the fighters come out and start we can sneak out behind most of them. They'll be trying to get as close to the cage as possible."

I wipe my sweaty palm on my pants. "Fine, but I need to leave before they start. I don't think I can handle it."

An announcer's voice floats through the air and the crowd simmers. "Ladies and gentleman the night you have all been waiting for. I would like to introduce our two competitors tonight. With $4,000 for the winner we have two undefeated men coming together in the ring for the first time." The crowd cheers, and screams can be heard from the women. "The first opponent is from right here in this town, standing at 6 feet 2 inches and weighing in at 200 pounds. He is the one and only Punisher!" The crowd erupts into cheers and the sound is a buzz in my ears. A large man comes barreling into the ring; his brown hair cut into a military style. The stone-hard muscles on his body look fierce enough to scare the other opponent away in my opinion. Shivering, I stand on my tiptoes trying to see over the rest of the crowd. "And the other opponent standing at 6 feet 3 inches and 195 pounds is the famous and mysterious Ghost!" The entire room cheers then settles to a low whisper as a man climbs into the ring. His rippling back is facing us. He stands there, head bowed for a split second then he lifts it, facing his opponent.

"You ready to go?" Jumping, I turn my attention to Phil.

"Um…yeah in a second." My eyes feel drawn to the ring even though my mind is telling me to leave. I can't shake this feeling I'm right where I'm supposed to be and I need to keep watching. The crowd is pushing towards the cage, blocking my view of the ring. Standing on my toes, I still can't see anything over the mass of people. Mia climbs up onto the bar to watch the fight. She holds her hand out patiently waiting for me to decide if I'm going to join her. Do I really want to do this? Without a second thought, I climb up onto the bar and stand next to her.

As the bell rings I watch as the Punisher lunges and clocks the other guy in the jaw. The Ghost barely moves with the force of the hit. The next punch he blocks carefully and he circles the Punisher. He looks like a predator circling his prey. As he turns, his hair hangs in his eyes, obscuring part of his features from the crowd. He swings out, clocking the man with a left hook then catches him with an upper cut. The Punisher flies back, landing on the mat dazed and confused. I squeal watching the impact but the crowd cheers, drowning out my voice. The Ghost's head turns in my direction and he lifts his face, staring right at me. My heart drops to my stomach as the room spins. Sucking in short breaths, I try to pull in as much oxygen into my lungs as I can. Phil's hands are lifting me off the bar and the last thing I see of the Ghost are his ice-blue eyes. "Colton?" I cry.

"Ashley! What's wrong?" Phil, Trent, and Mia all crowd around me. I scramble past them, trying to get back onto the bar. "Whoa! Ash, calm down. You had a panic attack." Phil wraps his arm around me again.

"Let me go!" I yell. My only thoughts are focused on getting back to the bar so I can see if what I saw was real. I have to know if that was him. A loud bell rings in the background and the crowd starts scattering.

"Ashley, we have to go!" Mia yells into my ear. Her green eyes come into view and it's enough to pull me back into the now. The entire basement is ringing loudly with an alarm. The crowd is scattering out a side door, people are stampeding over each other.

"What's going on?" Panic rises to the surface.

"That's our alert system that the cops are here. We need to go now! Can you follow me?" Mia shouts. I nod my head and grab her hand. "Follow close to me and don't let go until we're out of this mess." She pulls me along to the other end of the bar. Phil and Trent are following us. I glance back at the mass panic of everyone scattering. In the middle of the cage he stands searching through the crowd, his eyes frantic. They land on mine and with just that glimpse recognition sets in. Colton stares back at me for the first time in ten years. He moves his mouth, but Mia pulls me through a door and he disappears from my view.

The long dirt hallway twists and turns; damp air mists my skin as we run along the corridor. "Where are we?"

Mia tugs me along behind her; how she can see where she is going is beyond me. "We're almost out of here, hold on." She turns one last corner and pushes open another door. This one leads into a small storage room. She stops as she peers through the crack into another room. Whispering, she turns. "Okay, it's clear. Let's get out of here, but stay quiet."

She pushes through the door into a small dusty room that hasn't been used in years. Heading for the front door she peers up and down the street. "When we get outside we're all going to pretend we were just heading home from a date." She opens a small drawer and grabs something out of it. Tossing them at each of us she grabs a shirt for herself puling it on over her uniform top.

The shirt smells musty as I slide it over my head. The

long sleeve blue shirt forms to my body covering the work shirt I was wearing. "Why do you have clothes here? Where are we?" I glance back to Trent and Phil as they zip up hooded sweatshirts.

"I'll explain later. We need to get out of here. Ready?" We all nod as Mia walks out onto the sidewalk. Trent slides out next and wraps his arm over her shoulders casually. They stroll down the sidewalk leaning into each other. It looks so natural.

Phil's warm hand slides into mine. Glancing down at our interlocked hands, my stomach turns. "Is this okay? It's just until we're out of range of the bar." He eyes me, waiting for my permission.

Biting my lip, I fight the urge to rip my hand out of his. "Yeah. Let's just get out of here." He smiles and opens the door, pulling me along with him into the cold air. As we stroll down the street the sirens sound only a block over. My stomach rolls with nerves. Shit! Colton is back there. What if he's being arrested? And since when does he fight? I have to go back to find him. "Um…I think I forgot something back at the bar. I'm just going to walk by and see if the coast is clear." Pulling my hand from Phil's, I turn to head back with only Colton on my mind.

A hand clamps down on my left wrist, stopping me in my tracks. "Ashley you can't go back. If you get caught by the cops or if someone sees you and recognizes you from—you know, your previous life it could be really unsafe for you." Phil turns me around, placing his hands on my shoulders. With a gentle squeeze he lowers his eyes to mine. "Please, I'm begging you to just stay here. We can grab whatever you forgot later or tomorrow. Just let the heat die down."

My chest feels like it's on fire with each second that ticks by. "Listen, if Matt is having the fights then I'm sure the police are okay with it. Something else must have happened for them to be called. Like someone got sick. I don't know. But I'm going back I have to…" Peering over my shoulder, I search for those blue eyes.

Phil chuckles. "Damn, Ashley…I knew the minute I laid eyes on you that you were an innocent. I swore I wouldn't let anything else bad happen to you." His fingers brush along my jawline, sending a shiver through my body. My eyes shoot back to his face. What the hell is he talking about? Sighing, he drops his gaze to my lips. "I just didn't realize how truly innocent you are." With a sad smile his hand reaches out to brush a piece of my hair behind my ear. "Matt holds illegal fights. The cops are not okay with them, trust me. Anyone associated with them will go to jail. They've been trying to bust Matt for a while now, but we're always too quick with our escape plans. The only reason I can think of why they showed up tonight is because of the Ghost being here. People tend to talk louder and more often when a legend that no one has actually seen shows up."

At the mention of his alias my heart clenches. He looked so dangerous stalking his prey in the ring. Each movement was methodical as he circled his opponent waiting to strike. I should have been scared shitless, but a small piece of me was excited. I loved watching him move gracefully around the ring and when he heard me he remembered me. The recognition in his eyes was enough to shatter me.

"Hello?" Phil snaps his fingers in front of my face. "Ash, where'd you go just now?"

Pulling myself out of my thoughts, I back up a step. Phil's face falls when he realizes what I'm about to do. "I'm sorry, Phil. I have to."

Turning, I take off running towards the end of the block. The cool air stings my lungs with each inhale and I pump my legs faster. As the street comes into view I slow up, panting to catch my breath. The sirens have stopped and the silence is deafening. Wiping my hands on my legs, I try to muster the courage to head around the corner. Fear of losing him a second time has me paralyzed. *Please, Lord, let me make it through this;* I close my eyes with the silent prayer. A renewed sense of determination settles in my gut.

I head around the corner and slowly walk towards the bar. There is one police cruiser left parked outside of the building; the officer is patting someone down behind the trunk, checking their pockets. Scanning the area, I look for any sign of Colton. He couldn't have gone too far. I slow my pace as the officer stands back and places the cuffs on the person; Colton stares right at me as the cold metal cuffs are tightened around his wrists. "No…" I breathe out.

My stomach feels like it's been punched as silent tears trace down my cheeks. His steel eyes watch me with every passing second. The officer pulls Colton over to the car door and places his hand on his head to help him into the cruiser. Collapsing onto my knees, I watch as Colton is placed into the backseat of the car and the door slams shut. My heart crumbles to a million pieces as they start to drive away and head towards me. As the car slowly passes, Colton's face is watching me from the window and he mouths one word. The only word that could break me even more than I already am. "Stay." I nod as he disappears from view.

CHAPTER 12

I DON'T KNOW HOW LONG I SIT HERE IN THE COLD WITH my arms wrapped around myself. Honestly, I can say I don't care if I stay here all night. Just the glimpse of Colton after all these years has brought me to my knees. The ache in my chest before is nothing compared to the nuclear war going on in my heart now. I never thought I would see him again.

It was Greg's idea to elope and it was him who told me I wasn't allowed to stay in touch with anyone from home. Once we moved away, he cut off all ties to anyone who might help me see that he was manipulating me. I never was able to find out what happened to Colton. The thought of Greg is the only sane thing making me get up and head back to the shelter. My legs have become numb from the cold. Slowly standing, I pull my cell out of my shirt and check the time. It's one in the morning.

"Shit. What the hell am I supposed to do now?" Holding back the tears threatening to consume me, I try to think of where I could possibly go. A noise across the street pulls me out of the self-pity, and I watch as Matt exits the bar and locks up. "Ugh. I guess this is my only option?" I glance up to the sky asking for some sort of sign. "Yeah, that's what I thought." Wrapping my arms around my chest, I walk across the street.

Clearing my throat, I shift on my feet, an old habit that soothes my nerves. "Hey, Matt…"

Matt jumps. "Shit!" He spins around grabbing his chest. "Ashley? Is that you? What are you doing out here so late?"

"I uh…I." Looking at my shoes, I stumble for the words.

Glancing at his watch he mutters, "Shit, the shelter is closed for the night isn't it?"

I just nod, unable to form any words.

"Hey, if you need a place to stay you're more than welcome to stay at my place. I have a spare room if you want." He tilts his head sideways. There he goes with that damn pity look on his face. I'm so tired of feeling helpless and having to rely on others for help.

"No…" I make a show of glancing around. "I just wanted to see if I left my jacket here. I have some place I can stay tonight." Crap, why did I just say that? I wish my fat mouth would shut up for once.

He eyes me warily. "Listen, how about I leave you the key to the bar. You can find your jacket and if you get too tired to head out to the place you're staying, then you can sleep on my couch in the office." He takes the key off his key ring and hands it to me.

"I really do have some place to stay... I just wanted to grab my jacket." Staring at the tiny key of hope in my hand, I blink back a tear.

He gently places his finger under my chin, tilting my head to his eye level. "Ashley, take the key and stay. If you need to. You don't have to say anything else about it." He smiles as he pats me on the shoulder. "Have a good night and lock up behind you." He waves as he walks off down the street.

Gripping the key, I watch as he disappears from view. The chill sinks into my bones, causing my teeth to rattle against each other. Sliding the key into the lock I push open the door and rejoice at the heat encompassing me; my limbs tingle with the warmth. I shut the door, flipping the lock just in case and walk over to grab my jacket from under the counter. The silence of the bar has me feeling antsy; I head back to Matt's office and shut myself in. It doesn't feel as lonely back here in the small space. Curling up on the small couch, I flick on his desk lamp to keep the darkness at bay. The day's events play over in my mind on repeat. The fight, the cops, and Colton. After all these years he still melts my heart with just a look. Breathing out, my mind slows and all I see are his blue eyes as he pulls away in the police car.

A soft scraping noise pulls me from my dreamless sleep. Squinting, I listen to the silence; my eyes close and sleep nearly drags me under until my ears catch another odd creaking noise. My eyes shoot open as I lunge from the couch. I'm wide awake now. My heart is pulsing in my ears, drowning out any sounds around me. I feel my hands around Matt's desk searching for anything to protect myself with. My fingers wrap around a stapler and I tighten my hold on it with each silent second that passes. I tiptoe over to the door, my sweaty palms causing the death grip to slip on my only weapon. The weight of the stapler settles in my hand; the only thing it would protect me against is something as small as a mouse.

Tugging the door open, I peer out into the hallway. The darkness obscures everything and I strain my ears to wait for another sound. My feet shuffle into the hallway as I hold the stapler above my head. With each passing second my pulse quickens and my stomach turns. *Maybe it's just the wind. Get yourself together, Ashley.* I stop at the end of the hallway and glance into the dimly lit bar area. There is no sign of anyone around or of what could have made the noise. Sighing, I drop the stapler and clutch it against my racing heart.

With one last glance I turn around to head back to the office. My body slams into a hard wall and I tumble backwards, reaching out blindly I try to catch my fall. Just before impact a hard arm wraps around my waist preventing my imminent faceplant. As the shock wears off my panic rises. The arms holding me pull me closer, never losing their grip. I struggle and try to wiggle free. "Let go of me!" Yelling, I kick my foot out, impacting with something on the intruder.

A low groan slips past their lips. "Shit. That hurt. Ashley, calm down."

The sound of his voice stills the beast inside of me. *It can't be.* "Colton?"

His hands twitch on my sides as he pulls me upright. The darkness fades and his blue eyes come into view. "Ashley." His breath fans over my face with the barely audible whisper.

Reaching out, my fingers trace his jaw line, the stubble pricking with each stroke. He stiffens with my touch. "Colton. I…I can't believe you're here."

His cold eyes roam over my body, soaking in every detail as mine do the same to him. His body is harder, deadlier than I remember. The last few years have been good to him. His jaw line is more prominent, making his eyes stand out against them. There are multiple tattoos peeking out from under his shirt sleeves.

Leaning my forehead against his chest, I wrap my arms around his body and pull him into a hug. Grabbing onto him, I pray he won't disappear from my arms like in all my dreams. "I can't believe it's you." I squeeze him tighter. The tears fall freely, running rivers down my cheeks. "This can't be real." I sob into his shoulder.

Clearing his throat, he breathes out into my neck and his arms stiffly wrap around me for a second before he pulls out of my grasp. He lets his arms drop from my sides and I can sense the second he shoves the distance between us. With hardened eyes, he runs his hand through his hair. "How is that husband of yours?"

The bitter words he throws at me crack my heart into two. Flashbacks of the past Colton are no longer reality, I see before me the boy who broke my heart on my doorstep years before. I don't know what came over me, but this man before me doesn't reflect the image I've been thinking about all these year. His scent lingering on my clothes assaults my lungs, reminding me of home. If I thought I was lonely and broken before, this moment has proven me wrong. A heart can still break even after being smashed to oblivion by someone else. "Things are fine." I say more to convince myself than him.

He crosses his arms over his chest and I can feel his eyes searching for answers to the unasked questions floating between us. Neither one of us wanting to break the silence. "Hmmm. I didn't see him around earlier. Does he know you're here?" He shrugs like he's just talking about the weather and not our lives.

A small tear slips down my cheek as I see the broken boy hiding behind the mask of anger on the man before me. "Colton…I…"

"Jesus." He runs a hand over his face as he cuts off my words. "This has to be some sick twist of fate." A dark, tormented chuckle slips from his lips. "After all these years, I run into you here?" He shakes his head as he laughs to himself. I must be missing the punchline to a joke. I squint my eyes in confusion as I try to read his thoughts.

"What are you doing here, Colton?" I cross my arms and try to hold myself together. This is not the boy I remember standing in front of me. No, this man is harder around the edges.

"I could ask you the same thing." He crosses his arms in front of his chest mimicking the same pose as mine, but his stance comes off more foreboding. His hard eyes bore into me, waiting for answers.

"I work here," I whisper.

He shakes his head. "That's not what I meant and you know it." I can feel the anger radiating off of him, the tension in the room as thick as the blood in our veins.

He pushes from the wall in frustration and starts to pace the small space.

I flinch out of instinct and jump back a step. The movement causes him to stop dead in his tracks and that's the moment realization dawns in his eyes. His gaze goes to the corner of my face where the makeup covers the truth. My secrets, the ones I've been trying to hide from, are now splattered against the walls between us. The lies and reality mingled in a chaotic mess of our fate. His eyes glance down taking in the cast on my wrist. "It seems to me we're both not telling the whole truth." He grits out through clenched teeth. The anger burning in his gaze.

Jumping at his tone, I yank my wrist to my chest and cradle it out of habit. "I fell. It's just a sprain." The excuse slips past my lips without a second thought. Years of lying about my bruises has now become a habit I can't seem to escape. I pull my gaze from his and take another step back, putting more distance between his anger and myself.

He asks slowly, like he's talking to a child, "You fell?" His gaze flashes in disbelief. "The girl who used to do gymnastics religiously and could walk across a balance beam without effort?"

I fiddle with the Velcro on the cast, avoiding eye contact. "I just fell on the wet floor. I'm just clumsy. It's nothing." Holding my breath, I wait for his reaction.

"Hmm…" He watches me.

"Hmm? Hmm what?" I glance up and regret the moment I do. My heart betrays me with its erratic beating in my chest.

His eyes rake my face and settle on the bruise by my eye. "It's amazing how well I still know you and I know when you're hiding something from me."

"I'm not hiding anything. I really did fall." Crossing my arms over my chest, I challenge him to call me a liar.

A sad, flat chuckle slips from his lips. "I don't doubt that you fell, but you are hiding something." His hands intertwine behind his head as he leans back, staring at the ceiling. I can barely make out the words he whispers to himself, "You used to trust me enough to tell me anything. I used to think we would never lose that. Man, I was a stupid kid."

The finality in his tone scares me, but it doesn't stop the anger from burning in my veins. "You left me," I seethe. "Don't give me that bullshit line, I was there. If anyone was stupid, it was me for ever trusting you. I gave you everything and you destroyed me." My chest rises and falls rapidly with each anger fueled breath. "And just so you know, I'm not with Greg anymore," slips past my lips before I can stop the truth from tumbling out. My eyes widen and I bite my lip to hold back anymore secrets from spilling out.

He holds his breath and slowly drops his arms to his

side. He looks at me waiting for more. "Why?" is the only thing that he says. The wall is still up between us and another secret is staining our path back to each other.

I shake my head. "It doesn't matter. You don't get to come in here, demanding answers after ten years. You lost that right when you walked away from us." My words crack as I swallow over the lump in my throat. I wrap my arms around my waist to try and hold myself together. The sadness slowly engulfs me and I feel the dark thoughts swirling in my mind again.

"Huh, well, you sure didn't seem too heartbroken. You sure shacked up with him pretty quick and then disappeared from everyone's lives back home for those ten years without a single phone call." His words are laced with hurt and betrayal.

He isn't lacking any truth in his statement; to the world it probably did seem rushed. Selfish even. In reality, I was just too scared to own up to my mistakes and let others know how badly I had failed once I realized how doomed I was with Greg. "That's none of your business. If you want to talk about the past and who hurt who, fine let's do it. There's a couch in the other room we can sit on because it's going to take hours for me to remind you of how bad you tore me apart. You want to go have a talk?" I half-yell, half-cry.

He doesn't say anything and after a few moments of

silence I'm starting to regret my question. He shakes his head, breaking the trance between us. "I can't. Not right now. If you had asked me ten years ago I would have said yes, but right now…" He trails off with a sigh. "I need to go." He turns and starts to head towards the back stairway without another word.

"Colton, wait." My voice cracks as a lump forms in my throat. Regret consumes me.

He hesitates on the top of the stairs, his hand hovering over the railing. His head hangs as he takes a deep breath. I hold my own breath while praying this isn't how this ends. As his shoulders tighten and his back stiffens, a tiny crack runs along my heart. "I can't." Is all I hear as he disappears from view.

I slide down the wall next to me, tears blur my vision and a sob falls past my lips. The shattered pieces of my heart are floating in the center of my chest and I'm unsure if they will ever fit back together again. As the tears blur my vision and my world crashes around me again, the dread and realization of what happened between us all those year ago settles in my gut. The only boy who could have saved me, broke us both.

CHAPTER 13

THE PAIN SHOOTING THROUGH MY NECK AND BACK IS enough to make me wish death had taken me in my sleep. Slowly rolling over, I stretch the kinks out of my muscles and stand. Each movement is more painful than the last. "Shit." I roll my head and try to loosen the tight muscles. I am never sleeping on this shitty couch again; I'd rather sleep on the floor. The emptiness of the room is apparent with each passing moment. Remnants from last night's interaction with Colton play through my head. The ache in my chest intensifies.

Shifting off the couch I stretch out my legs getting the circulation flowing again and something flutters to the ground with my movement. A tiny piece of paper lies on the floor beside my shoe. Grasping it with my shaking hands, I bring the words to my face.

Ashley, if you still want to talk I'll be at the bar later tonight. I'm not promising anything, but I'll try.

-Colton

His words wash over me and a tiny sliver of my heart falls back into place. I'm feeling an emotion I haven't in a long time. Hope. Closing my eyes, I squeeze the letter to my chest. "Please don't let us screw this up again."

I tuck the piece of paper into my jeans pocket and pull my cell out. It's almost time for the shelter to be open. Mia is going to be so pissed I didn't come back last night. Ugh. Throwing my jacket on, I head out to brave the storm called Mia.

The short walk up hill was just long enough that by the time I reach the shelter the doors are open. I slip into the day area and quietly try to sneak into the cot section. I feel like I'm doing the walk of shame through a college dorm.

"Where the hell were you?"

Jumping, I whip around and see Mia curled up in one of the chairs. "Hey. I'm sorry I got locked out last night. I slept at the bar."

Mia's eyes widen in shock. "Wait! How did you get into the bar? And what do you mean you were locked out? I thought you and Phil took off together. Are you okay?" She scatters off the chair and moves towards me.

"I'm okay. I promise." Smiling, I can't help but laugh at the motherly side of her. Her concern means a lot to me. "I went back to the bar for my coat and Matt was locking up. He realized how late it was and offered to let me stay at his place." Shuffling my feet, I brush my hair behind my ear. "I told him I had a place to stay, but he gave me the key to the bar. He said to lock up when I left and he went home."

Her jaw drops. "He actually gave you the key to the bar? He doesn't trust anyone to lock the place up but himself. I can't believe he offered to let you stay at his place too." She paces while mumbling to herself.

The heat races to my cheeks. Why would Matt trust me to lock up the bar? He must have felt sorry for me. "I just slept there last night. I couldn't come back here."

"What happened to Phil? Did he ditch you? What a freaking jackass. I'm going to kick his ass tonight," she seethes.

"Mia. Phil didn't ditch me…I sort of ditched him." She stops her internal murder plan and stares at me. "He just…I wanted to get my jacket and he didn't want to go back to the bar. So I took off without him." Shrugging, I wait for her explosion.

She watches me with narrowed eyes. "He hit on you, didn't he? I knew the idiot liked you. I just didn't think he'd be stupid enough to try something with everything going on last night. What an idiot."

"He didn't hit on me. Didn't you hear me? I left him." Throwing my hands up into the air, I pause the conversation. "You know what, never mind. I really don't want to know. I'm back and it's over. I just want to get a shower and change my clothes."

"Go get your shower. We can finish this conversation later. Especially since I know you didn't go back just for your jacket." She stares at me, challenging me to disagree. My pulse speeds up with the guilt of lying to her. "I saw how you looked at that guy in the ring. You knew him. I mean I can't blame you for staring; he's one fine, sexy man." She fans herself. "You don't have to tell me who he is right now, but you will and soon. Go get your shower while I plot revenge on Phil for being an idiot and letting you leave." She shoos me away as she paces the hall.

The normalcy between Mia and me is comforting in a way. Another tiny piece of my heart goes back into place and happiness settles in my gut. For once in my life I can see the light at the end of the tunnel, with a normal life possible. Grabbing my stuff, I head off into the shower with a renewed spirit.

After my shower, my muscles are less tight and the ache in my neck is almost gone. I head back into the day area in search of Mia and find her sitting in the chair from earlier playing with her puzzle piece necklace absentmindedly. Lost in thought, she doesn't notice me sitting across from her. "What are you thinking about?" I gently nudge her leg with my foot, pulling her out of her mind.

"Huh?" Startled she drops the necklace. "Sorry, I didn't see you walk up. You ready to head into work soon? We can grab some lunch." Standing, she stretches. Her clothes are looser on her than normal. I'm also stunned at how prominent her cheekbones have become.

"Yeah, let's go get some food in us." We both head out lost in our thoughts.

Walking into the bar, I pray that Phil isn't working. I'm not in the mood to face him tonight and I'm a little afraid of how Mia is going to react. It's not even an issue to me, it's just something I don't want to deal with at the moment. Searching the bar, I relax when I see Trent behind the counter.

"Good afternoon, ladies. How're you doing after all the excitement last night?" Trent smirks while placing two sodas in front of us.

"Exhausted," Mia states matter-of-factly.

Shrugging, I take a sip of soda to avoid the question. My leg taps impatiently against the barstool. I wonder what time Colton will be back tonight. Or what if he doesn't come back? Shit, I wouldn't put it past him.

"Ashley. Yo earth to Ash." Trent waves a hand in front of my face, pulling me from my destructive thoughts.

"Hmph. Leave the girl alone, Trent. She had a long night." Mia yawns.

Perplexed, he looks between the two of us. "How did you have a long night? You were back early enough to get some sleep. Did something happen last night at the shelter?"

Biting my lip, I stare at the bar while tracing my fingers along the smooth grooves of the counter. "She didn't make it back last night did ya, Ash?" Mia grins at me while winking.

"Umm…" What does she want me to say? Geez, nothing like throwing me on the spot.

"What? Where did you stay? Didn't Phil walk you back in time?" Trent crosses his arms over his chest, which causes his muscles to bulge from his shirt sleeves. I glance at Mia, noticing her slightly drooling over him. Shaking her head, she averts her eyes sitting up straighter on the stool. I roll my eyes at her and glance back at the bar counter avoiding all eye contact.

"Well, actually, Ashley decided to be a damn idiot and took off to the bar leaving Phil behind. She stayed here last night. Apparently Matt was locking up and offered her a key and a place to stay," Mia states. She rubs her eyes and the exhaustion is evident on her face.

"He gave her a key? And why didn't you just go back to the shelter with Phil?" Trent looks between the two of us perplexed.

I shrug while playing with the straw in my cup. "It's not a big deal. I just needed to grab something."

"Huh." Trent looks to Mia and I see her shrug her shoulders out of the corner of my eye. Grabbing a towel, he starts wiping down the bar. "What's this about Matt letting you stay here? He never lets anyone in the bar without him."

"I know, right. That's what I said. I can't believe he just handed her a key. But to be fair, Ash is pretty likeable. I think we all took her in as family the moment we met her." Mia lays her head down on the bar and closes her eyes.

"Umm, I'm right here. I can hear you," I mutter.

"Sorry, Ash. I'm just so tired. I was up late and when I did sleep I didn't sleep too well." Another large yawn racks her body.

"Mia, why don't you go home? You know it's going to be extra slow the next day or two until the heat dies down." Concern laces Trent's voice.

Shaking her head, she groans, "No, there's no way I'm hanging around that depressing hell hole without Ash. It's fucking miserable there when you have nothing to do. I'll be fine, just give me something to wake me up a little."

Trent places a red bull from the fridge in front of her while eyeing her warily. "I still think you should go back and get some sleep. But for now drink that. It should kick you in the pants a little."

She lifts her head, cracks it open, and starts chugging. "I don't mind working alone tonight if you need some sleep. You do look exhausted," I chime in.

"Nah, I'll be fine once this kicks in. Besides I want to hear all about Mr. Sexy pants." She chuckles. Trent cocks his eyebrow at her remark.

"Don't ask," we both state at the same time.

A few hours into the night I'm disappointed to see Colton hasn't shown up yet. My nerves over the situation cause the burger I ate earlier to toss around in my stomach. The fear of him taking off and me never seeing him again is enough to paralyze me.

"I'll be back, Trent. I need a breather." Setting down the notepad and tray, I head out front into the cool breeze. The street is filled with a few patrons from the bar, smoking and carrying on in their drunken stupor.

"Hey, purty lady…what ya doin out here? You want some company?" One of the men stumbles as he tries walking across the sidewalk towards me.

"Come on, man. I think it's time to get you home." His buddy, who is stone-cold sober, catches his friend as he starts to fall forward. "Sorry about that, miss, we'll be out of here shortly. Have a good night." Nodding towards me, he hooks his arm under his friend's and carries him over towards the parking lot.

CHAPTER 13 | 155

I wrap my arms tighter around me to control the shaking. I swear this night couldn't get much worse. Walking around the corner, I step into the alleyway for a reprieve from any other drunken idiots. The cool brick wall I lean against presses into my back as I stare up at the darkened sky. The laughter from out front dies down and fades from my ears. I close my eyes and inhale the cool air; the burning sensation from each breath entering my lungs is a reminder that I'm still alive.

A bottle clanks on the ground a few feet into the alley and the sound pulls me from my meditation. Hushed whispers drift to my ears. Normally I'm not one who walks into a dangerous situation or any situation that's suspicious, but something about the voice feels familiar. I push from the wall and glance down the darkened alley. Two shadows huddled together stand out next to the dumpster. Curiosity gets the better of me and I head towards the two people to make sure they are okay.

"You got the rest of the money? Let's see it." A deep voice drifts to my ears.

"Here, I told you I had it. Now pay up, I don't have all night," a female whispers in return.

My pulse picks up speed as they hand each other something. As I get closer one of them turns, heading down the opposite way of the alley, and the other one heads towards me, stopping me in my tracks. Backing against the wall, I stand there waiting until the stranger passes, hoping they don't notice me. Staring up at the moonlit sky, I pretend to gaze at the stars.

The girl stumbles over an empty bottle and drops an envelope from her hand. I reach out to help her up when she snatches the envelope off of the ground and shoves it into her pocket. "I got it. Mind your own business, will you?"

My heart stops. "Mia?"

Her eyes widen with shock as she brushes the dirt from her pants. "Oh! Hey, Ash." Her eyes dart around her, refusing to make contact with mine. "How long have you been out here?"

"A few minutes. I needed a breather from everything. Who was that you were talking to?" I fiddle with the brace on my wrist.

"Who was who?" She turns heading towards the front of the alleyway.

I follow after her. "That guy who gave you the envelope. Who was he? And what's in the envelope?"

She pushes her shoulders back and flips her hair over her shoulder. "I have no idea what you're talking about, Ash. I was just out here catching my breath. The envelope has my money in it from my paycheck. You know they say you shouldn't leave anything personal at the shelter when we aren't there."

Just before she can reach the edge of the alley, I grasp her arm and pull her to a stop. She turns, her gaze burning with anger. "Listen, Ash, just drop it. Some things are better left alone and this is one of them."

A sharp pain shoots through my wrist as she snatches her arm from my grip. "Shit." I pull my brace closer, trying to alleviate the pain.

"I'm sorry." Mia's hand reaches out.

Backing away out of her reach, I watch as her gaze falls to the ground in defeat. "Mia, I don't know what's going on with you and maybe you're not ready to talk about it. Just know I won't judge you. I just want to help you. That's what you would do for me."

"Some people can't be saved, Ash. No matter how hard we try they are already drowning and it's just too late." Her eyes fill with unshed tears as her hand reaches up to grasp her necklace.

"I don't believe that at all, Mia. And you shouldn't either. We all can be saved, we just have to want it. I won't pretend to know your full story and I won't pretend to know exactly what you're going through. But we both have been on a destructive path that led us to each other. Now we just have to trust ourselves to pull us out of the despair. To keep surviving. Even on days we want to let it all consume us. We have to put down our vices and learn to cope together." Nodding to her back pocket, I stare her down. "That won't save you. It's only a temporary solution that will turn into a bigger problem with time."

Mia shuffles on her feet and turns her head up towards the sky. We both stand there in silence as the minutes tick past. "Do you believe in a higher force? That someone or something out there is greater than all of us?"

I look up to the sky and watch the thousands of stars in the galaxy shine brightly above us. "Yeah, I do. I have to believe in something. If I don't, I'm afraid of what will happen to me. My beliefs get me through the darkest days."

She stands there silently gazing at the sky for so long I fear I've lost her completely. "I used to believe. Years ago. Then after everything that happened to me, everything I lost, I couldn't imagine a world where anyone or anything would allow such evil into our lives. I just gave up hope and became bitter."

Pulling her dull eyes back to mine I see the shell of Mia. The deepest, darkest version of a girl who has been through hell and is still living it. "That's the thing, Mia. We can't give up hope or faith. Whatever you want to call it. The moment you give up is the moment the evil truly wins."

Shaking her head, the corner of her lips turn up in a crestfallen smile. "Ash, no matter what happens to me, always keep that faith and innocence. The world has been cruel to us all, but never lose your faith. If anyone can survive this, it's you." She turns her back and heads out of the alley, stopping just at the corner. "I appreciate you sticking around for the time you can. When you showed up with the bruises gracing your face and your head held high for everyone to see, you set a tiny spark of hope in me. Hope for a better tomorrow and that we can heal from our past. I know it's too late for me, but not for you. My hope is you, Ash. You and your survival." Without looking back she whispers, "You can't save me, Ash."

My heart cracks with each despondent word, her defeat and surrender evident in every sentence. Wiping the silent tears from my cheeks, I watch the corner she disappeared around hoping she will come back as the feisty Mia I have come to know. As the minutes pass dread settles in my gut. If Mia wants to run herself down a self-destructive path then I will just have to stop her each chance I get. I will remind her of who she is and why we all love her. Why we need Mia in this world. First, I'm going to figure out what was in that envelope so I know exactly what I'm up against.

Pulling my shoulders back, I take a deep breath of cool air, hoping for the courage to finish out the night without losing my mind in the process. With a renewed sense of purpose, I head back into the bar, the loud chatter from the patrons a comfort to my buzzing nerves.

As the last few hours dwindle down Mia becomes more distant. I watch as she shuffles from a table of chatty business men, her eyes glazed, staring off into space. Walking over I gently lay my hand on her shoulder. She jumps and inhales a breath, her eyes slowly focusing on me. "What's going on, Mia?"

Her eyes slowly glance down at my hand and back up to my face. "Nothing really. Just trying to finish up the last few rounds at my tables."

I pull my hand back and watch as she stares off into space again. Snapping my fingers in front of her face I try to draw her back to me. "Earth to Mia. You feeling alright?"

"Yeah, I'm good, Ash. Please don't worry about me." She exhales and turns towards the kitchen, disappearing behind the doors.

"Hey, what's going on? You seem a little distracted tonight and so does Mia," Trent comments.

Placing the empty tray on the counter, I pull off my apron and sigh in exhaustion. "I'm just tired. Nothing a little sleep won't cure. Mia's another story." The clock above the bar reads a little past ten. I know I can't wait all night for Colton to show. I'll eventually have to head back. And the possibility of him showing is getting slimmer and slimmer with every second.

Matt struts over from the table he was chatting with. "Ash, you and Mia should head back. You both look like you've been hit by a truck. You're starting to scare the customers." He winks.

"Har, har, har. How original Matt." Mia sneers while walking behind the counter.

"I think I will head out if that's okay with you, Matt. I'm feeling a little wiped." Grabbing my jacket, I pull it on while absently staring into space.

"I think I'll head out too. Only so Ash doesn't have to walk alone. Not because you told me to." Mia takes off her apron while pointedly staring at Matt. Her sassy side is starting to slowly reemerge.

He throws his hands up in surrender. "Hey, whatever you want to tell yourself, Mia." Turning, he heads back to mingle with the patrons.

"Let's get out of here," she mumbles as we both stumble through the exit.

Silently walking, both of us are lost in thought. An eerie chill shoots down my spine as thoughts of the monsters in the night swarm through my brain. Pulling my jacket tighter around me, I search the street for any signs of danger. I can't shake the feeling someone is watching us. "Mia, do you feel odd? Like something's off?" My teeth chatter; a little from the cold but mostly from the fear gripping my chest.

She slows her steps and peers around us silently scanning the street. "I don't feel anything except tired. Maybe the last few days have you on edge." She loops her arm through mine, comforting my nerves a little. "Come on, let's get inside and get some rest. We'll both feel better tomorrow." Glancing behind us one last time before entering the shelter, I can't shake the feeling that something's wrong.

Mia must be psychic because once my head hits the pillow my shaky hands and tumbling stomach calm. I feel the depths of sleep pulling me under without a second thought.

CHAPTER 14

A LOUD CRASH JOLTS ME UPRIGHT FROM A DEAD SLEEP. My heart pounds against my rib cage. Voices rise slowly, shattering the silence in the room. "Sir, you can't come in here." The mousy female staff's voice carries to my ears.

"I don't give a fuck what you say. I'm looking for my wife and if you don't get out of my way I'll move you myself." What sounds like Greg's voice pierces my heart and fills me with panic.

"Sir, the lady asked you to leave. Either you walk out the door by yourself or I'll help you. But you are leaving," Brad's steady voice demands.

"Hey," Mia whispers into my ear, causing me to jump. Turning, I stare right through her, rooted in my fear-induced coma. Her hair hangs in a wild mess around her cheeks and her green eyes are wide from fear. "Hey, Ash!" she whispers again while snapping her fingers in my face. Adrenaline courses through my veins and my fight or flight instinct kicks in. My eyes widen as the reality of what is happening settles in my gut.

"I can't be here." I tremble.

Another loud crash and the sound of footsteps sound from the other room. "Ashley, where the fuck are you?" He bellows and his words pierce right into my heart.

"I know the back way out. Come on." Mia's soft hand grabs my forearm, pulling me to a standing position. "Hurry, this way," she insists while pushing her wayward hair out of her face. Her hand gently tugs me along the back hallway away from the dayroom and past the communal showers towards a small set of stairs.

"Where are we going?" My voice shakes. My legs become weak as I stumble into the wall.

"Ashley, come out here right now!" Greg screams from a distance. "Get the fuck off of me. I'm a lawyer and I can have you thrown in jail for assault if you don't get your hands off of me."

Mia helps me back up to my feet. "Just a little further. There's a back door that heads out into an alleyway a block away from the entrance." She pulls me down the stairs and we follow a dimly lit hallway with damp floors.

"Is this another underground tunnel?" Gently

swiping the wall, I feel clay against my skin. The sounds from the shelter fade the farther we travel in them.

"Yeah, the city is full of them. When the current owner of the building bought the place, he decided to keep the tunnel intact just in case of emergencies. I just know this will bring us out far enough away where that asshole can't find you."

Shivering at the mention of Greg I peer behind us, expecting to see him rushing down the hallway. The menace in his voice ripples through my mind. Turning a corner, we ascend another set of stairs. Mia drops my arm and cautiously peers through the crack in the door. Silence greets our ears. She throws the door open and pulls me up the rest of the steps out into another alleyway. Because I'm only wearing a t-shirt and jeans, the cold air seeps into my skin straight to my bones intensifying the shivering.

The ice-cold fear pumping through my veins slows as the adrenaline wears off. Taking a deep breath, I stumble as the walls spin in my vision. Nausea creeps up my stomach and bile rises into my throat with each inhale. I place my hand on the brick wall and try to steady my weak legs. "Mia…I don't feel so well." I suck in another breath and try to get enough oxygen into my system, but my breathing becomes shallower with each inhale. I take a step forward and collapse against the cool wall, sliding down to the hard ground. *Please, I don't have time to be in shock.*

"You're safe now, Ash. Take a deep breath. Come on, don't pass out on me." Mia's cool hand shoves my head between my knees.

"What the fuck happened?" A person bellows and we both jump.

"She had a slight panic attack. Whoa, wait a minute. Don't you go near her!" Mia snarls and places her body between the person's and mine.

He stops walking and places his hands in the air. "Hey, it's okay. I'm not going to hurt her."

Taking another deep breath, I slowly relax and let go of my fear. He's here. He came back.

Mia scoffs. "And who the hell are you?" She plants her feet and crosses her arms over her chest as if daring him to come closer.

He slowly tries to move around her, but she blocks him again. "I'm Colton, and I promise I'm not here to hurt her. I just want to make sure she's okay." The soothing tone in his voice relaxes some of the tension in Mia's shoulders but she still doesn't budge. "What's your name?"

She stays silent for a moment. I shift, leaning back against the cool brick. "Mia, it's alright."

She eyes me, looking between us. "You hurt her and I won't have to call the cops because you won't exist anymore. You understand?" Narrowing her eyes, she shifts out of the way.

"I understand," he says as he cautiously approaches. Colton drops down to his knees beside me, his eyes roam over me, taking in every inch. I have a feeling he's not checking out my sexy body. As I snort at my own silent joke his eyes rise back to my face, his eyebrow cocked with confusion. "Ashley, what happened? Who did this to you?" he calmly asks.

"No one. I-I just had a…p-panic attack," I push out through chattering teeth.

"Damn, you're freezing. Where's your jacket?" He slides his arms out of his coat, revealing a sweatshirt underneath. "Never mind, save your strength. Here put this on." His hands gently help me lean forward as he slides the coat over my frozen arms. Pulling it tighter against me, I revel in the warmth. He stands and pulls his sweatshirt over his head, tossing it to Mia. "Put that on before you freeze too."

She narrows her eyes while sliding it over her head. The sweatshirt is three sizes too big on her, but she snuggles it closer to her body. I can't blame her; he's like his own mini-heater. "Thanks," she clips out.

He nods at her, a mutual understanding between the two. Rolling my eyes, I slowly try to stand, but my wobbly legs make the feat harder than expected. Colton wraps one arm behind my back and the other arm under my legs and swings me up to carry me.

I glare at him and spit out, "I can walk. You don't have to carry me." Honestly, I don't think I could walk too far, but I don't want to inflate his ego.

He pulls me closer and turns. "I'm sure you could. Just humor me and let me help you." And that's that: there's no room for arguing. Resting my head on his shoulder, I breathe in his earthy, musky scent. How I've missed that smell.

"Why didn't you show up earlier? And where did you just come from?" I glance around us, trying to figure out where we even are.

Colton shifts his arm under my legs and pulls me closer, adjusting my weight evenly. "I got held up in my meeting with a local scout. There's a fight they want me to do, but I told them no. There were some other previous obligations I had today that ran longer than I expected."

I open my eyes and watch him. "Why did you say no?"

His jaw clenches as he peers at me through lowered lashes. "It was out of town and I'm not ready to leave the area yet. We haven't had a chance to talk and I did tell you I'd try."

My heart skips a beat with the thought of Colton leaving. I knew he wasn't going to stay here forever, but I haven't had time to process him actually moving on to other cities.

"So where are we going?" He looks between a silent Mia and me.

"Umm..." Mia stumbles over her words. Since I've met her, Mia hasn't been known to be short for words.

Colton gazes down at me, his blue eyes piercing. I bite my lip and shift my eyes to his chin, avoiding his scrutinizing gaze. "Okay, well then we have to get out of the cold. We can head back to my hotel for now." He starts walking towards the street.

"No!" Mia shouts. Colton falters in his footsteps. "Sorry, it's just, let's go this way instead." She points down the alley away from the shelter, her face a steel mask.

Colton narrows his eyes at her. "Is there a reason we can't go that way?" He points to the street he was walking towards seconds ago. Mia's eyes widen, a glimpse of fear showing through. Colton stiffens underneath me at her expression and clenches his jaw. Watching her, he turns and heads the way she wanted to go. "All these secrets and lies have me thinking the worst. When we get to the room you both are telling me what's going on," he states matter-of-factly.

"Nothing happened, Colton," I lie.

"Don't. Do not lie to me again," he sighs. "If you

keep lying, Ashley, how can I trust anything you tell me?"

Jumping at the truth in his words, I cower into his arms. A slow sigh slips past his lips. "I'm sorry, Ashley. But I don't think I'm asking for too much."

I wiggle out of his grip and stand on my own two feet, the strength slowly returning to my legs. The moment his arms leave my body I feel an ache in my chest. "I told you the truth last night, it's not my fault you didn't believe me." I say like a spoiled child. I know I'm being defensive and I know he has a point, but I did tell most of the truth last night. I just happened to omit certain things from the conversation. His eyes harden and I can see he's not budging. Shit. "I'm sorry. I just don't want to talk about everything right now." A shiver wracks my body, whether it's from the cold air or my nerves I'm not sure.

He continues heading toward the end of the alley. "Fuck." He mumbles to himself. "Fine, but think of how this looks to me. I stumble on you cowering in an alley barely able to breathe at God knows what time, any time I ask you what's going on you give me evasive answers…" He stops and his gaze lands on my bruised face. "And you keep lying to me. There's something scaring you two and there's obviously more going on than you're saying. I'm not stupid, Ashley." He continues walking and mumbling under his breath. Mia and I exchange a glance before following after him. I decide it's best to just stay silent the whole way back to the hotel instead of pointing out to him that he's the asshole who was evasive ten years ago.

When we finally make it to the hotel a wave of exhaustion and relief settle over me as Colton locks the room door behind us. I take in our surroundings as I wait for the warmth of the room to start thawing out my hands. There's a queen-sized bed to the right of the door against the wall and a TV set at the end of the bed on the opposite wall. There's a large window overlooking the town and the view is amazing even at this hour. Mia stands by the door, fiddling with her necklace. Her blonde and blue hair is hanging wildly in her face and a few dirt streaks line her cheeks. I notice how ragged we must look to Colton. I guess that explains the tense look currently adorning his face.

"Sit down." He gently coaxes Mia and I out of our thoughts. She glances at him as he points to the edge of the bed. I sit down and am instantly engulfed by the soft mattress. Wow, this is way better than those cots we sleep on.

Mia glides over on autopilot and flops down next to me. Scooting over we lean into each other, helping hold the other one up. "Thank you," I murmur.

Colton grabs a long-sleeve t-shirt and slides it over his head, his muscles rippling with the movement. He only nods at my comment. He leans back with his hands interlocked behind his head staring at the ceiling silently. He has the same tell as years ago; the only way I know he's furious about something. We sit in silence, none of us wanting to break the calm. With a deep sigh, he moves to the bathroom and I can hear the water running through the door.

Mia glances at me with haunted eyes. I wrap my arm through hers and lay my head on her shoulder. "Thank you, Mia. If it wasn't for you…well, I might not be here right now." My voice hitches.

She squeezes my hand. "Any time. To be honest I was just as scared as you. I was so afraid I was going to lose you." She rests her head against mine.

A clearing of the throat pulls us from our bond. Colton stands there with two glasses of water, his shoulders stiff. Handing us each a cup he pulls a chair over and sits directly in front of us, his elbows resting on his thighs and his fingers steepled under his chin. His blue eyes assessing both of us. "Are either of you hurt or injured?"

We both shake our heads 'No' and I can physically see him relax at our answer.

"Thank God," he whispers and holds his head in his hands. He runs his hands down his face and sits back in the chair. "Can you tell me what happened?"

My pulse starts to race with his question. I don't

think I can do this; I can't let him see how broken I am. A soft whimper slips past my lips as a tear traces the edge of my cheek.

Colton reaches out and cautiously swipes it away. The pained expression on his face breaks my heart even more. "I can't take much more of this. Please tell me what happened, I can't help you if I don't know what's going on," he says.

The calming tone of his voice is easing my resolve, but I'm not quite ready to trust him yet. I shake my head and place the glass of water on the nightstand with trembling fingers.

"Okay. Let's start with some simple questions. If you don't want to answer one we'll just skip to a different question. What do you think?"

I nod my head as I pull my legs to my chest, holding them with my arms.

"Alright. What's your friend's name?" Colton sits back further and runs his hand through his hair.

"Mia," I mutter. She gently rubs slow circles on my back, giving me the strength to face the man of my past.

He nods. "Nice to meet you, Mia. I'm Colton Graves." He holds out his hand waiting for her to take it.

She slips her hand into his and shakes. "Nice to meet you, Colton," she mumbles.

"Okay, next question. Why were you outside this late at night in the alley?" He scrutinizes my face.

My eyes fill with tears; Mia's hand stills on my back. Biting my lip, I shake my head and place my face into my knees.

He groans. "Okay, okay. Next question. Why are you working at the Groggy Inn?"

I turn my mouth away from my legs, but refuse to make eye contact with him. "I needed a job. They were hiring, so I took it." There. I answered one of his questions without freaking out. Score 1 for me, anxiety 0.

Sighing, he leans forward in the chair rubbing his face. "Ashley, if you keep being so evasive how am I supposed to know what's going on? I thought you wanted to talk? That's what you said last night."

"Chill out," Mia snaps. "She's had a rough night. Give her a break." Colton stands and folds his hands behind his head again. I silently watch the internal struggle he's battling float across his facial features.

He closes his eyes and takes another deep breath. I feel like since we saw each other for the first time last night, that's all he's been doing. Battling mixed emotions between anger and need.

"I'm sorry, to both of you. I can see on both of your faces that something bad has happened. I just wanted the truth for once."

Mia straightens and glares at him. "Who the hell are you anyhow? I saw the way she looked at you last night, she obviously knows you. But she hasn't seen you in a long time. How can you expect her to trust you, just like that?"

He sits back in the chair, the exhaustion evident on his face. "Who the hell am I? That's a good question," he mumbles. "I'm no one, not anymore. But if either of you are in trouble, I'm willing to listen and help you find a solution."

My body shudders with his words and every breath feels like it's tearing out my lungs. The tears fall freely with his admission of being no one, it's not true. To me he's been everything, even after he destroyed me. After all these years of picturing him to escape my reality, he's here but doesn't know the truth. How much he still means to me. What a cruel world we live in. Mia and Colton's voices ring in my ears and their calming words are driving me insane. I don't deserve their pity.

"Stop," I whisper while clamping my hands over my ears. "Stop! Just stop! Please…" I scream.

Silence falls around us. Mia looks away remorsefully. Colton steps back, eyes wide at my outburst. "I can't take this anymore." I hug my legs tighter, trying to keep the demons at bay.

Mia stands. "I'm so sorry, Ash. I didn't mean to upset you. Please, forgive me." She wraps her arms around her middle.

I reach out and pull her down to me, grasping her in

a hug. "It's okay, Mia. I just…I think I need some time to talk to Colton alone."

She pulls back with a sad smile gracing her lips. "I'll head out. Will you be fine here?" I nod.

"Wait a minute before you leave," Colton speaks up. "I want to check on something, stay here for just one minute." He strides over to the door and closes it behind him.

"Well, that wasn't awkward at all." Mia nudges my shoulder and rolls her eyes sarcastically.

I smile. "Yeah, I forgot how observant he can be." I swipe the tears from my cheeks with the shirt sleeve.

She pats my shoulder. "I can see the concern he has for you. I don't think you're getting rid of him anytime soon. Which is a good thing with you-know-who out there somewhere."

A fresh shiver of fear lands in my stomach. "I hope Colton doesn't go anywhere. I've missed him but I also kind of hate him right now."

The door jiggles and swings open. We both jump as Colton strolls into the room shaking his head at our skittish behavior. "Here, Mia, I rented you the room across from us. You can stay there tonight, that way you're close in case Ashley needs you. Plus, it's not safe for you to be walking back alone at this time of night."

She gently takes the key out of his outstretched hand. With a shaky voice she murmurs, "You didn't have to do that. You don't have to spend money on me. I can stay somewhere else."

He slides his finger under her chin, lifting her eyes to his. "I know I didn't have to. I wanted to, Mia. It's not safe for you out there and anyone who protects a friend as fiercely as you do has earned my respect."

Her eyes glass over, but not a single tear falls. Her voice hitches. "Thank you." She turns and leans down near my ear. "He's a keeper, Ash. Let him in," she whispers for only me to hear before she turns to leave.

Colton watches from the doorway until Mia is safely locked inside her hotel room. Shutting the door, he throws the lock into place. Yawning, I stretch and curl up on my side settling into the pillows. The shock has finally worn off, but is replaced with my need to be near Colton. Mixed feelings race through my mind. I can't trust him, he left me, but he's here now.

"Do you need anything?" Colton crosses his arms as he stands beside the bed.

My pulse quickens with the impending conversation. "No, but thank you for everything, Colton. I just want to get some rest. I can sleep on the chair tonight." Rolling I start to sit up from the comfortable mattress. I guess the chair won't be as bad as the alleyway ground.

"How about you take the bed, I'll take the chair. It's not a problem." He grabs a pillow and an extra blanket from the other side of the bed.

"Are you sure?" The thought of sleeping on an actual mattress makes me feel happy, but guilt consumes me with the thought. "I don't feel right kicking you out of your own bed. It's no big deal if I sleep somewhere else."

He shakes his head and settles into the chair. His long legs are stretched out in front of him and crossed at the ankles. He can't be comfortable at all. "Get some rest, Ashley. It's late." He closes his eyes and puts an end to the argument.

Closing my eyes, I settle on top of the blankets feeling safe for the first time since Greg showed up at the shelter.

CHAPTER 15

The sky crackles with lightning, the electricity flowing through the night air. Colton grabs my hand and we run for cover as the sky pelts us with rain. He squeezes my hand as he pulls me under the awning of the gazebo. Panting, we both draw in short breaths from our sprint across the field.

"Well that was fun," I sarcastically say while ringing the excess water from my hair. Colton's heated gaze roams over the shirt that's plastered to my skin. "Like what you see, Graves?"

His gaze rises to my face and with lowered lashes he moves forward, closing the space between us. His black t-shirt pulls tightly against his muscles and it only accentuates my desire for him. "Sweetheart, not only do I like what I see, but I love who I see," he huskily breathes against my lips.

Goosebumps spread along my skin, bringing each tiny nerve-ending to life. I run my hand over his hard chest, up his neck, and give his hair a gentle tug. His sharp intake of breath gives me the reaction I crave. My legs shake with anticipation. His arms wrap around my waist and pull me into his body. His hardness presses into my core and sets off fireworks in my heart. My eyes roam over his features and settle on the thick lashes covering his electric-blue eyes. Pushing myself on my tip-toes, I brush my lips against his. Tiny electric waves pass between our light touch.

He closes his eyes and clenches his jaw. "Ash, if you keep pushing me I won't be able to stop. There's only so much a guy can take before he needs more." His strained voice sends excitement through my body.

The control I have with just one touch empowers me. Gently, I swipe my tongue along his lower lip. He shudders in my arms. "I don't want you to stop," I entice.

His eyes flare open and his hands fist into the back of my shirt. "Don't. My control is slipping and with words like that you're testing my strength. I promised you I wouldn't do anything until you were ready. I'm not breaking promises, Ash."

A frustrated moan slips past my lips, causing his face to fall in pain. His control is slipping fast; if I push a little harder it will completely collapse. Is this something I'm ready for? Am I ready for that commitment? I freeze, lost in thought.

His hand moves along my side, settling in my hair. Tilting my head sideways, he watches me. "I can see it in your eyes, Ash. I know you're not ready and it's okay. I'll wait until the end of time for you. Please don't push yourself to do something just because you think that's what I want." He places a gentle kiss on my forehead and traces kisses down my cheek. If I move just a millimeter our lips will fuse. Biting my lip, I try to stop the urge to turn into him. Desire and hesitation battle in my mind.

His breath fans over my cheek as he turns to whisper in my ear, "I love you, Ashley Andrews. Don't you ever forget that. We're still so young; we have our whole future ahead of us. Don't rush it; I'll always be here."

A booming clap of thunder pulls me from my dreams. My senses are skewed and I glance around trying to remember where I am. The sound of snoring from across the room pulls me back to reality and scenes from the previous day flash through my mind: Greg, Mia, Colton. Rolling over to my back, I stretch and try to relax. A burst of lightning lights the room. Colton is sound asleep sitting in the chair across from me; his tattoo-covered arms lay on his chest. How this man has changed so much from the boy in my dream amazes me. Darkness falls over the room again as I close my eyes, chasing the dream I was pulled from.

His voice crawls over my skin, the pressure from his body on mine is suffocating. His rancid breath spreads across my tear stained cheeks, causing vomit to race up my esophagus. I lash out and scratch at his arms where they pin me down.

"Bitch!" he screams as his hand falls against my face with a deafening slap. Greg's black pupils bore into my soul, draining all the fight I have. "You are mine! Don't you ever forget that!"

I kick out as a guttural scream rises from my throat. "No,

Greg! Never again will I be yours," I spit out, fighting with all my might. His hand closes on my throat, trying to still me. Closing my eyes, I search for the comfort in his blue ones, but I can't find him. All I see is emptiness and I know this is it. My fate has been decided. Stilling, I stop fighting fate and Greg wins.

"Ashley!" My body is being violently shaken, my head rolls to the side. "Ashley, wake up!" Colton's voice drifts to my ears from somewhere in the distance, calming my fears of what's coming. His hands encompass my face. I breathe in his scent as he embraces me.

"Colton, I can't believe you're here," I sob.

"Ash, wake up please. Open your eyes. You're having a nightmare," his voice pleads.

Opening my eyes, the remnants of Greg disappear and Colton's face comes into view. His glossy eyes are crinkled in the corners with worry. "Colton?" Reaching up I gently glide my fingers over his jaw, the stubble prickling the pads.

"You alright? You had me worried for a minute." He lets out a relieved breath and tucks a stray strand of hair behind my ear. Butterflies flutter in my stomach with his light touch. He backs away and sits on the edge of the bed, putting distance between us again.

My chest shatters with pain. "I'm sorry, Colton. I didn't mean to upset you." I scoot up in the bed and wipe the sweat from my brow.

"Please, don't apologize for something you have no

control over." Resting his forehead in his hands he leans forward. "Ashley, please tell me what's haunting you. What happened to you?"

As I lay there watching him struggle with the situation, I think about telling him the truth. It sits on the tip of my tongue. "Colton...I..."

He turns towards me and I avert my eyes from his steady gaze. "You said you wanted to talk, but yet you can't get the words out. I don't get you, Ashley. What happened to the strong confident girl you used to be?"

I lift my gaze to his in irritation. "What happened to the guy I used to love and left me behind like an unwanted piece of trash? You can't just show up in my life and expect me to tell you everything. You lost that privilege years ago." Tears threaten to fall, giving away the hurt that's lacing my anger.

He frowns while rubbing his hand behind his head. "I'm...I know I hurt you." He shifts his face away from me. "Fuck." I watch as he battles whatever silent war is waging in his mind. I almost feel guilty for the harsh words that spilled from my mouth.

I close my eyes and try to summon all the courage I can. Biting my lip, I glance down at my clasped hands. I can't stand to see the pain I've caused this man reflected back at me, even if he does deserve it. "I...I don't even know what to say. I thought about this moment so many times and now that it's here I'm at a loss for words."

He doesn't turn or even acknowledge my words with more than a grunt.

Shaking my head, I glance up at his back. "I've thought about you a lot over the years." I snort internally at the truth to that statement. God, how I wished this man would come riding in on his majestic, white horse and save me: how stupid and naïve I was. He can't even stand to look at me still.

"Me?" he whispers. "You shouldn't have, I didn't earn that right."

My mouth dries with his words. I can't tell him my secrets; he wouldn't understand. Just like he doesn't understand why I needed to believe in him for so long. Chasing away the thoughts, I shift a little closer and cross my feet under me. "Where have you been, Colton? These last ten years what have you been up too?"

He turns his burning gaze back toward me. Everything stills around us as the moments pass with unspoken words. His pain, and what looks like regret, washes over his features. What has happened to you, Colton? A wall falls over his face as he stares at the ceiling. The moments tick by; did I lose him already? I shouldn't have brought up the past. "I was just wondering. It's okay, we don't have to talk about it, yet."

Sighing, he crosses his arms in front of him. "It's not that, Ashley." Clearing his throat, he stares over my shoulder lost in thought. "When I left you…let's just say

I wasn't myself. I had what I thought were good reasons for an 18-year-old boy, but I know now I caused more damage than good." He shakes his head while running his fingers through his hair, causing it to stick up in random places.

"Why did you leave me? I never understood. Things were great between us. What did I do?" My voice cracks.

He stays silent and I watch as his Adam's apple bobs a few times. He clears his throat. "You did nothing, it wasn't you."

I twiddle with the blanket between my fingers, but refuse to pull my gaze from his features when I ask him my next question. I need to see the truth on his face. "Did you leave me for someone else?" My throat swells and a rock lodges in my stomach as I wait for his response.

His head whips to face me and he stares at me without flinching. "No," he asserts. "I would never leave you for someone else. I loved you." The truth in his words and displayed on his face cracks my heart.

"Then why?" I cry. I scramble to my feet and move to the chair to place distance between us. I'm afraid if I sit too close, my heart might burst into ash from the pain. "If you loved me, you wouldn't have left without an explanation. People who love each other don't hurt each other." I fold my arms over my chest, wrapping myself in a hug.

"Nothing I say will make up for what I did, Ash. I..."

"Try," I seethe, not letting him get away with a piss-poor excuse. No, not after wondering for all these years, he doesn't get to avoid my questions.

"I got into some serious trouble. Something happened that I'm not ready to talk about, and I ended up getting arrested that day. That's why I was late to meet you at work." He breathes out and I can see him struggle with finishing.

"What happened?" I hold my breath, too scared that any noise will cause him to stop.

"After I was released, I realized you didn't need the burden of me and my problems dragging you down." He stands and starts pacing the short area beside the bed. "I would have held you back from going out of state to school. You had your whole future ahead of you, and I was staring down the barrel of a loaded gun. One that would destroy any future I had planned." He stops pacing and turns to me with tears in his eyes. "I couldn't do that to you, I wouldn't do that to you. So I made the decision that if you hated me you wouldn't stay by my side and fight with me. You could have your happy future without being dragged under with me."

The silence in the room feels deafening. My heart pounds in my chest and I swear he can hear it bouncing off the walls around us. "Jail?" I breathe out to no one in particular. Before the shock wears off a burst of anger spreads through my chest, igniting the flame I was afraid would burn me. Maybe my heart will burn to ash. "You had no right," I seethe. I jump to my feet and move closer to him, his eyes widen, and he backs away a step. Good, let him feel my anger. I push a finger into his chest. "You had no right to make that decision for me. That was my choice to make. I would have fought beside you. I loved you, Colton. I wasn't just some high school chick who didn't care what happened to you in the future. You were my future. You. Not some jerk I met in college because you decided you weren't good enough for me."

He captures my hand in his and I begin shaking. I don't know if it's from everything that happened tonight crashing around me or his touch. "I'm sorry, Ash. I'm so sorry." His forehead leans against mine as a salty tear lands on my lips. We stand there, both panting, our pain mixing with each breath.

If that fateful night would have happened differently, I never would have met Greg. I wouldn't be here right now hiding in fear. A shudder wracks my body. No, don't do that. I can't blame Colton for my decisions. I could have fought him, I could have demanded an answer, but I didn't. I left, defeated and broken. "I need some time. To absorb all of this." I gently pull my hands from his and back away a step. He watches me with an intensity that sends a chill down my body. He nods and I crawl back into bed, exhaustion tugging at me. I'm mentally drained and I don't want to feel anymore.

"I'll be over on the chair if you want to talk some more." He hesitates. "I really am sorry, Ashley. I didn't mean to hurt you the way I did."

I swallow and the tears threatening burn my throat and eyes. I don't say anything. What more is there to say? We both are fighting our way through hell right now and words aren't going to save us from it. I hear him shift in the chair as he pulls the covers off the floor. Once he settles down, the silence of the room pushes in on me. My thoughts run rampant and I know I'm not going to be sleeping anytime soon. After what feels like hours I sit up in defeat. "Colton," I whisper. "You awake?"

"Yeah, I'm awake." His voice sounds exhausted even to my ears.

"Can't sleep?" I pull the covers over my shoulders and sit against the headboard.

"No, can you?" I hear him shift to another position in the chair trying to get comfortable.

"No." I sigh. My head is telling me to let him stay there, uncomfortable and miserable, but my heart is torn. "You can sleep in the bed if you want. Or you can just, I don't know sit with me over here and maybe talk if you want." My pulse races as I wait for the rejection I know I'm going to hear.

A deep sigh greets my ears. "I'm not sure that's the best idea. You need your space from me right now."

"Shit, Colton. Stop telling me what I need or want to do. If I didn't want you to sit here I wouldn't have offered. Let me make my own decisions for once." I know it's harsh and after our conversation earlier it probably felt like a knife to the heart for him, but I don't care. I'm a grown-ass woman, I can make my own decisions.

He doesn't say anything and for a moment I think he's just going to ignore me. The chair rustles and his heavy footsteps pad across the room. I feel him standing at the side of the bed, hesitating. I grab the covers before I can change my mind and pull them back for him. "Get in, it's cold."

He crawls under but keeps his distance from me. If I wasn't so confused I'd probably laugh at how ridiculously close he is to falling on the ground right now. I flip on the small light beside the bed and breathe out a sigh. "After everything, what happened? What did you end up doing?"

"A few years later when I went home, I drove my poor parents crazy with my antics. They didn't know what to do with me…" His jaw hardens as his eyes meet mine. "I tried calling you. Asked around, but you were just gone. That was when I knew I'd fucked up." His eyes shift back over my shoulder. "I was so angry. Furious at the world, you, myself, and the shitty fate we had." Shaking his head, he leans back against the headboard.

"What did you end up doing?" I whisper, scared of the answer I would hear back.

"I drank a lot for a while. At least, until my parents threatened to kick me out." He says it so nonchalantly, without even a hint of bitterness.

With a held breath, I urge him to continue. "What did you decide to do?"

He sighs. "Does it matter?"

I glance down at his arms so he can't see the tears welling in my eyes. Through the blurred vision I notice a tattoo across his forearm. It's of an eagle sitting with its wings spread on top of the earth, an anchor behind the earth. My heart races as I recognize the symbol. "You joined the Marines?" My voice shakes.

His eyes follow my path and land on his tattoo. "You always were observant. Probably why you did so well with your psychology classes." A short, strained laugh slips past his lips. "I could see what I was doing to my parents. The pain in their eyes was too much."

The tears brimming in my eyes blur his face in my view. "You could have been killed," I breathe.

A sad smile curves at his lips. "At that moment in time, I honestly didn't care. I just accepted it as an option."

Tears stream down my face as I imagine a young,

hopeless version of Colton running into battle. My fists clench and my teeth grit as I realize what his stupid decision years ago could have caused. I nod my head, but inside I'm still waging a war with myself. "What were you doing at the bar and the fight?" Changing the subject is the only thing holding my anger back.

He shrugs. "After the fight got raided by the police, I missed my check in at the hotel. Matt offered to let me stay there for the night. He said something about feeling guilty that I was arrested at his place." The nonchalant attitude he has is pissing me off. "It's just a hazard of this job. I know the dangers of it all."

I replay the fight in my mind, the way his lithe body moved around the other person stalking his prey. The brutality behind the fights makes me queasy. My pulse races with the replay and I realize I don't know this new Colton as well as I thought. "But, why do you fight? Do you enjoy hurting people?" I scoot back towards the headboard and pretend to rub my eyes. I don't want to hurt him with the distance, but I need some space.

"I never enjoyed hurting people." His eyes harden as he sees through my thoughts. "The people who cage fight are all willing participants. We know we can get hurt and we know we're going to hit each other. But we don't go around hurting others. My hands would never hurt anyone who wasn't in the cage with me."

I pull my knees to my chest and lean back, closing

my eyes for just a second. Exhaustion is quickly overcoming my strength. "I don't know how I feel about that honestly. I guess I'm just glad you're safe." Shaking my head, I yawn. The stress from the day finally setting in.

He shifts off the bed and turns off the light next to the bed. "Get some rest, we can talk more tomorrow if you feel like it."

I hear him walk back to the chair and shifting the covers around. My eyes are heavy as I settle into the covers. Colton's voice breaks through the fog in my head. "Why are you here sleeping in my hotel room instead of going to your home, Ashley?"

My eyes slowly close, the sleep tugging me under. Colton's words wash over me, humming me to sleep. "I had no place else to go," I mumble.

"What do you mean? Why didn't you go home?" he coaxes.

I try to fight the exhaustion, but my mind has lost the battle. My mouth moves without my brain understanding what it's saying. "I don't have a home…" Yawning, I curl up into the pillow and let the darkness consume me.

CHAPTER 16

A GENTLE KNOCK STIRS US FROM SLEEP. UNTANGLING myself from the comforter, I swipe the sleep from my eyes. "It's probably Mia." I mumble as I crawl to the edge of the bed. I get up to answer the door, just as Colton's hand wraps around my wrist, stopping me from moving any further.

"I'll get it, just in case." He places his hand on the doorknob as I step out of his way. Colton opens the door and Mia walks in past him. Her eyes a little less baggy with a little more color to her cheeks.

I greet her scowling face with, "Good morning, Sunshine. You look like you slept well." Stretching, a large yawn slips past my lips.

"You look exhausted," Mia retorts. She flops down in the chair Colton slept in next to the small table. "I actually slept pretty well, one of the best nights of sleep I've had in a long time."

"Good morning, Mia." Colton shuts the door and flips the lock.

"Morning," she mumbles while crossing her arms over her chest.

I can tell she's still on guard with him and his motives. "Hey, what time do we work today?" I ask.

Her eyes pull away from the stare down she's giving Colton and relax a little. "At two." She glances at the clock on the desk. "We have a while still before we start. I didn't realize it was only seven. I hope I didn't wake you two."

"No worries, I'm used to waking up early. Part of my job when I was in the Marines. Now it's habit." Colton grabs a bottle of water off the table and takes a drink.

Mia watches him and I can see a little of her resolve breaking through. "What are your guys' plans today?"

Colton turns and looks at me. Obviously I'm the one intruding on his time, but I'm not ready to leave him just yet. "Did you want to get some breakfast before I work?" My heart skips with my own question. Breakfast with Colton? What if he says no?

He's silent for a little too long and I'm starting to rethink how comfortable I thought we were getting together. "Yeah, we can grab some food. I know a place that makes good homemade breakfast. Mia, you're more than welcome to join us if you want."

"Nah, that's okay. You two go and catch up. I was going to head back to the shelter and grab some clean clothes." Her eyes widen when she realizes what she said. "Shit."

I hold my breath as I try to think of an explanation to give Colton. Damn it. I wasn't ready to tell him yet.

Colton stiffens, but says nothing at her confession. I guess he's letting this slide. It makes me curious about why he's not asking a thousand questions right now though. Sighing, I sit on the edge of the other chair and face Mia, ignoring the tension in the room. "Can you grab my bag under my cot and bring it to me? I really don't want to go back there."

Taking off her sweatshirt, she hands it back to Colton. "Sure thing. I already showered so I'll just grab your bag after I change my clothes. I'll meet you back here in twenty?" She places her hand on the door knob.

"Thanks, Mia."

Colton heads over to the door with her. "I'm going to walk you back, just to be safe." He hands her back the sweatshirt. "Wear this. It's cold outside, you can give it back later."

Mia's eyes widen. "I'm fine walking by myself. It's no big deal."

He shakes his head. "Just humor me, will you? It'll

make me feel better." Pulling open the door he gestures for her to go through first. Turning, a tight smile pulls at his lips. "Lock the door behind me, I have a key to get back in. Also, feel free to take a shower if you want, I have some shampoo you can use in there. I'll bring your bag back with me then we can head to breakfast."

Biting my lip, I walk over to the door. "Thank you, Colton. For everything."

He nods stiffly and closes the door behind him. "Lock the door." His muffled voice carries through the wood.

I flip the lock into place and the silence of the room surrounds me. I head to the bathroom and jump in the shower hoping to be done before he shows up with my bag. After a quick five-minute wash, I rinse and shut off the water. "Colton?" I call out and silence greets my ears. I dry off and pull on the clothes from last night as I hear the door opening and closing.

"It's just me. I have your stuff out here for you." Colton's voice carries through the room.

I open the door and head out while towel drying my hair. His back is turned to me as he slips his shirt over his head. His muscles ripple along his back with each movement. I suck in a sharp breath and turn away, giving him his privacy. "Sorry, I didn't know you were changing."

A chuckle bursts from his lips. "It's fine, Ashley. I'm dressed; I was just changing my shirt."

"I should have called out before I opened the door. I didn't mean to invade your privacy." Biting my lip, I chastise myself for wanting to see him shirtless again. My stomach tumbles with the picture of his back floating through my mind.

"Hey, don't beat yourself up. It's just a shirt. You can turn around now." His hand gently tugs on my shoulder, spinning me to face him.

The towel drops from my hands and my wet hair cascades over my shoulders. I need to think of something, anything to keep my mind off of what I want right now. I focus on random things to distract me: baseball, balloons, those annoying little ankle-biter dogs.

"What are you thinking about? You have a disgusted look on your face." He bends down and grabs the towel I dropped.

Butterflies race straight to my gut and flutter, reminding me of the effect he has on me. "Honestly? I was thinking of anything that I can't stand to try and tame my thoughts." I look him over and groan inwardly as his muscles bulge under his t-shirt.

He chuckles at my confession. "Why would you need to tame your thoughts?"

Glaring at him, I contemplate if he's serious or not. The gleam in his eyes tells me he knows exactly what I'm thinking about.

"What were you thinking about that you can't stand?" He holds back a laugh.

Crossing my arms, I sigh. "Oh you know sports, balloons, and annoying little dogs. But I should have thought about your cocky attitude and it would have worked too."

A tiny smirk tugs at his lips, breaking the angry facade he's had the last few hours. "Seriously? Balloons and dogs?" He chuckles. "Those things should bring happiness."

I roll my eyes and snatch my bag off the ground. "Yeah, well they annoy the crap out of me. I'm going to get dressed."

"I didn't mean anything by it. It just caught me by surprise." He shoves his hands into his pockets and looks at the floor. "It's funny how in one day my life is completely shifted. This thing," he waves his hands between us. "Whatever this is, I'm not sure if I'm ready for it."

My breath hitches with his brutal confession. Before I can say something I might regret later I back up a step. "I'm going to get dressed and then we can head to breakfast if you're still up for it."

His arms fall to his side and a wall goes up, blocking his emotions from my view. "Sure, let's get out of here. Mia put your jacket in there and she said you could use her makeup. I'm guessing to cover that." He nods towards my face while his fist clenches at his side.

I knew it was going to take a while to get through to him, but now I'm not sure if there's any hope that it will happen. "Thanks. I'll be out as quick as possible." I head into the bathroom to get dressed and cover the bruises from his view.

CHAPTER 17

TEN MINUTES LATER WE ARE HEADING OUT INTO THE cool air. The sun is shining and birds are chirping in the distance. I pull my jacket tighter while looking at the area around the hotel. There are a couple of small consignment stores, two coffee shops, and a Laundromat. Only a few people are on the sidewalk with us, mostly businessmen and women rushing off to work with their coffee and bagels. "So where are we going? There are some coffee shops I know of around here." Colton doesn't respond so I glance sideways. He's typing something into his phone, oblivious to anything I said.

Clearing my throat, I watch as he pulls himself out of his texting and turns to me. "Huh? Did you say something?" He seems distracted as he slides his phone into his pocket

"I was wondering where we're going. Who were you texting? Am I keeping you from something? If I am we can skip breakfast, I don't mind." I rub my hands together to calm my nerves.

"Are you cold?" Reaching out, he slips my hand in his to try and warm them.

I'm not even sure he meant to do it or if it just felt right. Either way, I think I'm okay with it. The tiny gesture brings on good memories from our past. A slow smile curves my lips as I remember the first time he held my hand. His hand was clammy and he was so nervous when he asked if he could hold mine.

"What're you thinking about?" His thumb rubs the back of my hand in slow circles.

"Just the first time you held my hand and how nervous you were." Smiling, I glance down at our intertwined fingers.

Snorting, he slows his pace. "Not only was I nervous, I felt like I was going to pass out waiting for you to answer. As the minutes ticked by I was mortified I even asked. I should have just went for it and hoped you didn't throat punch me."

Biting my lip, I remember my internal debate. Even back then I was so worried about falling too hard and too fast for him. "We were young, things seemed less complicated back then," I admit.

He nods, but loosens his grip on my hand. "They feel

a little warmer now." He pulls a pair of gloves from his pocket, "Put these on and you should stay warm."

My chest tightens, but I slip the gloves over my fingers. "Thanks," is all I can manage without breaking into tears again.

He nods and slides his hands into his pockets. "We're here."

Looking up, I see a small mom and pop diner in an area of town I've never been to before. I didn't realize how far we had walked. Colton pulls the door open for me and the heat from the diner engulfs us. The aromas of home-cooked food assault my nose. Fresh baked bread mixes with the scent of bacon. There are a few booths along the walls and a small bar with stools in the middle of the room.

"Feel free to seat yourself, I'll be right over with some menus for you both," an older lady wearing a pink and white uniform announces without looking up from her pad of paper.

"Let's sit in a booth." Colton leads the way to one tucked in the corner of the restaurant.

I slide into the teal colored bench seat and admire the 50's style diner. "I've never seen this place before. How did you find it?"

He slides into the bench seat across from me and pulls his jacket off. "Every town I travel to, I look for the best diners around. Nothing beats a home-cooked meal when you're traveling. When I arrived to town I saw this place on one of my walks and decided to try them out."

I look around and take in all the cheesy and nostalgic decorations while smiling. "I love diners. I've loved them for as long as I can remember."

"I know," he states without any explanation.

My eyes dart back to him. "You remembered?" I whisper.

"Of course I remembered. You used to light up every time we went out and ate at one. You would count the different decorations and compare them to the other diners you've visited." He shifts in his seat and leans back against it. "Kind of like how just now your eyes lit up for the first time since I saw you the other day in the bar. A little bit of the old Ashley is still in there, you just have to find her."

"Why did you find a diner in every town you traveled to?" I already know the answer deep in my heart.

"I just wanted to surround myself with memories. Eventually, it became like a silent form of torture and healing all in one." He leans back with a sigh.

A silent tear trickles down my cheek and I swipe it away while looking out the window. "Memories have a way of either healing us or destroying us."

The waitress appears at our table and slides two menus in front of us. "Sorry for the wait, I brought you both some waters," she states, freeing us from the awkward conversation only a moment before.

Colton grabs a menu and holds it up, blocking his face from my view. Sighing, I grab a menu too. "Thank you."

"No problem, Hun. Can I get you all something to drink?" she asks.

I glance up and notice her name tag says Bonnie. "Can I have some coffee please, Bonnie?"

"Of course, dear. How about you, Sugar?" Bonnie turns to Colton.

"Coffee for me too," he grunts.

She glances between us and a small smile curves her lips. "Would you like a minute or two or are you ready to order?"

"I'm ready."

"A few minutes," Colton states at the same time.

Bonnie looks between us, not sure who to listen to.

Colton places the menu down and relaxes. "I'm sorry, we can order. You can go first, Ashley."

I watch him waiting to see his wall go back up, but he leaves it down and lets me see the hurt he feels from our conversation. "I'll have blueberry pancakes, please." I hand Bonnie the menu and glance out the window away from Colton's stare.

"I'll have the same with a side of bacon and scrambled eggs please."

She takes his menu and scribbles our orders down on her pad. "I'll leave you two alone and will be back with your coffee shortly," she calls as she walks away with our orders.

I notice the amount of people on the street has doubled since we first left the hotel. There are a few moms pushing strollers looking frazzled as they weave between everyone. A man is walking while talking on a phone, his wife silently texting away at his side. "How can people do that?"

"Do what?" Colton turns and looks out the window.

"Be in each other's company, but on the phone. Not paying attention to each other. It just doesn't feel right. If you're with someone your attention should be on them, not on a phone." I scoot closer to the window to get a better view. "Who could be so important that they're texting them while they're with other people?" I watch as a few more people walk past fiddling with their phones.

"That's pretty normal for today's standards. They're probably playing on a social media app or something. Checking in where they're at so their friends can see. I never understood any of it personally."

I pull my eyes from the passerby's and see Colton staring out the window. "What's a social media app? And how are they checking in?" I imagine them calling their friends to tell them where they are and what they're doing at that exact moment. I giggle at how ridiculous it sounds.

"You haven't heard of social media? Where have you been living and how have you not seen it somewhere? Even businesses use it now-a-days to build a customer base."

The waitress, Bonnie, brings over two cups and a carafe of coffee. "There you go. Let me know if you need anything else. Your food should be ready shortly."

I watch as she leaves and wonder if she's ever used a social media app. Probably not. Bonnie looks like an old-fashioned type who calls on a landline. I pour myself some liquid caffeine and savor the first sip. It's been a while since I've enjoyed coffee. We never had any at home and anytime I bought it Greg complained about me wasting money so I just stopped buying it.

"You look at peace when you sip your coffee." Colton grabs his cup and mixes in four packets of sugar along with three small containers of creamer.

"Would you like any coffee with that sugar?" I tease. I like my coffee black and strong. I cringe as he stirs his and it's almost the color of milk.

"Actually, I prefer my sugar and creamer with a dash of coffee." He says as he takes a long sip. "Delicious. Sweet, just the way I like it. You want to taste it?"

I curl my lip as I imagine the taste of his. "I'll stick with my black coffee, thanks."

He chuckles and places his cup on the table. "Do you at least have a cell phone?" He asks, changing the subject back.

"Yeah, I have a cell phone. It's just not one of those fancy dancy ones other people have." I look back out the window. "It's usually in my pocket so I have it when I'm at work."

Colton pulls his out of his pocket. "Can I see yours?"

I reach into my jeans pocket searching for it, but it's not there. "I guess I forgot to grab it this morning. It's at the hotel in my bag I bet."

He places his back in his pocket. "Remind me later to program my number in your phone and I'll put yours in mine. Just in case you need me again."

My pulse quickens with his underlying meaning. Just in case whatever or whoever I'm running from shows up. "What have you been up to besides fighting and searching for diners over the last few years?"

It's his turn to look uncomfortable at the subject change. "Um…well I volunteer to teach some self-defense classes in the towns I travel to. You know, show others how to defend themselves."

"You volunteer your time to teach the classes? That's really generous of you. Who do you normally teach?"

"I usually find local colleges to volunteer at, but sometimes the towns I'm visiting know in advance and special programs will reach out to me asking me to volunteer." He shrugs his shoulders. "Right now I'm volunteering for a place called Sacred Heart. It's a women's shelter. They meet me at the local gym with a few women who wanted to learn self-defense."

I'm tracing the rim of my coffee mug, but my finger stills when he speaks. "Sacred Heart?"

His heated gaze roams over my face. "Yeah, have you heard of it?" He takes a long sip of his coffee without his gaze wavering from mine.

I swallow over the lump in my throat. "Actually…" My mind is begging me to stop talking, but my heart is telling me to let it out. "That's where I'm supposed to be staying." I clasp my shaking hands beneath the table to steady myself for his response.

He nods as he watches me. "I was wondering that. I had a feeling."

I suck in a sharp breath. "How did you know?"

He sits silent for a moment. I wonder if he is even going to answer when he finally breaks the silence. "I didn't know until you just verified my suspicions. But I just took into account the little bit you've told me so far. You're running from something, your face has a prominent bruise along side it, and you admitted last night in your sleep you had no place to go. Also, add in the night terrors and Mia staying there and it all makes a little more sense."

My heart beats wildly out of my chest. He knows,

and I didn't even have to tell him anything. But he only knows part of it, not who I'm running from or why. "That's very observant of you. Did they teach you to figure things out like that in the Marines?"

"They do teach you to be observant of your surroundings, but also being surrounded by trauma victims you tend to pick up on key behaviors." He sets his coffee cup down. "Are you ready to talk about it yet?"

I shake my head and I can see the disappointment in his eyes.

Bonnie stops at our table and places two large plates in front of us, breaking the tension yet again. I'm going to leave her the biggest tip I can afford for saving me twice now. My blueberry pancakes are larger than I expected, covering the entire plate and coated with a heap of fresh blueberries. Colton has the same along with another plate overflowing with eggs and bacon. I'm not sure how he's going to eat all of that in a sitting, my stomach hurts just from looking at it. "Enjoy, you two." Bonnie smiles and heads off to her other tables.

Colton pulls the plate closer and stares at it. "I should have thought this through better. I didn't realize how large their portions would be."

As the tension eases, a giggle slips past my lips as I take my first bite. The sweetness of the pancakes mixed with the tartness of the blueberries erases the last few tense moments. "This is delicious. Probably the best blueberry pancakes I've ever tasted."

Colton shovels some of his into his mouth and a quarter of his plate is already clean. "They're pretty good. I've never had blueberry pancakes before."

"Why did you order them then? I would have let you taste mine instead." I take a few more bites.

"You've always been obsessed with blueberry anything so I thought I'd give it a try and see what the fuss was all about. It's not bad." He grabs a piece of bacon and bites it while smirking at me.

"I'm not obsessed with blueberry foods. I just enjoy them." I pretend to pout.

"I remember on your 16th birthday I took you to a bakery to pick out a cake. The minute your eyes landed on those blueberry muffins you insisted you wanted that instead of cake for your birthday. I bought a dozen muffins for you and you refused to share with me. I think it only took you three days to finish off that dozen." He laughs while finishing up his eggs.

This. I can do this. Talking and joking about the past is easier for me. "I couldn't help it. They were fantastic muffins. They were the best muffins I had ever tasted. I think I gained ten pounds in those three days too." I actually ate them all in two days, but no need to let Colton know that. Maybe I do have a blueberry addiction.

"Huh, you wouldn't have gained that much had you learned to share with others." He winks as he pushes his empty plates to the side.

I eye my half-eaten pancakes and feel my jeans tighten with the thought of eating anymore. "Would you like the rest of mine? I'm full." I push my plate away and relax back into the chair.

"Nah, I'm good. I think if I ate anything else it'd be overdoing it." He rubs his stomach.

"I think you may have already overdone it. I could barely finish my pancakes and you ate all of yours plus eggs and bacon. I feel sick just imagining that amount of food in my stomach."

Bonnie returns to check on us, her eyebrows raise as she sees we're already finished. She grabs Colton's plates out of his way. "How was the food? Would you like a box?"

I smile as I hand her my plate. "No, thank you. It was delicious."

"I'm glad to hear it." She places the check on the table, "You can pay at the counter whenever you're both ready. No rush. Have a great day you two." Bonnie smiles and heads off with our plates balancing on her arms.

Colton glances at his watch. "Well I suppose we have a little time before you need to be at work."

"Really? I'm not sure what to do before my shift

starts. Mia and I usually go window shopping or we eat lunch at the bar." My heart drops with the realization that I'll have to leave Colton again while I'm working. Snap out of it, he's the one who left you, stop depending on him to be there all the time now.

"Come on, I'll go pay then we'll take a walk together." He slides out of the booth and holds his hand out to help me up.

"I invited you, so I should pay." I pull my cash out of my pocket.

"Don't worry about it, I ate three times as much as you. It's only fair I pay for the food." Slipping his jacket on, he walks over and pays our bill without another word.

As we head outside, the air has warmed up enough to make our walk comfortable. A few shops have their doors open, letting the fresh air in and I glance into the windows as we pass, admiring the antique furniture and artsy clothes. "I've always loved antique pieces. The story and history they must have seen in their long lives has to have been interesting." I point into the window. "Like that desk, most people would see a worn piece of wood which has seen better days. But when I look at it I imagine people of all ages and decades sitting down and writing letters to loved ones at war or family halfway across the world in their home country. Each nick and dent in it is a piece of its history. A story that will last forever."

Colton stops and stares in the window with me. "I never thought of it like that. But then again you never see something as it looks on the outside, you've always found the story within it."

I shrug my shoulders. "I have to believe there's more to this world than what we see on the outside. Everything has a story and a soul. Some are more scarred than others, but they still hold memories good and bad."

His hands slip into his pockets. "And no matter how scarred they are they're still beautiful. Come on, I saw this shop yesterday and I bet you'll love it. They have all kinds of antiques with lots of stories." He smiles at me as he heads down the sidewalk.

He wasn't exaggerating; most of the items in this store were made over a century ago. I run my fingers over the Remington No. 10 typewriter and I try to imagine the books the writer created with it. "This place is amazing, Colton." I move around the shelves and a large smile curves at my lips. On a table sits a plush teddy bear with a missing eye, it's once soft brown fur is now bare in spots. "This bear has seen better days I assume, but imagine all the children's lives it's witnessed. The laughter and sorrow of multiple generations. How it's still intact is beyond me."

"It doesn't look like it's intact there, Ash. It's missing

an eye. It probably plucked it out itself after some of the things it has witnessed through the years."

I smile as we fall back into old routines, joking with each other like it's normal. Colton picks up the bear and I can't help but giggle at this masculine man holding a tiny teddy bear so gingerly.

"What?" He cocks his head.

"Nothing. I think that teddy bear suits you."

His grin widens and his eyes glisten with mischief. "Hmm…you think so?" Holding the bear out, he scrutinizes it. "I don't know, I think maybe if it had another eye it would look a little better."

"Yeah, but I think that's what makes it perfect for you. A scarred teddy bear for a hardcore fighter."

"He does look like some of my opponents when I finish with them." He tucks the teddy bear under his arm. "I'm sold. This little guy belongs with us. Besides, I can't let him rot his days away here in this store. No offense, but the potpourri smell is enough to make this little guy want to jump ship. We can't let him suffer any longer."

Chuckling, I shake my head. "Well, let's go buy it, then we can head out of here. The smell is giving me a headache too."

After Colton purchases the teddy bear we head back out onto the street and the reality that our day together is coming to an end is breaking my heart. It's felt like nothing has changed between us and I have to remind myself that we still don't know each other that well. "I guess we should head to the bar, I have to work soon."

He turns toward me and pulls his hand out of his pocket. "I have something for you first." He holds out his closed hand.

I slowly reach my shaking fingers out. "You didn't have to do that."

"Don't be nervous. It's just something small." He drops the item into my hand.

As he moves his away I can't help the tears that form in my eyes. In the palm of my hand lays a small blue and red thread bracelet that I made for him our senior year. I gave it to him with the promise that I would always be there for him, even when I was away. "You kept this all these years?"

He takes the bracelet out of my palm and ties it gently around my wrist. "I never let it go. I think I kept it to remind myself that even when things in life change, you can still find some good things in the memories. I'm actually surprised it's still intact after my tour overseas."

A tear drips onto our hands as I admire the bracelet gracing my arm. "I don't know what to say."

"You don't have to say anything. I just wanted you to know that whatever is in your past that you're afraid of, there's always good memories and people there to help you fight through it." He runs his hands through his hair.

"That sounded way cheesier than I imagined. I just meant that you have friends that are willing to help you and listen."

"Thank you, Colton," I whisper.

"You're welcome." Turning away, he breaks our eye contact. "Let's get you to work before you're late."

CHAPTER 18

THE CROWD AT THE BAR IS SLOW TONIGHT, WHICH SEEMS to be becoming the new normal since the fight was busted the other night. I wipe off the table and grab the tray full of dirty dishes. As I drop them off in the kitchen I catch a glimpse of Mia walking back in from outside. She cautiously glances around the room as she tries to slip unnoticed behind the bar. If she thinks no one has noticed she's acting different lately, then she really is oblivious. She grabs her notepad from her pocket, brushes the wrinkles from her apron, and heads toward one of her tables to check on the customers. I would ask her what's going on, but the last time I did that it ended up not going so well. Blowing out a sigh, I grab my own tray and toss it on the counter.

"Easy there, no need to take your frustrations out on the counter," Trent goads.

But I'm not in the mood for his joking and teasing tonight. I haven't heard from Colton since he dropped me off earlier, Mia's up to something that I'm sure is going to get her into some serious trouble, and honestly I have no idea where I'm going to stay tonight. Add on the fact that Greg is somewhere out there lurking in the night and I'd say we have a pretty great recipe for a fucked up life. "I'm sure it'll survive," I snap.

His eyes widen with my outburst then narrow to two, probing slits. "Okay, that's it. What's going on with you? You're acting completely opposite than usual." He crosses his arms over his chest and continues. "In fact, you're acting like Mia and that's even more worrisome. Spill it."

I roll my eyes so hard I see little spots in my peripheral vision. "You know I don't have to be a meek and innocent person all the time. I do have other emotions." With a quick flick of my wrist I toss my notepad behind the counter next to the register.

"Shit, I didn't mean anything by it. I'm just a little worried about you, Ash. I've never seen you this angry before." He doesn't move. He's probably too scared of what I'll say if he does.

"I'm fine," I clip out. "In fact, I'm just peachy." I untie my apron and crumble it into a ball. "I'm going to take a break, I'll be back in 15." Trent just stands there speechless as I walk out the door.

The street isn't too crowded, but standing there so exposed I shiver with fear. Wrapping my arms around myself, I slowly walk around the corner to the alleyway. As soon as the voices out front fade, I can finally breathe easy again. Guilt is eating at my conscience for snapping at Trent and for being such a coward when it comes to Mia. How can she not see what she's doing to herself? I'm not even sure exactly what it is that she's doing, but it's not healthy from the way her body is slowly shrinking.

Blowing out my frustrations, I lean against the cold alley wall and slide down to the ground. I close my eyes and count my breaths to try and erase the stress. One… Two… Three. The hard cement behind my back digs in just enough to keep me aware of my surroundings, but still focused in this moment. Four… Five… Six. A shadow falls over my face and my eyes pop open out of fear. All I can see is a shadowy figure standing over me, as my heart beats out of my chest and I sit there frozen in fear.

"Is that seat taken?" Colton's voice rings out as he nods to the ground next to me.

Thank God, I was sure I was going to be murdered or attacked in the alley and no one would hear me. I shake my head 'No' and try to will my voice to work again. He shifts to the side and sits down next to me against the wall, his long legs laying straight out in front of him amongst the dirty walkway. Gross. I didn't realize how nasty this alley was before I sat down. "You don't have to sit if you don't want to, it's actually pretty disgusting out here," I say, breaking the silence between us.

A low chuckle emerges from him. "Trust me, I've been in worse environments than this. Nothing a little soap and possibly bleach can't kill."

I glance over at him and see he's serious. "You know you can't bleach blue jeans, right? You'll look like a hippie from the 70's if you do."

He glances down at his jeans that are pulled tightly around his upper thigh muscles and tilts his ankle from side to side. "You don't think I'll look good in tie-dyed jeans? I think I could pull it off."

I can't help but laugh at the image of him wearing blue and white tie-dyed jeans all while sporting his tattoos. "Yeah, I don't think it's a super macho look. You're probably better off just burning those pants tonight."

"Probably," he smirks. Leaning back, he stares at the moon shining above us. I pull my legs closer to my chest and rest my chin on my knees. We sit there in silence, the only sounds around us are the few people passing the entrance a couple of feet away.

CHAPTER 18 | 223

"What're you doing out here?" I ask, my curiosity winning me over.

"I stopped by the bar to pick up some of my payment from Matt when the bartender told me you were out here." His shoulders shrug as he continues to watch the stars. "Figured I'd see what you were doing."

"Oh." Freaking Trent, always trying to fix things.

"So, what are you doing out here? It's not exactly the most relaxing environment."

I lean back against the wall and sigh. "I was trying to just find a moment of silence away from people."

I see him eye me from the corner of my vision. "Huh. I can leave if you want me to."

I shake my head, "No, I don't mind you being here. I just wanted a break from the people in the bar."

"Hmm…" is the only thing he responds with.

"What?" I roll my eyes and wait for him to comment about how I'm not behaving normally, like everyone else has tonight.

"Nothing really. I'm just curious if you're trying to hide from the patrons or your friends."

I roll my head to the side and glare at him. "Why would you think that?"

A small smirk tugs at his lips, "Your bartender friend may have mentioned you seemed off tonight. I figured that probably pissed you off."

"I wish Trent would give it a rest. He's always trying to

fix everyone, but not everyone needs to be fixed." I do adore Trent, but I wish he'd stop trying to analyze everything. "He should be more concerned about Mia than me. I'm fine."

"Why's that?" he asks.

I debate if I should tell him more, not that he'd really care or go back and tell Mia what I said. My need to talk with someone about it wins out. "I saw her meet up with some odd guy in the alley the other night, when I asked her about it she got really defensive." I fiddle with the hem of my shirt as I avert my gaze. God, I'm a shitty friend right now. "I dunno what's going on with her, but I'm worried. She's lost a lot of weight and she's acting weird. Maybe I'm just being paranoid." But deep down I can't shake this feeling that I'm not.

"Did she say anything when you asked her about it? Anything that might put your mind at ease or explain a little of what's going on?"

I shake my head and tilt my gaze back to the sky. The moon is almost full tonight and the stars are peeking through the city haze.

Colton shifts next to me. "I wouldn't worry too much about it. Just keep an eye on her and see if things get worse."

"I guess," I mumble, not entirely thrilled with the idea. After a few more minutes of silence I push myself to standing. "I guess I should get back to work, my breaks been over for at least ten minutes now." I brush as much dirt from my jeans as I can.

He stands beside me and stretches his arms above his head. "Listen, I know we haven't exactly found our footing again, but I just wanted to make sure you had a place to stay tonight." He places his hands behind his head and closes his eyes. "Shit. What I'm trying to ask is, are you safe going back to the shelter or did you need somewhere else to stay?"

My lips curve up at his concern. "I'm thinking I'll just stay here at the bar tonight. Matt won't mind." Tense silence reigns for several seconds. I have nowhere else to stay, but I feel like it is my job to take care of myself, not his.

"Hmm..." He drops his hands and crosses them over his chest. I can see his jaw clenching as he tries to work out something in his head. With an exasperated sigh, he looks back up at me. "You can stay with me again tonight."

My eyes pop open at his suggestion. I can't stay with him. It looked like he was in pain when he asked me to and I know he's not ready for me to intrude on him anymore. "You don't need to feel like you have to take care of me. I'm completely capable of taking care of myself. It's not a big deal." I shrug. "The bar is safe and I can lock up after myself." His jaw clenches with my words as he runs his fingers through his already messy hair.

His eyes narrow and his features hardened. "I never said you couldn't take care of yourself. I'm offering you a place to stay that isn't in a secluded bar, where if something happened to you no one would know until tomorrow afternoon." His voice lowers. I can see the struggle in his eyes as he tries to stay calm. "You have two choices. Either you can stay with me and we will walk back to the hotel together."

My heart thunders in my chest as I know where he is heading with this conversation. He always was so damn stubborn. "What's option two?" I breathe.

"Or I'll stay here with you to make sure you're safe." With a cocky smirk, he leans back against the wall, giving me room to breathe. "It's up to you really. I'm fine with either option."

I release the pent-up frustration since I know he has won the battle. There's no way I'm staying in Matt's tiny office with him and honestly, I don't feel like fighting with him anymore. "Fine. I'll stay at the hotel with you, but I'm sleeping on the chair."

His smirk turns into a full-blown smile and his eyes crinkle at the edges. "Good, because I really didn't want to sleep on the hard floors at the bar. And we'll discuss sleeping arrangements later." He shrugs, ending the conversation. "You should probably get back to work. I'll meet you here at the end of your shift and we can walk back together."

A frustrated grunt rumbles at the back of my throat. "Fine. I'll see you later." I turn to head back inside while grumbling to myself. How the hell did I end up staying with him again for a second night? At that thought, my heart does a happy skip and my stomach does a flip. I glance down at my body and whisper, "Traitors."

The remainder of the evening flies by, not that there was much time left to my shift. My fifteen-minute break ended up being over thirty minutes. Thank goodness no one seemed to care I was missing for so long. Mia comes over and flops down in the chair next to me at the bar. "Hey, I'm getting ready to head back. Are you staying at the shelter tonight?"

I shake my head as I untie the apron from my waist, "No, I don't exactly feel comfortable enough to stay there anymore. I'm sorry, Mia."

Her green eyes have large bags under them as she lays her head down into her arms on the table. "I don't blame you. Do you at least have somewhere else to stay?"

"Sort of. Colton is letting me stay at the hotel again tonight." Only because he's stubborn and I didn't really want to stay at the bar. No offense to Matt, but it's freaking creepy in here at night.

"Huh. He offered you to stay there?" Her head perks up and her eyes sparkle with mischief.

"Whatever it is you're thinking, it's not like that. It about killed him to spit out the words and ask me to stay there. I think he'd rather be rid of me, but he can't stand knowing someone in danger may need help and not doing anything about it." Standing, I grab my coat from off the back of my chair and shrug it on. "He's not the same person he used to be and I'm not really sure where we're at right now. I'm just thankful to have somewhere to stay where Greg won't find me."

Mia clears her throat while staring behind my shoulder. Shit. I can feel his presence standing behind me. I groan inwardly as I try to figure out how much he just heard.

"Nice to see you again, Mia." Colton shifts next to me into view.

"You too, big guy." She hops off the barstool while grabbing her jacket. "Well, I'm out of here. Got places to go and peeps to see. You two have a goodnight." She winks at me, causing me to roll my eyes. "And Ash, if I don't hear from you by tomorrow afternoon I'm coming to find you."

"I'll be fine, Mia. Don't worry about me." I glance out the door at the dark street. "Do you want us to walk you back?"

"Nah, I'll be fine. I'm used to the walk." She heads to the front door where Trent is standing.

"I'll walk with her and make sure she gets there safe," Trent says as he holds the door open for her.

Her eyes narrow in his direction. "I don't need your protection. You don't need to bother."

He shakes his head, but doesn't move. "Yeah, well no one said you did. I'm just being a friend and making sure you're fine walking the darkened streets back to the shelter. No need to get all girly on me. Besides, it's on my way."

She huffs at him and whips the hood to her jacket over her head. "Whatever," she mutters as she brushes past him out the door.

"Have a goodnight you two," Trent calls out in exasperation as he follows her outside.

"Is she always that feisty?" Colton asks in disbelief.

I chuckle, because honestly since I've met her that's her normal attitude. It's just Mia. "Goodnight, Matt. See you later," I call out.

Matt pops his head out from the hallway. "See you. I'll close up tonight, I'm going to be working a little late. Can you just lock the front door on your way out?"

"Sure thing. Don't work too hard." I pull the key Matt gave me the other night out of my pocket. As we walk outside I slip the key into the lock securing Matt inside. The cool air brushes against my bare hands, sending a shiver up my arm. It's way too cold for this time of year. Frick. I huddle into my jacket further trying to generate more heat.

Colton is silent most of the walk back. I steal glances his way every few minutes, but he's too lost in thought to notice. I shove him with my shoulder playfully as we approach the door. "What's going on in that head of yours?"

He looks over toward me as he inserts the key into his room. We both enter, the warmth encircling us and a large shiver courses through my body. He heads over to the thermostat on the wall and turns it higher. "I'm wondering what your story is from the last several years, but I'm also worried I'm not ready to hear it yet." He sighs as he shrugs off his jacket. "I've been through war and seen grown men die out there. And this..." He waves between us. "This scares me more than that ever did."

"Colton...I'm not trying to keep secrets. You have to know that." Sitting on the edge of the bed, I prepare myself to let him in.

"Do I? Why should I know that, Ashley? I haven't seen you in ten years, which was my own fault. But at every turn, I try to help you and you refuse to give me more than a vague answer." His rage and words wash over me. He falls into the chair across from me and holds his head in his hands. Through his fingers his muffled words come out, "I know I don't deserve to be trusted. Just forget it."

The fact that he wants to forget us breaks my heart. Fine, he wants to know my story I'll give it to him. Fuck him and his aversion to feelings. With a deep breath I begin, holding nothing back in the process. "Remember that night you left me on my front steps in tears and alone?" His deep grunt is enough to let me know he remembers. "Well, I went off to college earlier than I planned. I met Greg in my Psych class my first day at school. He was charming and sweet. He made me feel comfortable on campus and took it upon himself to show me around. The moment I met him he pushed all of my thoughts of you and honestly my family out of my head." Colton glares at me as he clenches his fists against his knees. "Hey, you're the one who insisted I tell you. I tried to warn you I didn't think we were ready for this, but it's too late to stop now." I cross my arms over my chest and find the strength to continue. "As I was saying, he invaded my senses and my mind. He would call me multiple times a day to tell me he thought I was beautiful. He had flowers delivered to my dorm room along with balloons once a week just because. It seemed like a dream come true and a blessing when I didn't have to focus on the pain every waking moment."

I glance at Colton to see if he's still listening. The pain on his face and clenched fists in his hair cause my heart to speed up, anxiety trying to claw its way into my thoughts. Closing my eyes, I push the anxiety down. I have to finish this and lay it all out. "We dated steadily for 3 years, everything just seemed normal and perfect. We were the most popular couple on campus I was working towards my Psych degree and he was working on his degree in law."

"Did you graduate?" Colton interrupts.

I think back to that time, the early stages and the years after marriage. It took six years for me to obtain my Master's degree and that was with graduating early. How I even managed that during our first years of marriage is beyond me. "I did. I have a Masters in Psychology."

"That's good," he mumbles to himself.

Rolling my eyes, I continue, "After that Greg became more desperate and pushy with marriage. I wanted to wait until after we both graduated to make our studies easier, but after a few months of asking, I finally said yes." I absentmindedly rub at my ring finger where my gold band used to sit.

"The night before my wedding I found one of the notes you had written me during high school. I was reading it when Greg walked in. He ripped it out of my hands and told me I had to cut all ties to you and anyone else back home. That he loved me too much to allow a high school asshole to ruin our future. He must have forgot you were already out of the picture. He would tell me that I was beautiful and that he would give me the world. That if I left, no one else would love me as much as him." A dark chuckle slips past my lips at the irony of that statement. Greg definitely knew how to woo me. Colton shifts off the chair and begins pacing the room, intertwining his fingers behind his head in his messy hair.

"Well, you know the rest of that story, it's pretty straight forward. Greg and I married the next day. It was great for a few months and then little things started to change with him." Staring at the ceiling, I allow the memories of the screaming matches and broken glass bombard me. "He became more controlling, angrier with me over little things. One night I remember I made a chicken and overcooked it by accident. I thought he was coming home right after work and when he didn't show I left it sitting on the table thinking he'd be home any minute. Two hours later he stumbled in the door smelling like perfume and booze. When he saw the table, he sneered at the cold meat and chucked the plate across the room, shattering it against the wall. He walked out of the room without another word, leaving me there sobbing and cleaning up the shards of glass."

"Seriously?" Colton snaps. His jeans sit low on his hips from his hands tightening in his pockets, his rigid posture causes his chest to rise and fall violently with each tense breath. "You had to know that's mental abuse, you were getting a degree in psychology. Why didn't you leave?"

I sit up against the headboard and pull my legs to my chest. I should have left then, things would have probably been a lot easier if I had.

Hanging his head, Colton stands there silent for a moment and I wonder what he's going to do next. Running his hand through his hair, he closes his eyes. "I'm sorry, Ash. I won't interrupt again. Please, go ahead and finish." He clenches his jaw with each word.

My stomach flips at hearing his nickname for me slip past his lips so easily. Murmuring I continue, "Well, that went on for a few more months and continued throughout the entire relationship. He started coming home later and later smelling of other women. I had no one to turn to or talk to. I was fired from my job because of his strict rules and my own mother cut me out of her life." Colton's pacing stills. "I stayed in the house all day cleaning and trying to find things to keep myself busy. After he left for work one day I noticed his email open. I saw he had been writing another woman telling her he loved her and that she was his soul mate. It didn't hurt like I thought it would to see the messages. Actually, it solidified my decision that I had to get out. I couldn't be there anymore." Hugging my legs closer, I pull myself deeper into the memories. "I started hoarding a little bit of cash here and there from what he would give me for groceries. I was biding my time before I could leave and never look back. Then…well I had an awakening and I took off one morning. I took the little bit of money I had saved and called a cab after he left for work. I didn't know where to go so I told the driver to take me to the shelter and when the cab pulled up I almost told him never mind."

Staring at the ceiling, I'm thrust right back to a few days ago, the anger and hurt a fresh reminder. "I knew of it from when I worked at the hospital years before. I've been there for a few days now." Looking over, I watch Colton's face and wait for his reaction.

He walks over to the edge of the bed and turns on the bedside lamp, crawling across the mattress he sits next to me. He gently swipes a tear from under my eye with the pad of his thumb. I didn't realize I had been crying. His fingers trace over the still lightly bruised area. "He did this to you, didn't he?" He doesn't wait for my answer because he knows the truth. He drops his hand and scoots back against the headboard, staring at the ceiling. "Ash, is he who you were running from the other night?"

It's funny how when things get uncomfortable neither of us can look at each other. I sit there, not sure where to go from here. I told him my darkest secret and he didn't run. Telling him the truth, that Greg was there that night, makes it all seem even more real. My stomach flips, as the lie spews from my lips. "I'm not sure. There was a commotion at the shelter and I ran out of fear."

"You're not sure?" He glances down at me.

I avert my gaze so he can't see the lie about to cross my lips. "No. I don't think it was him, the fear that it could be him just caused me to run."

His shoulders relax as he releases a deep breath. "I'm glad to hear it wasn't him. Right now, I'm not sure what to tell you to do." He runs his hands down his exhausted face. "Let's get some rest. We're both exhausted and we can figure something out tomorrow." He stands to head over to the chair.

My pulse pounds in my ears and my heart is waging a war with itself. "Colton…" I wait for him to turn his attention back to me. "You can sleep in the bed if you want. It's a big bed, and I think we could share it without getting into each other's space." I trace the stitching on the comforter with my fingers to try and ease my erratic heart. Does he know I need his company right now? The thought of his response causes fear and regret to settle in my stomach.

His eyes close at my question, and a look of pain crosses his face. The silence consumes me and I want to retract my offer immediately. "I don't think that's a good idea. Get some sleep, Ash." He flips off the light and I can hear him shuffling the blankets onto the chair.

My heart sinks and tears well in my eyes. Just when I thought we made a break-through, he goes and shuts me out again. As I fight the tears that are burning my eyes, I make a silent promise to myself that I'll never depend on anyone again to help me feel safe. That thought is the last thing I remember.

CHAPTER 19

THE LIGHT FROM THE SUN PEERING THROUGH THE curtains warms my face. I go to swipe the sleep from my eyes and feel a dried spot of drool on my chin. Heat flushes my cheeks as I quickly wipe it away, I glance over at Colton and pray that he didn't see. The chair where he was sleeping is empty and the blankets are neatly folded on top. I wonder what time it is for him to be up already. The little clock on the nightstand shines 8:00 a.m. Ugh. Flopping back onto the bed I stare at the speckled ceiling. If someone would have told me a few weeks ago that I'd be sleeping in Colton's hotel room I would have laughed in their face. Then again, that would have required me to have actual friends so the chances of hearing that would have been slim.

The door handle jiggles, causing my heart to race.

The subdued anxiety I've been carrying for the last two days, now skyrockets to levels reaching DEFCON 1. I jump up in bed, ready to bolt towards the bathroom when the door swings open. I freeze like a deer in headlights as Colton strolls in holding two steaming cups of coffee.

He stops mid-step when he sees me. "It's just me, Ash."

His calm tone soothes the fear from my veins and I loosen my grip on the edge of the bed. "Sorry, I didn't know you had left." I fall back onto my knees and wrap my arms around my center to try and ground myself to the moment. I count the flowers on the hideous bedspread and repeat them in my head: one ugly red rose, two wretched vines wrapping around each other, heading towards three depressing pink carnations. The pattering of my heart evens out as I study the blanket. Whoever thought this bedspread was a good idea for décor was obviously out of their minds.

I feel Colton's presence shift next to me, and the coolness from his shadow causes a shiver to course through me. He squats down next to the bed and I avoid eye contact. He doesn't need to see me like this, he doesn't need to see how scarred I am. I trace the outline of the thorns on the vines. His warm finger slides under my chin and pulls my gaze to his. His blue eyes search for answers I already gave him. After a few seconds of neither of us talking, a slight frown tugs at the corners of his lips. He stands and the second his finger leaves my chin I ache for his touch again. My pulse races, but this time from a dash of excitement mingled in with confusion. I haven't felt this in years; my chest aches slightly and my palms are sweaty. What is this feeling called again? I wonder.

A cup of coffee is pushed into my line of sight and with shaky fingers I wrap my hand around it. "Thank you," I whisper so quietly I can barely hear it. His frown deepens, but he doesn't speak as he sips his coffee. I put the cup to my lips and the heavenly scent is almost enough to make me forget everything before this moment. My eyes close involuntarily as I take the first sip.

"So that's all I have to do to get you to relax after a panic attack? Give you a little coffee?" Colton's deep voice washes over my senses confusing me even more. "I should buy bulk in this stuff."

I open my eyes slowly. How dare he think I'm such a hot mess that he needs to buy bulk. I narrow my eyes, but relax when I see him smiling. "That's not funny."

His smile grows as he turns away to try and hide his laughter. "It's a little funny. You should have seen your face when you took the first sip. A fire could have broken out and you still would have been sitting there in your own little world as happy as could be." He rummages through his bag searching for something.

I roll my eyes and take another sip. "I doubt coffee could keep me calm during an actual emergency, but I'm not going to lie it's a great stress reliever for me."

He shakes his head, but continues to chuckle. "I see that." He pulls whatever he was looking for out of the bag and flips it in his hands inspecting it. I scoot closer to see what it is he's holding. He looks over at me and smiles, holding out a small roll of what appears to be an ace bandage like thing. "It's a hand wrap." The look on my face must have clued him in to my confusion because he continues to explain. "Fighters use it to help protect the joints in their hands. When you hit something hard you don't want to fracture anything. It's pretty easy to do, especially if you have small hands and are learning to fight."

I raise an eyebrow at that. "But you already know how to fight."

He eyes me mischievously. "Who said it's for me? It's for you."

"Me?" I squeak out. He can't be serious.

He laughs, "Don't look so scared. You're not fighting anyone. I'm taking you today to the gym with me. I'm going to teach you a few self-defense moves."

I scoot off the bed and gently take the wrap from his hands. It's lightweight and feels like a stretchable fabric.

It seems so unimportant, but the lethality behind its use frightens me. "You don't have to do that."

He takes the wrap and plops it into a small backpack along with some gym clothes and tennis shoes. "I know I don't, but I want to. It'll be good for you to learn some self-defense and how to throw a proper punch. Just in case." He shrugs. "Plus I have a class I'm teaching today so if you wanted to you could stick around for that. I'm sure some of the girls in class would enjoy having you there."

"What kind of class are you teaching? It's not for Sacred Heart is it?" I bite my lip, everything seems to be happening so fast.

"No, it's a self-defense class for a local charity here. They help teens who've been victims in the past." He peers in his bag again, rummaging through it. "The charity sets up life skills classes for them to take along with a training like mine to help them feel safer as they transition into safer environments. I teach them what to do if someone attacks them and how to get away to find help." He turns and gives me his full attention. "The main thing I teach them is to run to safety, but if they can't there's a few moves they can use to disable their attacker to get free. But they need to remember to always run from the danger." He emphasizes the last statement and I can't help but think he's directing this to me.

"I do run." I cross my arms and glare him down.

"Didn't I just tell you I ran the other day? I'm not a fool, I won't stick around if someone's trying to hurt me."

He raises his eyebrow at my words; the silence around us is deafening. "Really?" he says.

I think back on the last few years. Okay, so maybe I didn't run for the first few times, but I did eventually leave after *the incident*. But Colton doesn't know about that, and I'm not telling him just yet. "Really. I may not have run the first time things went to shit, but I did eventually run. And I've been running ever since."

His mouth opens, but closes before he says what's on his mind. He picks up my bag from the table and hands it to me. "Here, go get changed into something you can work out in. If you don't have anything don't worry, there's a store by the gym we can grab you some clothes from." He walks away, effectively ending the conversation. This is going to be a long damn day, I think to myself.

An hour later, we are both standing outside the gym doors. A new bag of, in my opinion, too expensive workout clothes sits in my hands. He insisted on buying them for me, using the fact that he sprung today's activities on me and I didn't have time to prepare for our outing. Whatever, he can pay $60 for a pair of workout pants and tank top if he's so inclined. It serves him right after our argument earlier. I am not a pushover, at least not anymore. Greg will never hurt me again. As we enter the gym, the light scent of sweat and rubber mats rushes through my nose. It's kind of soothing in an odd way, it's a reminder that I'm alive to fight another day.

"The women's lockers are through there," he points at a door located on the left side of the open gym concept. "And past the mats are the men's lockers. Let's both go change and meet over by that climbing rope hanging down against the wall."

I nod my head and walk towards the women's lockers. There's a few large rings dispersed throughout the middle of the gym, on the outskirts are stations. Some weight benches grace the right side of the gym by the men's lockers. I see some punching bags lined in a row along the far wall and jump ropes hanging next to them. This gym is not for the beginner, that's for sure. Nervousness and fear overwhelm me as I begin to realize Colton may have more of a workout in mind than I'm ready for.

After quickly changing, I head over to the hanging rope. I stare up at the ceiling; that's a long way to go using your arm strength. The rope rubs roughly through my fingers and I give a gentle tug on it.

"Trust me, that rope can hold a 350-pound man without a problem."

Hearing Colton's voice, I jump. "It looks difficult. We aren't doing this today, are we?" I glance up one last time and it solidifies my decision that there's no way in hell I'm climbing that thing, ever.

He chuckles, "No, not today at least." He starts walking over to the large sand-filled punching bags. "First, we're going to stretch then I want to see your form so we'll use the bags."

We set-up on a mat next to the bags and go through a series of stretches. I think I stretched muscles I didn't even know existed. I lie back on the mat with sweat dripping from my hair. "Are we finished? Is that the workout for the day?" I pant.

"That was just the warm-up. You haven't even started the hard part yet."

I glance up at him through narrowed eyes to see the smirk pulling at his lips. He's enjoying this a little too much. "I feel like I've ran a marathon already," I sigh.

He leans over and holds a hand out for me. "Come on, I'll help you up. You don't want to sit still for too long. You want to keep your muscles warm, there's less chance for injury that way."

I slide my sweaty palm into his and he tugs me up to my feet. They wobble like jello for a few seconds. "I don't know how you expect me to do too much, I can barely walk already."

He laughs while shaking his head. "You'll be fine. You're stronger than you think. Come over here and let's see what kind of stance you have before we get into the lesson."

I walk over next to him, wobbling every few steps,

but after a few seconds my legs relax and they feel normal once again. "What am I supposed to do?"

He positions himself directly in front of me. "Put your arms up like you're trying to block someone from hitting you."

I stand there, feet together and put my hands up on both sides of my face.

He shakes his head and circles around me. "No. First you want to make sure your feet are a little bit apart." He pushes his foot between mine and repositions them a distance from each other. "Move your right foot back some and bend slightly at the knees."

I shift at an angle and adjust my feet, making sure to keep them close to the same distance apart that he told me too. Now I'm standing at a slight angle from him, my left hip closer to him than just standing face to face. "Like this?"

"Yeah, but make sure you're not bending too much in the knees. It should feel natural, like you could just bounce in that position for quite a while from foot to foot, without getting tired. Try it."

I start off with a weak side to side bounce on my feet, and adjust my feet again to make it feel more comfortable. Once they are in the right placement, I can feel the difference. I could stand like this for a while and not feel uncomfortable.

"Good. Now let's fix those hands. Put them up again like you're going to block someone."

I place my hands by the sides of my face again. His eyes narrow in concentration and he wraps his hand around mine, closing it into a fist. He positions it down, more towards the center by the side of my mouth. He does the same to my other hand. I'm now standing in a fighting stance, just like I saw him do the other night in the ring.

"This is where you want to keep your hands, and make sure your shoulders are tight. It will give you more of a chance to block any blows to the head or face depending on which side the person is swinging at you." He stands in front of me, mimicking my stance so we look like a mirror image of each other. "If someone comes at you and swings at the right side of your head, I want you to roll to the side with your shoulder like this." He bends slightly to the side at his waist and his shoulder blocks where someone would have struck him. "Now you try."

I mimic his move and roll to the side just like he did, but I keep my feet planted for stability. "How's that?"

He smiles. "That was pretty good for your first try. I'm impressed." He shifts back into position. "Now practice the shoulder roll, but with both sides. Roll to the right, then to the left. Like this." His body rolls like it's second nature, from the right side and back to the left in one solid movement. "Keep your fists by your face to protect it and use your knees when you roll, bending them slightly. Your back heel will also pop up slightly depending on which side you go to."

I do exactly what he says and after a few tries it starts to feel like a normal movement. I shift back and forth, the burning sensation in my abs a sign I'm doing it correctly. "This is pretty easy."

"You're a fast learner. I think you'll pick up pretty quick during class." He looks over his shoulder toward the clock on the wall. "In fact, it will be starting here in ten minutes. Why don't we take a short break, grab some water, and then we should be ready for the students when they show."

We both grab our water bottles and fill them up. The sweat is dripping down my face again, but I'm starting to feel lighter. I haven't felt a single moment of worry since we started exercising. In fact, my mind felt clearer when we walked in here.

The doors open and a couple of young girls come walking in. They both have on t-shirts sporting the gym's logo and a pair of shorts. "Are they in your class?" I ask Colton.

He looks over and nods. "Yeah. There should be a few more showing up soon." He turns back to me. "Ready? Don't look so nervous, they're all pretty friendly."

I glance back at the two girls who are quietly sitting on a mat and stretching. Two boys and another two girls come walking in. None of them look older than sixteen. One of the boys is sporting a deep black eye, he turns slightly to hide it from view. "Does your class practice hitting each other?" I whisper.

"Never. Why?" He asks.

I nod towards the boy who now has his back toward us. "He has a pretty big shiner on his eye. I wasn't sure if it was from class or not."

Colton's jaw hardens as he covertly glances back. "Hmm. Let me go talk with him." He heads over and nods toward the boy. The kid jumps up and slowly follows him over to the side out of ear shot. I watch as Colton assesses the kid and tries talking with him out of concern. The care and worry is evident on his face. After a few moments, he heads back over to me. "He didn't say much, except he had a problem with someone at school. I'll talk to him more later if he's willing." He picks up a towel and his water. "Ready? You can be my partner during class."

Colton heads over and stands in front of the students. "Good afternoon. This here is Ashley, she's going to be joining us today for our lesson. I hope you all can show her the respect you show me." He has a serious look on his face, but I can see the slight smile at the corner of his mouth. No one answers him, but all six pairs of eyes land on me. "I see you're all starting your stretches, let's do those for five more minutes, then get into your defensive stance. We'll practice some blocking again," he continues.

They all resume stretching and get ready for the class. I sure hope I can keep up with them all and I hope he doesn't want to make this a daily routine. I don't think I'll make it through every day with this intense of a workout. I start stretching and get ready for the next hour of torture.

CHAPTER 20

An hour flies by and I learned more moves than I could possibly remember. There was a block, right hook, switch kicks, or was it a side kick? Anyway, I could effectively get out of a hold and block a punch now. The kids all wave bye as they head out carrying their bags. My hair is stuck to my face and I'm still breathing pretty heavy, my knees are weak and my arms feel like they may just fall off. "Well, that was fun. I'm not sure how you workout like that everyday though. I'm afraid I'd dissolve into a puddle of sweat eventually."

Colton stands in front of me and runs his fingers through his hair. "It's invigorating, actually. And after a while, you enjoy it. Your body starts to crave the endorphins it releases during a workout."

"Huh, well my body better not get used to it because

I'm not making that a habit." I roll my neck to try and get the stiffness out. I see Colton grinning at me through my lowered lashes. "You may think this is funny now, but when I can barely move tomorrow are you going to carry me to and from work? I think not."

"I would if you needed me to," he says to himself, but I hear.

My legs feel even weaker now, but it's not from the exercise. I take a sip of water and change the subject. "I know you said after the war you decided to take up fighting, but why? I mean why fighting?"

He stands there eyeing me, and I can see the internal struggle he's battling. He takes a towel and dries off his forehead while speaking, "When I was overseas, I lost a lot of good men. When I came back home, the transition to civilian life just didn't make sense to me. It was hard finding a day job when just months before I was pulling my remaining men out of a bombed Humvee." I take a deep breath to try and suck in more oxygen. His words stab right through me and the haunted look in his eyes shatters my heart. "The things I saw and people I lost replayed in my mind constantly."

"Did any of your friends make it back?" I whisper and I'm not sure if he even heard me.

He sighs. "Only two of them. But civilian life isn't easy for all of us and Josh couldn't control his demons." He swallows before continuing. "When I got the call about him, that was the night I found my way into the underground fighting ring. It was the only way I could keep myself alive at the time."

"You mean he took his own life?" Shock courses through my body.

He puts his hands behind his head and leans back with his eyes closed and I know the answer without him saying it.

My eyes fall and my heart skips a beat. He blames himself for what happened to Josh. "You have to know it's not your fault. If someone was that determined to take their own life, there's not much you could have done to stop them. He would have kept finding ways to do it. PTSD is an awful disease that a lot of men and women in our country face daily." I walk over toward him; his body is tight and rigid with each of my words. With a gentle touch of his arm, I bring his attention back to me. "Colton, PTSD can affect anyone. Even those who we look up to. It's a silent killer. You can't stop something like that by yourself, and I think Josh knew that."

His blue eyes bore into mine, searching the depths for answers to questions I'm not even sure he knows he's asking. "I know. Somewhere deep inside of me knows that. But damn is it hard to accept that I couldn't have stopped him." His shoulders heave as the emotions flicker across his features. Anger settles on his scowled face and his fists clench at his sides.

I slowly move my fingertips down to his closed fist and encircle his hand. He tenses with my touch and my heart cracks once again. This man is going to splinter my heart into so many pieces I won't even know how to start putting them back together again. "Can I suggest something?" His jaw remains clenched, but with a slight nod of the head he encourages me to proceed. "Something that can help with the anger is to breathe deeply."

He eyes me like I'm crazy with this suggestion. "I think most people know that."

A small smile curves at my lips, "Just hear me out. I know it sounds like some hippy-dippy bullshit, but if you do it right it works." I shift to stand directly in front of him. I have to tilt my head up to meet his eyes, I never realized how much of a height difference is between us. His brown hair hangs in his eyes and sweat drips from the ends. As I reach up to gently brush a strand to the side he stiffens. "I'm just going to move your hair so you can see clearly," I coax as I continue. "Okay, now look me in the eyes and with each deep breath, as you exhale I want you to name off one thing that has you so angry. It can be a feeling you have inside, something that happened, or even a person."

He eyes me curiously, but does as I suggest. With a deep breath in, he closes his eyes on the exhale and speaks, "Being oblivious to the fact that Josh was so desperate he had to take his life." His fist clenches tighter under my hands.

"Good job. Take another deep breath," I encourage.

He watches me with clouded eyes on the inhale and closes them again on the exhale. "I'm angry I let my own problems drown me and keep me from seeing that he needed me."

I gently squeeze his hand to urge him to go again.

Deep breath. "I'm angry that I could see myself in him and I understood why he did it."

My chest aches with his admission.

Another deep breath as his eyes remain closed. "I'm angry that I let myself feel so weak, that even I would have welcomed the cold barrel inside my jaw over the pain I had to fight daily."

A tear slips down his cheek and my knees wobble at the sight. I have to stay strong, for him. He needs me to stay strong while he crumbles. "Now, I want you to take a deep breath and on the exhale, explain why you're not to blame. Just trust me."

He watches me through glassy-eyes and takes a ragged breath. "I always made it known I was there for him. I called him daily to check on him. He made his own decision, and even though he knew he wasn't alone he still went through with it."

His fist loosens in my grip.

Deep breath. "I drank to fight my own demons,

which in a way is like pulling the trigger but without the immediate consequence. And even still I made sure I called him to talk every day. I even spoke to him the day he..." His words trail off as he focuses on the space behind my shoulder.

"One more time, Colton. It's okay." My voice aches as I talk over the lump in my throat. The burning sensation with each word is almost too much to bare.

With a final deep breath, he exhales. "I coped the only way I knew how and I'm thankful I found an outlet for my anger. Otherwise I would have ended up beside him in the ground. And I know that all of this anger towards myself, is actually fear of what I could have been. I saw myself in Josh and it scared me shitless." His fists unfold as he entwines his fingers with mine.

I watch through blurry lashes as his shoulders relax and the weight he's been carrying around with him slowly disappears. I don't move, I'm too scared of seeing his walls go back in place once he realizes he let me in.

"Thank you," he whispers.

I blink and let the tears fall. Swallowing past the lump I try to force the words past my lips. "I did nothing, it was all you."

He shakes his head. "No, I never would have admitted that without you helping me through." As he rakes his hand through his tousled hair it sticks straight in the air from the drying sweat. "It feels good letting some of that anger go finally," he admits.

"I can't imagine it's been easy holding that in for the last few years." As he let's go of my hand, I back away and cross my arms over my chest. The chill is starting to sink in with each passing second. My body is exhausted from the emotions whirling around us.

"No. No, it hasn't." He breathes. Turning he grabs his sweatshirt and hands it to me. "You can wear this, if you want. It'll help you warm up as we walk back to the hotel room."

The soft cotton between my fingertips gives me a sense of comfort. "We're going back to the hotel?" I glance down at the faded symbol on the front by the zipper. It's a skull with the words 'To Fight is to Live' circling around it. My fingers trace the words.

"Well, yeah. We could both use a shower and I just figured you could stay with me again." He looks to the left, avoiding eye contact. "I kind of like having you around for company. It's a nice change from my usual lifestyle."

I hold my breath with his words. "What's your usual lifestyle like?" I'm not sure I want to know the answer to this, but my brain decided to spit the words out without letting me think it through first.

He smirks. "Fighting my opponents then going back

to a quiet hotel room and fighting my inner thoughts, alone. It's nice having someone around to talk to."

It's not exactly what I was hoping for, but I can handle that for now. Friendship. Is that what this is between us? "Okay. I'll stay with you again," slips past my lips without a second thought. My brain must not want to think the consequences through, or it could be my heart doesn't. I pull his sweatshirt over my head and the instant I'm surrounded by his scent my heart sighs in content. Yup, it's definitely my heart calling the shots tonight.

Colton bends over and grabs his gym bag, without a thought he slides his hand into mine and leads me towards the door. "C'mon. Let's go get cleaned up before we smell up the gym too much."

Yes. I think to myself as his thumb rubs circles against my knuckles. Apparently, his brain isn't thinking this thing through too hard either.

CHAPTER 21

By the time we make it back to the hotel I'm exhausted. I curl up on the bed for a few moments to try and regain my energy. The last few hours I spent with Colton has been the most excitement I've had in a while. The heaviness of my eyes pulls my lids closed and the last thing I see is Colton pulling the blanket over my shoulders.

"Are you awake?" Colton's muffled voice vibrates through my dreams.

I slowly open my eyes and feel the weight of sleep hanging around me. I turn over to face him and see he's sitting at the table, papers surrounding him. "Sorry, how long was I out for?"

He smiles as he shuffles some papers into a stack.

"About an hour, I would have woken you sooner, but you were dead to the world."

I slowly inch myself up onto the bed and rub the sleep from my eyes. My muscles are screaming with the slight movement. "Holy shit am I sore."

He chuckles. "Yeah, you'll be sore for a few days after the workout. Especially if you haven't worked those muscles in a while. I placed two aspirin next to the bed for you." He nods to the nightstand where there is a glass of water and two pills sitting in a small cup for me.

I can't believe he took the time to think about me and leave me medicine for my aches and pains. I smile at his kind gesture and I can feel my heart caving to the man sitting across from me. My brain is fighting for control, but my heart is slowly hammering its way to the top. "Thank you." I quickly swallow the pills with the water.

"You're welcome." He watches me with hooded eyes and my stomach flips. Our eyes are locked, neither of us moving, just the sounds of our breathing surround us.

I bite my lip and slowly pull my gaze from his. "What are you working on over there?" I whisper, effectively breaking the cord between us.

From the corner of my eye, I see him shake his head slightly and glance back at the papers on the table. "Just some documents I have to fill out for charity." His eyes soften as he signs another form.

My nervousness fades and intrigue replaces it. "What kind of charity? The gym that you teach at?"

He shifts in his chair. "It's nothing. I just like to donate some of my winnings back into the communities I have my fights at. Nothing major."

The no big deal attitude of his makes me think it's more than he's saying. "That's really sweet of you." Every moment I spend with him, the more he surprises me. "What charity are you donating to here?"

"It's no big deal really." He places the papers in a stack and stands from the table. "If you're not too tired or sore, I was thinking we could go to something this afternoon together."

The fact he wants to spend time with me shocks me, but I try to hold back from showing it to him. The more time I spend with him, the more I feel like my old self. "I'm not too sore. What did you have in mind?"

"It's just a little surprise. I'm going to hop in the shower really fast then we can head out." He grabs his bag from the floor and heads towards the bathroom.

"I'll get dressed out here." The door shuts and all I hear is a deep sigh from behind the door before the water turns on.

Slowly standing from the bed, I walk over to where my bag is next to the table Colton was sitting at only moments before. My eyes glance at the papers on top and the word "donation" is printed in bold letters across the top page along with Sacred Heart Shelter below it. My breathing picks up and my hands start to shake as realization kicks in. I pull my eyes away, but not before my brain processes what I just read. Out of all the charities in the area, he chose the shelter I was at to donate to. A tear falls and for the first time in ten years, I feel hope. Maybe Colton doesn't hate me as much as I thought he did. With a lighter heart I get quickly dressed before he's done with his shower.

The wind stings our faces the minute we walk outside of the hotel. It's only been a few blocks and my cheeks are already becoming numb to the wind. I shove my hands into my pockets and try to get some feeling back into my fingers. "Where are we going?" I say through chattering teeth.

He hunches his shoulders to fight off the wind. "It's right up here, I didn't realize it would be this cold out." He slides his arm around my shoulder to try and have our body heat warm us both. I'm too cold to think about how he doesn't hesitate to touch me anymore. As we round the corner, a red barn-like building with no windows or signs announcing what it is stands before us.

"Finally, we're here." He drops his arm and opens the door for me. It isn't much warmer in here, but at least there's no wind. Before us is a large plexi-glass wall surrounding a stadium. I push closer to the glass and peer at the sheet of ice in the middle of the floor that glistens beneath a row of fluorescent lights. My palms become sweaty as excitement courses through my veins. How did he remember?

Colton shifts closer to stand next to me and his heat soaks through the side of my jacket. "You know, if we go out there you can see it better."

I peel my eyes away from the glass and anxiously look around for the entrance. "We can go out there?"

He chuckles and wraps his fingers through mine. "Come on, Ash." He pulls me behind him as I watch the ice, dreaming about being out there again.

It's been too many years to count since I last skated, but my body still vibrates with excitement at the idea of starting again. I had taken skating lessons as a child and every time I stepped out onto the ice I felt like a different version of myself. Of course, that all changed when I was 12 years old. During a routine, I attempted to perform an axel jump and broke the growth plate on my right leg. Apparently, a fractured growth plate takes longer to heal than we all thought and by the time I could walk without any pain it was a year later and I had given up on my dream. I haven't been out on the ice since that day, but standing here I can't wait to throw on some skates and try again.

Colton stops before me. "What do you think?" He shifts to the side to reveal a small table at the edge of the entrance. There's a few sandwiches from the local deli sitting on top and on the floor are two pairs of ice skates: one for me and one for him.

"You did all of this?" I run my fingers over the pure white skates. Picking them up, I notice the laces are fitted perfectly through the eyeholes and ready to be worn. "Colton, you put this all together?"

He sits down in the chair beside the table and grabs his skates. "It's no big deal, I just wanted to do something today that you might enjoy. You were such a good sport about class earlier, that I decided to see if they were open. Besides, I was starving so I figured we could eat while we're at it." He shrugs, like he didn't just do the kindest thing anyone has done for me in a long time.

I sit beside him and start to put my skates on too. The effort he's put into this day has my heart racing and my mind confused. I don't know what's going on between us and that scares me.

He smiles and his eyes drift off in the distance, remembering the past. "Remember when we'd pack a picnic lunch and find a quiet place to eat outdoors away from people? You always felt claustrophobic if we went to a busy area." I watch as he comes back from the memories in his mind and his eyes reach mine. "This kind of reminds me of that, there's no one around and you noticed too. When we walked in you immediately relaxed a little."

My breath hitches with the intensity of the moment.

He breaks the tension as he stands. "Let's go skate for a bit then we can eat."

I finish tying the laces and stand; my legs wobble from my uneven balance. This might be more difficult than I remember. A sudden burst of fear and uncertainty latches onto my nerves. I glance up at Colton ready to tell him maybe we should eat first, but the look of excitement in his eyes holds me back. "Let's do this," I say with a renewed determination as I slowly make my way to the entrance of the rink.

As I glide out onto the ice, my first few movements are rocky. But with a little time, my feet remember the moves and I glide across the ice with confidence.

Colton follows beside me and gives me enough room to practice. "This is fun." He skates ahead and turns around to face me. As he skates backwards, he smiles. "Show me some of those fancy moves you used to do."

His words push my fears to the side and my feet start picking up speed. The need to feel the air blowing through my hair and the ice gliding under my feet is too much. I push myself forward as fast as I can. Circling the rink, I lean as I round the corners and I imagine soft music playing in my mind. I close my eyes and feel the music in my soul as the ice scrapes beneath my skates with each move. Almost as if I had willed it into existence, a classical song caresses my ears from the speakers around us. I open my eyes and see

Colton staring at the front desk as he gives them a thumbs up. His mischievous eyes turn back to me as he watches me move fluidly across the ice. My smile spreads across my mouth as the chords to the song soak into my skin and the energy I feel has my eyes closing.

The moves from my last performance years ago start replaying in my mind and my feet follow suit. I push off into a spiral, my left leg lifted into the air behind me. As I round the corner I lower my leg and I push off into an axel jump, landing without an issue. The adrenaline pumping through my veins has my fingertips tingling and as the crescendo in the music reaches my ears I push all my hurt and anger into each move as I glide across the ice. Every spiteful word and punch ever inflicted on me is forgotten with each second passing me by. Greg forcing himself on me and the trust he destroyed in me are exercised out. As I land the twirl, I finish with a spiral and as the music's last chords come to an end so does my anger. I feel lighter and for the first time: free.

Colton's hand slides beneath my chin and lifts my gaze to his. His eyes shine with pride. "That was amazing, Ash." He stares at me, both of us breathing erratically. His finger slides against my cheek to catch a tear. As he caresses my neck, I bite my lip. He closes his eyes and leans his forehead against mine. His breath slides against my skin, sending chills down my arms.

"What are we doing, Ash?" His breathing picks up as his lips move a centimeter from mine.

The need to feel his lips against mine is overwhelming. My hands tingle and my legs feel weak from need. "I don't know, Colton. I really don't know," I whisper.

His breath fans over my cheek as his hand slides into my hair. "Since I saw you the other night, I've been fighting a battle in my heart. I'm tired of fighting this." His eyes search mine, but all he will see in return is desire and need.

"I know. So let's stop fighting it." I move closer and brush my lips against his. The spark from the gentle touch sets me on fire. I don't move, I just let them linger there out of fear. My heart picks up speed with each passing second. Please, don't let him pull away. His eyes close and he doesn't move. I lay a gentle peck against the side of his mouth, begging him to let go of his fear. With a deep inhale of breath, he pulls me tighter against him and fuses our lips together.

Desire and need rush through me and shove all my reservations out of my mind. Leaning closer, I throw all my fears and pain into the kiss--chasing the demons away. He stills for a moment, before he lets go too. His teeth scrape my bottom lip, causing tingles to shoot through my body. I can feel his hands move down my waist and he guides me off the ice. We both break the contact to quickly remove our skates. My fingers shake with need as I try to get them off with warp speed. With the last skate removed his hands find my waist as he lifts me into his arms. I wrap my legs around him as he slows the kiss and we explore each other as my back rests against the cool glass wall.

I'm not ready to break the contact with him yet. I run my hands down his chest and stop just at his hips, feeling his muscles tighten with each breath. My body wants more than just this kiss, but my mind is fighting against it. I feel his tongue swirl around mine and his hands tighten their hold on my hips to keep me in place. Any dark thoughts are pushed from my mind. He shifts closer between my legs and a small moan slips out at the pressure on my core. Grinding my hips against his, I try to ease the burning need that is consuming me inside. His weight, that first felt secure and safe, begins suffocating me. The pressure of the glass at my back holds me in place between his arms. *"Hold still, you will give me what I want. Do you hear me, bitch?" Greg sneers beside my ear.* I struggle against *his* hold, trying to push him off of me. My pulse races and spots form before my eyes with each forced breath. My hands tighten around Colton's collar as I push him off. I try to stay rooted in the moment with Colton, but my mind keeps flashing back to that awful night.

He pulls back panting, breaking our contact. "Ash. What's wrong?"

His voice breaks through and reality comes crashing back around me. I unwrap my shaking legs from his back. *How am I going to explain my reaction to him?* Bending down, I put on my shoes while I stall for an explanation.

"Please tell me what I did wrong." The raw pain in his words tear at my heart.

"You didn't do anything wrong, Colton." I lean my head back against the cool glass with my eyes closed. How did we get here? After all these years, I finally find him and I'm just a broken shell of who I used to be.

"Something happened and you can't deny it." I feel his hand cup my cheek as his thumb rubs circles along my temple. "Open your eyes, Ash. Let me in."

I squeeze my eyes tighter, hoping that he will just drop it. If I tell him the truth, he won't understand.

His fingers slow. "How about instead of telling me, we do the breathing exercise you taught me. Take a deep breath, Ash."

My eyes pop open with his words. He's watching me with cautious eyes, his hands slide down to mine as he puts a little space between us. He takes a deep inhale and I do the same. We both breathe out and as I exhale I push out my thoughts of Greg. I take another deep breath and exhale my fear of what's happening between Colton and me. With my third and final deep breath I exhale my anger with everything. "I'm sorry," I whisper.

He lets out a deep breath as his fingers intertwine

with mine, "You have nothing to be sorry for. We both let our emotions take over." He squeezes my hand. "Do you want to talk about it?"

I shake my head. "Not really."

"Okay." He runs his fingers through his hair and takes a step back, giving me some more space. "When you're ready, I'm ready to listen."

I bite my lip to stop the truth that wants to spew from my mouth. It's safer this way.

"Did you want to keep skating?" He slides his hands into his pockets and glances back out at the rink.

"I'm sorry. I just kind of want to head back to the hotel if that's okay with you." Wrapping my arms around my middle, I try to hold off the chill that's sweeping through me.

"You don't need to apologize for not wanting to do something. Never feel bad about telling me how you feel." He bends down and picks up our skates from the jumbled pile on the floor. "Let me go return these and then we'll head back. We can eat the sandwiches in the warmth of the room." His smile eases my worries. It may be tough to find our way onto stable ground together, but in this moment I know that there's nothing I want more than this.

He heads back over from turning in the skates and scoops up the food into one arm. "Ready? We better walk quick if we don't want to turn into popsicles out there." He reaches out and holds my hand like I just didn't have a mini-meltdown only moments before. His thumb runs along my wrist as we walk outside towards the hotel.

Five minutes later we enter the room shivering. The temperature dropped significantly over the last few hours. Colton grabs a pair of clean sweatpants out of his bag. "Here, why don't you change into these and then crawl on top of the bed. We can watch a movie and hopefully warm up some."

I head into the bathroom to change. I slip out of my jeans and pull his warm sweats over my chilled legs. Everything seems so normal at the moment and it's driving me to over think the entire situation. We're just two friends hanging out, we're going to watch a movie and eat sandwiches. Nothing to be stressed about. This is what friends do. I'm not so sure my internal pep talk is helping. I open the bathroom door as I toss my hair up into a bun.

"Hey, what kind of movie do you want to watch? There's a new romance movie we can order or something else you might like. I'm not sure what kind of movies you enjoy now."

I crinkle my nose at the thought of a romance movie, hell no. "How about a comedy? I could use some laughs." He chuckles and flips through the channels. One of the movie titles catches my eye. "Hey, what about that Will Ferrell movie Step Brothers? I love that movie."

He stops on the movie title and hits order. "Your choice in comedy is right up my alley. I love Will Ferrell."

Excitement courses through me as I jump onto the bed and sit cross-legged against the headboard. "Come on and sit down before it starts. You can't miss the beginning, it explains the jist of the storyline." I pat the seat next to me on the bed as I watch the opening scene.

Colton shakes his head as he grabs two paper plates with our food on them. He hands me one and sits next to me cross-legged on the bed too. "I don't think I've ever seen this movie. What's it about?" He takes a huge bite out of his sandwich as he intently watches the movie.

"You've never seen Step Brothers?" I giggle. "If I explain it, it won't be as funny when you watch it. You have to experience it going in blind. You won't regret it." I take a bite of my sandwich as we both sit there engrossed in the comedy.

An hour later, Colton busts out laughing at the scene playing on the television. "How have I lived my life without ever seeing this? It's hysterical." He chuckles again as the two characters are bickering.

"It is pretty great." I smile as I slide down on the bed some to rest my head against the pillow.

"You tired?" He glances over at me.

I shake my head, but the yawn that overtakes me shows that I'm lying. "I guess maybe a little, but I don't want to fall asleep yet."

"Why don't you get comfortable under the covers, and you can rest your eyes for a bit."

"If I do that, I'll fall asleep for sure." I smile. This is what friends do, I remind myself over the pattering of my heart.

He scoots down on the bed too and faces me while resting his head on his hand. "It's okay to fall asleep. It's been a pretty busy day."

The tightness in my chest constricts with his nearness. I prop myself up onto my hand. "What about the movie? You paid for it and it's a good movie, you can't miss the ending."

He gazes at me. "I'm not worried about that, I can watch it anytime. You shouldn't worry about that either. You need to take care of yourself."

I suck in a deep breath as he inches closer. His hand tucks a piece of hair behind my ear and electricity shoots from his fingertips onto my skin awakening me. Before I can think about it, I close the distance between us. My lips find his and I gently thank him for everything he's done for me today. For healing my heart piece by broken piece.

With a sharp inhale he pulls away. "Ash, I can wait. Don't do something you might regret."

He's not being malicious or hurtful with his words, he's sincere. Something I'm not used to. "I don't regret anything we've done today, Colton. Earlier, I...I wasn't thinking straight. I trust you. I know we have a lot to work on together still, but my feelings for you are growing and fast."

He runs the pad of his thumb across my bottom lip. "I feel the same. It's all so damn confusing, but I can't stop it."

"Then let's not. Let's just see what happens." I hold my breath, hoping he feels the same.

A low moan slips past Colton's lips as he leans over me. His need for me pushes against mine. Instead of fear like earlier, desire shoots through me. With sleep no longer on my mind, need and desire consume my entire body. I tighten my leg around his and place a gentle kiss to Colton's throat.

He stiffens over me. "Ash."

I trail kisses along is jaw line and run my hands along his chest.

He shudders under my assault, letting out a deep breath. "Are you sure you want this? I don't want to push you into anything."

"I've never wanted anything more than you right now, Colton. Take me if you want to. Please," I breathe.

Groaning, he shifts closer. "Ash, are you sure?" The pain from holding back is evident on his face.

"Yes, Colton. I'm sure." My head rolls back at the tiniest friction between our legs.

A low rumble bursts from his throat. "God, what are you doing to me?"

His lips crash into mine as he lifts my hips and pulls my sweatpants from my legs. My insides turn with each electric touch. Slipping his hands under the hem of my shirt, he pulls it free from my slick skin and frees me from all restraint.

"You are so beautiful," he moans as he traces kisses down my neck and across my chest. His stubble softly scratches my sensitive skin. Pressing into his lips I claw his back, needing him inside me.

"I need you, Colton. Now. Please," I beg.

Lifting his head, he closes the distance between us, relieving the ache between my legs and in my chest.

Rolling over, he lies next to me panting; both of us exhausted and satisfied. Colton reaches out and traces my chin with his fingertips. He watches me, waiting. I can see the questions in his eyes. The walls around my heart are slowly collapsing.

I open my lips, to ease his worries. "I'm okay, Colton. I'm better than okay."

A sad smile graces his face. "Ash, if you aren't ready to tell me everything it's okay."

Closing my eyes, I draw up the courage I need to let him in. "I'm just not ready to talk about it yet. I will eventually. Just not now. Let's just enjoy this moment."

He wraps his arm around my waist and pulls me into the crook of his arm. "Let's get some rest. There's always tomorrow." He places a gentle kiss against my forehead as I sink against his skin.

Closing my eyes, I breathe in his familiar scent. "I need you, Colton," I whisper into his chest for only me to hear.

"Get some sleep, Ash." He continues playing with my hair, causing me to drift further into unconscious bliss. As my eyes give in and sleep takes over I hear him whisper, "I need you too, Ash."

CHAPTER 22

A SOFT KNOCK AT THE DOOR WAKES US FROM A DEEP sleep. I roll to my side and glance at the clock; it's already after eleven the next day. I can't believe we sleep most of yesterday and today away. I rub the sleep from my eyes as another gentle knock rings through the room. Shuffling from the bed, I head over to the door and peek through the peephole. "It's Mia," I say to Colton who is climbing out of bed too. I pull open the door and run my fingers through my wild hair. I'm sure I look a hot mess. I glance down and notice I'm still wearing Colton's sweats from the night before and my shirt is hanging off my shoulder. I pull it back into place as I smile at Mia.

She eyes me and a smile spreads across her face like the Cheshire cat. "You didn't?" I bite my lip as heat flushes my cheeks. She claps her hands and bursts out laughing. "You, girl, work fast. I bet it was totally worth it too." She looks at Colton's shirtless body, taking it all in. He smiles uncomfortably as he searches for a shirt. Fanning herself, Mia turns to me. "Damn, girl. I'm slightly jealous of you."

I grab a t-shirt off the floor and toss it at Colton's head. "Put that on before Mia tries jumping your bones." I roll my eyes at her ridiculous attitude. It's a nice change from the moody version she's been showing lately, but still a little overdramatic even for her.

Snorting, Mia comes over and throws her arms around me in a hug. "I'm just teasing you. I'm glad to finally see the sadness gone from your eyes." She squeezes me and backs up.

Colton pulls the shirt over his head, hiding his body. Damn, I'm already craving another round with him. A small moan slips past my lips. He cocks his head with a heated look in his eyes.

"God, you two, chill it out for two minutes. I'm going to need a cold shower just watching you." Mia flops on the bed smirking.

Blushing, I pull my gaze from Colton's. "Sorry, Mia. I guess time got away from us."

"I noticed. You forgot to let me know you were okay yesterday. I didn't want to pry, but I stopped by today when it had been over 24 hours since I last saw you. I wanted to make sure you were safe." Mia looks between

Colton and I. "I can see you're better than safe at the moment. I'm glad I didn't stay up worrying all night about you two." She winks at me.

"Yes, Mia, I'm fine. I should have called the shelter to tell you I was okay. I just got a little caught up in the moment." Colton chuckles at my reference. "Anyways, I guess we should get ready. I just noticed how late it was."

Mia glances at the clock. "How about I meet you back here in forty minutes and then we can walk to work together? I missed hanging out with you yesterday."

"Yeah, that sounds good. I'll take a fast shower so we aren't late."

Snickering, Mia looks between Colton and me. "Maybe I better make it an hour." With that she heads out the door, shutting it behind her. I can hear her laughing the whole way down the hallway.

"I like her. She's a little brash, but perceptive." Colton walks over to me.

"Yeah, she's not normally so blunt." I roll my eyes.

He stops just in front of me with a wicked grin. "What do you think, Ashley Andrews, is an hour long enough?"

Jesus, he knows how to get me turned on with just a look. I close my legs and try to alleviate the pressure building between them. "Definitely."

Groaning, he reaches his arms around me and guides me to the bathroom. "Let's hurry up and get in the shower. I have an hour with you and I'm not wasting a damn moment of it." He kisses my shoulder and a shudder wracks my body.

After another round we finally clean ourselves up for the day. He wasn't exaggerating about wasting a minute. I pull my hair up into a messy bun and slip on the sweatpants since I left my clothes in the other room. Before I get dressed I need to find my phone for tonight. Searching through the twisted mess on the floor, I pull my phone out of the pile and check the screen. The battery is dead, shit. I'll have to charge it while we are at work.

"I'm going to be walking there with you two, just to be safe." Colton leaves no room for argument.

"Seriously, you don't have to do that. Mia and I have been walking there for a few days now together. I'm starting to think Greg doesn't know where I am." I toss my cell between my hands.

"Just amuse me. I'd rather be safe than…" His words trail off and the reality of what could happen encircles both of us.

"You're right. The other option isn't something I want to think about." I plug my phone into the charger.

"Honestly, I don't either." Colton throws on his shoes.

A soft knock at the door alerts me to Mia's return. I open the door before Colton gets out of the chair. Mia stands there in her Groggy Inn shirt holding her hands over her eyes. "Is it safe to open my eyes?"

I burst out laughing. "Yes, you can open your eyes." Turning, I grab my backpack off the floor. "I'm going to get dressed in the bathroom. Mia, try not to tackle Colton while I'm gone. And, Colton, be nice." I wink at them both as I leave the room; Mia rolls her eyes as she flops onto the small arm chair.

The mirror in the bathroom is still a little fogged up from our shower games. I wipe a small circle in it to look at my reflection. I'm finally starting to see a little of my old self looking back at me. The bruise is mostly gone, but best of all my eyes don't look as haunted and my face even has a slight smile to it. Pulling my eyes away, I rummage in my bag for a clean pair of work clothes. As I push the contents around, my journal falls out at my feet. My pulse picks up speed as I stare at the old memories. I snatch it up off the floor and throw it on top of my backpack. Quickly I finish getting dressed before the anxiety has time to settle in my gut. I don't want to taint the good day I'm having with the bad memories. I place Colton's sweats, that I neatly folded, on top of the counter and head back into the room. Mia is sitting in the chair with her eyes closed while Colton makes the bed.

"You do know the maid usually makes the bed, right?" I plop my bag on the table.

"Eh, I don't mind. Besides I don't let the maids clean my room until I check out. Trying to break in the sheets so they aren't so stiff is a pain in the ass." He tugs the comforter up onto the bed. I shake my head at him.

"You ready, Ash?" Mia sits up and stretches.

"Yeah, I guess as ready as I'll ever be." I shrug my shoulders and put my jacket on.

Colton grabs his sweatshirt and turns off the lights in the room, "You ladies ready? I'll walk you there." He holds the door open for us as we shuffle out of the room.

As we leave the hotel, I pay attention to the area around me. It's only a couple of blocks over from the shelter, but it looks like a completely different world. The street is busier with fancy little restaurants and shops lining the streets. The store where I bought my jacket and Mia's necklace is only four doors down from the hotel. "I didn't realize we were near that store we went to, Mia."

"Yeah, I didn't realize it either until I left the other morning. It's not too far from the bar which is nice." She pulls her coat around her tighter. The fall crisp air biting through our skin.

"What store?" Colton asks.

"We stopped in this little second-hand shop a few days ago. I got my jacket there and Mia's necklace." I hunch into my jacket further. How the hell Colton is not freezing with only a sweatshirt on is beyond me.

"I haven't really paid attention to this area besides the diners. Actually, the only other place I went was to the bar for the fight the other night." He shrugs and glances around the street, taking it all in.

"Yeah about that fight, you were pretty bad ass. You were toying with the other dude," Mia chimes in.

"I wasn't trying to be bad ass, just trying to give the other guy a chance to get a few hits in. I don't enjoy hurting others." He shrugs while sliding his hands into his sweatshirt pockets.

"I'm sure Matt will want you back again once the heat dies down. That's the biggest night of profits he's ever made. When everyone heard the Ghost might make an appearance half the town showed up. It wasn't too bad in tips either." She giggles.

Holy shit, I've never heard Mia giggle before. Maybe Colton coming back into my life was a good thing for her too. She looks a little happier.

"I'm thinking my fighting career is over, but if I ever decide to take it back up I'll keep him in mind." Colton wraps his arm around my shoulder and pulls me into him as he places a kiss on the side of my head. Smiling, he winks at me as his arm moves down to hold my hand.

"You two are so cute together." Mia sighs. "I'm glad you're retiring from fighting. Ash has had enough of the violence for a lifetime."

Sucking in a breath, my body stiffens. "Mia…"

"Shit," she mumbles.

Colton stops in the middle of the sidewalk. "Ash? You said he only hit you that once and you took off the next morning." His accusations float through the air.

"Um…. well I never said it was only once. I just said that night was the final straw." I turn to glare at Mia for her slip up. She mouths 'sorry' to me. The bar is within view and I see the moment she decides to leave me to fend for myself. She turns and walks to the bar, leaving me to deal with Colton's wrath. Traitor.

"How many times, Ash?" He slides his finger under my chin, pulling my gaze to his.

"It doesn't matter. Honestly, Colton, I'm safe now. You're here and he's out of the picture. Please, I don't want to think about it before going into work. Can we talk about it later?" Begging is my only option.

He sighs and glances down at the bar. "Yeah, but this conversation isn't over. We can't keep secrets anymore." He runs his hand through his hair. "Come on, I'll walk you to the bar. I have some things to take care of really quick, but I promise I'll come back later tonight."

"Don't be mad, Colton. You can still stay for a while at the bar," I plead. His eyes flare at my accusation.

"I'm not mad, there are things I just need to do. Come on, before you're late." He gently squeezes my hand to reassure me and walks me the rest of the way to the bar.

After a quick kiss good-bye, I head inside as Colton takes off to do who the hell knows what.

"Where's Mr. Dark and Dreamy?" Mia glances over my shoulder as I walk in alone.

I shrug off my jacket, tense and a little pissed at Colton for leaving. "I don't know. He was being evasive. He said he had some stuff to take care of." Throwing my jacket behind the counter on the rack, I snatch my apron off the counter tying it around me.

"Who's Mr. Dark and Dreamy?" Trent chimes in as I throw my mini hissy fit.

"You know that fighter the other night? The Ghost? Well, it turns out Ash here knows him." Mia fans herself.

"No way! That's so cool," Phil chimes in. He plops down at the bar fiddling with his phone. I guess the awkwardness between us was all in my head. Phil seems to be back to his aloof self already.

Rolling my eyes at Mia's obvious inability for secret keeping, I head over to the bar and grab a bottle of Jack down from the shelf. I flip over a double shot glass and fill it. Tossing back the warm liquid, I feel my anger dulling with the numbness. I throw the glass in the dirty dishes bin and place the bottle back on the counter. Without another word to the nosey twins, I head out to wait on tables.

"Shit, Mia. You pissed her off," Trent scolds.

"Dude, I didn't know Ashley could get mad. Way to go, Mia," Phil chides.

"I didn't mean to. I need to learn to keep my mouth shut." The hurt in her voice reaches my ears. I feel a little guilty for being so hard on her, but my frustrations with everything going on are too strong. I walk away and try to forget Greg, Mia's big mouth, but most importantly the foreboding dread in my stomach.

CHAPTER 23

The door to the bar swings open and a cold draft blows in with the entrance of a new customer. Don't people know how to tell time? The bar is closing shortly since it's a weekday. Mia left a while ago to head back to the shelter. Since the crowd was slow, she decided to get some rest. She looked exhausted. I had assumed I'd stay with Colton again tonight but he hasn't shown up yet. And as it gets later and later I wonder if I made a mistake in that assumption. Glancing up from the table I am clearing, I look to see who the idiot is that came in five minutes before closing. Colton stands there looking around the bar, his blue eyes fierce. My heart flutters at the sight of him and relief washes over me.

Trent moves down the bar. "Hey man, nice to see you again." He shakes Colton's hand.

"Nice to see you too, Trent." He turns and his blue gaze lands on me.

I feel the pull his body has on mine as I instantly ache to be held by him. My anger deflates the second I hear his voice. "I thought you weren't coming back. I was starting to worry."

"I told you I'd be back. It just took a little longer than I expected, I'm sorry about that." He walks over and stops inches from where I'm standing. The need in his eyes is evident and I feel the heat of his gaze wash over me.

"I'm almost finished up, then we can head out?" I move closer and close the distance between us. Wrapping my arms around him, I pull him into a warm embrace.

"Definitely," he sighs.

Pulling out of his touch, I untie my apron and finish clearing the table leaving him to stand in the middle of the room. Trent watches me with a raised eyebrow, silently asking if everything's okay. I place the tray on the counter and put my apron away. "I'm heading out, Trent. Do you mind locking up without me?"

"Nah, it's good, Ash. You okay?" He grabs the tray for me and puts it away.

"Yeah, I actually am. Thanks for checking though." Smiling, I wave to him as I grab my jacket. Colton is waiting by the door for me. He nods to Trent as we leave the bar together.

"Trent seems nice. I like that he watches out for you and Mia," he states nonchalantly.

"Yeah, he's been really helpful since I started working again. I like how he takes care of Mia, too."

"I noticed his protectiveness of her." Colton's hands are in his pockets as we walk back to the hotel.

"I think he has feelings for her, but I'm not sure. They both run so hot and cold I can't keep up." I clasp my hands together in front of me.

"Oh, he definitely likes her. Trust me. I just don't think he knows where he stands with her. Mia's a tough one to read." He chuckles as he slips his hand in mine, warming me.

"You can say that again. I'm sure one day she'll open up." I bite my cheek, at least I hope she will one day.

The heat from the room blasts over my chilled skin and the tingling warmth is a welcome feeling. "Holy shit is it cold out there." I take off my jacket and lay it on the chair.

"Why don't you change out of your clothes and get warm? You can borrow a different pair of sweatpants again if you want." Colton rummages in his bag, pulling out his pajama pants.

"It's okay. I left your sweats in the other room earlier. They're still clean, I'll just use those." I head into the bathroom and shut the door behind me, leaning against it as I contemplate everything that's happened recently. I can't believe I'm back with Colton again, if that's what this is. I'm not even sure anymore, but I'm not going to question it.

I turn on the shower just to warm up and to wash the smell of the bar off of me. Jumping in I soak up the hot water, my muscles relaxing with the heat pulsating over them. I grab the mini hotel shampoo and conditioner bottles off the ledge and lather them in my hair. After a few moments, I can't stand the wait to visit with Colton. I haven't seen him much today and we have a lot to talk about still. Turning off the water, I climb out and dry off. I throw on his sweats and t-shirt I slept in and brush my wet hair out. Glancing in the mirror, I try pump myself up for the talk we're about to have. If I want this to last, I have to trust him. That means letting him in completely. Taking a deep breath, I calm my nerves as best as I can and head out to find Colton.

His back is to me as he stands in front of the small table. "Hey, I hope you don't mind I took a quick shower. I was freezing and I wanted to wash off the smell of the bar." He doesn't move or acknowledge me. Dread settles in my stomach. "Colton, I'm sorry about earlier. I should have told you the truth from the start."

Walking around the side of the table, I glance at his face. His jaw is clenched and there is a large hole in the wall next to him. My eyes widen as I look down at the table. Sprawled out on it are the pictures from when I was admitted to the shelter. Every square inch of the photo is filled with the bruises and damage Greg inflicted on me. The journal is open to my last entry from the night before I ran. My breath hitches as my vision blurs. With shaking hands, I reach out to take the journal off the table. Colton's hand shoots out and holds down the journal before I can grab it.

"You shouldn't have looked at that." Unshed tears make my eyes sting and as I try to speak, my voice shakes.

He watches me with hard eyes. "It fell out when I moved the clothes I set on your bag. Ashley, I knew you didn't tell me the whole story. But you didn't fucking tell me he raped you," he seethes.

I back up out of instinct, my mind racing with excuses. Did I purposefully leave it out of the story? Of course I did, I knew how he'd react. Fuck! The tears race down my cheeks as a sob tears from my throat. "I... didn't want.... I di..." I hiccup and try to catch my breath between each sob that wracks my body.

His jaw clenches as he turns towards the wall. He rests his hands against it with his head hanging. His shoulders ripple with each inhale of breath, the anger rolling off of him in waves. "You didn't tell me. And I... we had made love last night. Now I understand why you freaked out at the ice rink." The hardness and distance in his voice creeps back in. The crack I hear resounding in the room is my heart completely shattering.

"I didn't want you to worry..." I sob and collapse onto the edge of the bed.

"I shouldn't have slept with you last night. Jesus, Ashley." He turns to face me and the pain is etched on his face. "I should have waited, you're obviously suffering PTSD from what that asshole did to you." His voice shakes. "And I go and have sex with you for the first time without knowing, I'm so sorry."

I cringe and pull my legs into my chest, rocking myself back and forth. I would never intentionally make him have sex with me. I wanted it too. Maybe he wouldn't have wanted it if he knew how truly fucked up I am. Maybe that's what's wrong, he's pissed I didn't tell him how damaged I really am.

"Why didn't you tell me?" He shakes his head. "Never mind. There are so many secrets between us, I'm not sure we'll ever find our way out of them." With a deep sigh he stares at the ceiling.

I hiccup as another tear rages down my cheeks. I didn't think I had any tears left in me, that I was as broken as I could get. "I didn't want to hurt you...I didn't want you to be disgusted by me." I sob.

His bloodshot eyes turn to me. He strides across the room and kneels in front of me taking my hands in his.

"I would never be disgusted by you. I'm disgusted at myself. Ash, I should have known, and we should have moved slower."

The pain in his eyes is too much for me to handle, so I turn my gaze away. "It's my fault. All of this, everything is my fault." I wave my arm around encompassing the whole room and journal. None of this would have happened had I not made the decisions I made when I married Greg. Fuck, how stupid can I be.

"Don't, don't blame yourself. Look at me please, Ashley," he pleads. But I refuse to look at him. I can't. I don't want to see myself reflected back at me in his tearful eyes. "This isn't your fault, none of this is. No one deserves to be treated that way."

I turn with hardened eyes. "Maybe I do. They say everything happens for a reason. I've fucked up pretty bad in this life." A dark snort reverberates through my body. I know I'm being spiteful for no reason, but I can't stop the words from tumbling out of my mouth. I'm just so tired of fighting, tired of people feeling sorry for me. Maybe if I stop pitying myself, they will stop too. "Maybe everything that's happened to me so far I've deserved. There's nothing any of us can do about it."

He turns his tortured gaze to mine, a silent tear streaming down his cheek. Seeing me a shell of myself on his bed, his eyes narrow. "No. You're wrong, Ashley. I won't let him get away with this. I promise you that and I don't break promises." He stands and heads to the door. Resting his hand on the doorknob, his voice hitches. "I'm sorry you feel that way, but I refuse to believe you or anyone deserves any of this." And with that he walks out of the room and out of my life.

My chest aches with each breath I take and sobs wrack my body. The numbness tingles in the tips of my fingers with lack of oxygen. Rolling onto my side, I curl up and hug my legs. "He left me…" The tears pour from my eyes. "I'm sorry, Colton. I didn't mean to lie." Closing my eyes, I pray for the pain to disappear, for the hole in my chest to loosen. I cry myself to sleep while wishing Colton would come back through the door.

Opening my eyes slowly, I look around and try to figure out where I am. My body feels sluggish and heavy like it's filled with sand. The hotel room comes into view and chases away the fog in my brain. Colton is gone. With that one thought the tears start again. I slowly sit up, fighting the urge to vomit. My head spins with the slight movement. Wiping the tears from my cheeks, I slowly stand and walk over to the table.

My journal is upside down, the pictures scattered around. Averting my eyes, I grab my bag and clothes and throw them together. I slip on a pair of jeans and my shoes in a daze. I don't want to think about anything, if I do I may not have the strength to continue. Unplugging my phone, I turn it on and place it in my bra. This is starting to feel like déjà vu, except instead of running from danger, I'm running from the only place that ever felt like home to me.

I glance around the room one last time, making sure I have everything I need. The pictures and journal can stay here; I don't want that reminder with me. Grabbing one of Colton's sweatshirts, I slide it over my head smelling his scent on it. If only I had told him sooner, none of this would have happened. "This is all your fault, Ashley." I mumble to myself. "If you weren't so fucking full of yourself and learned to let others in, you wouldn't be standing here falling apart." The words I spew envelope me, becoming my truth.

If Colton doesn't want to be around me then there's no point in me sticking around here. As I pull his sweatshirt tighter, I imagine it's his arms holding me instead. I glance at the clock: it's 3 a.m. The shelter is closed. Fuck. Grabbing my backpack, I throw it over my shoulder and remember the key I haven't given back to Matt yet. I'll stay in his office tonight and find someplace else tomorrow to stay instead. Wrapping my shaking fingers around the doorknob, I head out without a glance back leaving Colton Graves behind me.

CHAPTER 24

Sometimes we all must fall to learn how strong we truly are inside. The strength comes from within at the darkest moments of our lives; when we think we can go no further we get up and trudge ahead, battling our inner demons. As I push my feet to keep walking, I realize this is my rock bottom. I've finally found it. It wasn't the abuse or that *night*. No, it was seeing a piece of happiness and having it ripped away from me. Again.

The eerie stillness of the street sends chills down my spine. Glancing over my shoulder, I scoot closer to the edge of the buildings and try to hide in the shadows. I pick up my pace and head down the block past the empty storefronts. It's after closing time even for the bars in the area and no one is left on the streets. Pulling the sweatshirt tighter, my eyes stay focused on the sidewalk below my feet; there's only a block left before I'll be at the bar. *It's going to be okay, Ash. You're almost there. The monsters in the night won't get you.* Turning the corner, I glance up as the Groggy Inn comes into view; the windows are dark and motionless. I pull the key out of my pocket and squeeze it in my hand as my pace quickens, my chest beats rapidly with each step I take. As I slide the key into the lock I slowly turn the doorknob open and push my way inside, taking a deep breath I try to relax my nerves. I'm safe now.

I go to push the door closed with my arm, but it doesn't budge. "What the hell?" My voice carries through the dead air. I try shoving the door again, but it won't close. Pulling it all the way open, I glance at the floor to see if the rug got caught under the track preventing it from shutting. A large object is in between the door and doorframe causing it to not seal shut. Stepping forward, I kick the object to move it, only it stays in place. The faint outline of laces on the object come into view. Unable to move, I watch as it moves toward me. Following the outline of the laces, my eyes rise from the leg until finally landing on a face.

A menacing smile forms on the face I most fear and the voice of my nightmares sneers, "Well, look who we have here."

My whole world crashes around me and the fear coursing through my veins is enough to paralyze me.

That voice, the one of my nightmares is standing before me. I knew this day would eventually come, I just didn't think it would be so soon or when I was alone without help. My mouth dries, and the pounding of my heart echoes in my ears. I'm sure he can smell my fear, he always could.

"I told you I'd always find you." He steps forward and my feet stumble backwards. As he stalks toward me, I summon the courage to move as far away from him as possible. I reach behind me and feel for the bar or anything I can protect myself with.

"You thought you could run from me? You thought I would just forget about you and go on with my life?" He chuckles. "I own you, Ashley. You're mine and no one else's."

The dim lighting behind the bar lights his face as we get closer. Greg's once honey colored eyes look dark and menacing. My back bumps into the bar, causing me to let out a small whimper.

He sneers in disgust. "Look at you. You look disgusting: cowering from your own husband." He moves slowly, stalking me like prey. "Don't you have anything to say to me, Ashley? It seems you're forgetting your place."

A resolve washes over me, calming the shaking in my legs. I refuse to let him have power over me anymore; I will not let him control me again. Shaking my head, I defy his request.

His eyes flare and as his hand rises I turn my cheek. I'm two seconds too late as his hand cracks against my ear and cheekbone. Stars flash before my eyes and vomit rises in my throat. Reaching up, my fingers gently trace where he hit me and assess the damage.

"Bitch! How dare you! You owe me an apology for the shit behavior you've been displaying. You made me look like an idiot when I had to tell people you weren't home or when I had to miss work to search for my ungrateful wife who took off." The man standing before me doesn't even resemble the Greg I met ten years ago.

He paces the space before me with his hands clasped behind his back: back and forth mumbling to himself. As he's distracted, I glance around for an escape route. If I can make it to Matt's office I can lock myself in and call for help. I slowly scoot along the bar, trying to put myself behind Greg and nearer to the hallway. His crazed eyes stare blankly at the floor, unnoticing. I continue backing up almost to the entrance of the hall. *Just a few more steps.* A loud crash sounds; I stiffen as I realize I knocked over the barstool.

Greg's eyes shoot up and zero in on me. The confused look on his face disappears within seconds as he sees the hallway directly behind me. He lets out a guttural growl the moment he realizes my plan. Turning, I run with all my might down the hallway, my chest pumping faster than my legs. In three short strides he's behind me. He grabs my hair and yanks hard to stop my momentum. The force of it slams me back into his chest. The blinding pain shoots up my skull as I tumble into Greg. The force of our collision causes him to stumble backward and trip over his own feet. We are both lying on the floor dazed. I scramble to my feet and take off again towards the back stairwell. The office is too close; he will catch me before I even lock the door. Running down the stairs, I hear him climbing to his feet.

"Get back here, you bitch!" he screams. I hear the pounding of his feet getting closer.

The head start I have might be enough to lose him. Turning the corner, I run past the fighting ring and aim for the underground tunnel Mia took me through a few nights before. I can't let him find me, I know he'll kill me. A shudder rushes through me. I hear Greg stomping down the stairs as I turn the corner and plummet into the darkness of the tunnel. I slow my pace and lean against the wall, listening as I pant.

"Where are you, Ashley? I'm not going to hurt you. I just want to talk." Greg's voice is muffled from the other room. The tunnel entrance is hidden from his view; I pray he won't stumble upon it.

The eerie silence sends my heart into a panic. Taking short breaths, I throw my hand over my mouth to muffle the noise I'm making.

The sound of glass breaking shatters the silence and

it's followed by a crash and the sound of wood splintering. "Look what you made me do!" he screams as more banging and crashing sounds reach my ears.

I pull my cell phone out of my bra and grip it in my hand. Slowly, I ease my way down the hallway and the crashing becomes more distant. Flipping open the phone, I stare at the lit screen as I scroll to my contacts and hover my finger over Colton's number. Taking a deep breath, I push the call button next to his name and the phone rings in my ear. My pulse races with each ring and I worry he won't pick up.

"Hello?" he answers.

A soft sigh slips past my lips. I hold the mouthpiece closer while covering it with my other hand to muffle my voice. "Colton? It's me, Ashley."

"Ash?" he breathes out into the phone. "Listen, Ash, I'm sorry for the way I behaved earlier. I was a complete dick. I shouldn't have left. I just couldn't stand myself, I should have known." He's silent for a moment.

"Colton, I need your help." I whisper, panic rising in my voice.

"What's wrong? Ashley, where are you?" I can hear the sound of him fumbling with something through the connection.

"I'm at the bar in the tunnels. He's here, Colton. He found me." My voice cracks as the reality settles in.

"Shit! Damn it! That motherfucker! Ash, Run! I'm

coming for you. But you need to run, as fast as you can and as far away as you can." Colton's breathing picks up and I hear shuffling, it sounds like he's running.

"Colton, I'm scared. Please hurry," I say as the phone is ripped from my hand. A scream rushes out of my throat.

"Ash! Ashley!? What's wrong?" Colton's voice travels through the phone in the air, the fear evident with each word.

Greg answers his question for me, his voice threatening and low. "I'm sorry to cut this short for you, but Ashley is mine. You won't see her again."

He pushes a button on the phone and Colton's words come out loud and clear through the speakers. "You better not touch her you motherfucker! I swear to God I'll kill you if you lay another hand on her." Colton's voice comes through as cold as steel.

Greg's fist collides with my face in a sickening crack and stars burst in front of my eyes. A sob tears from my throat as the metallic taste of blood fills my mouth.

Chuckling, Greg moves the phone toward his mouth. "Oops. Too late. She's mine and don't you forget it." Greg hangs up the phone and slams it shut. "Well, well. Who would have thought your whorish self would go crawling back to Colton? I told you to end it with him years ago. Have you been cheating on me this whole time?"

He grabs my hair and pulls me up off my feet. I bite my tongue to keep from screaming in pain. My vision blurs with every movement of my head.

"Have you?" he screams while shaking me. My head slams against the wall. He's going to kill me. This is it.

"No…" I manage to muster words to try and calm him.

His grip loosens as he pulls me into him, his hard length pushing into my abdomen. I swallow down the bile rising in my throat with his touch. "I've missed you so much, baby. I'm so sorry for scaring you. Why do you make me do these things to you? If you had just listened and did what I said none of this would have happened." He rubs his hands up and down my back, rubbing small circles on the sides of my spine. I try to fight the urge to recoil from his touch.

"Can we…move out of this small hallway, Greg? It's cold and dark in here," I murmur playing to his softer side.

"Sure, baby, come on." He slides his hand into mine and pulls me along the hallway back into the area where the fighting ring is.

As we enter the open room, I take in the damage he's created. There is scattered glass across the floors from broken alcohol bottles and the stools are smashed to pieces around the room. "Come here, baby. Let me look at you."

He pulls me over to the ring and sits me against the edge. His thumb swipes along my lip and a small bloody streak is on the pad of his thumb when he pulls away. He watches me and slides his thumb into his mouth, sucking the blood.

"You taste so good, baby." His eyes close as he licks his lips.

"Greg, we should go upstairs. There's a first aid kit up there." Anything to get closer to the front door, please let him buy it. I slowly stand and move towards the stairs.

"We can stay down here, baby. Your lip is ok. Nothing a little TLC won't fix." His thick fingers wrap around my wrist, pulling me back toward him. His right hand slides under the hem of my shirt while his lips caress my neck.

Shuddering, I hold the tears at bay. "Greg, please. Let's go upstairs, I'm not feeling so well."

"Shhh, baby. Let me take care of you." He glides his hand under the waistband of my pants.

I push his hand away while turning my neck from his lips. I refuse to let this man take what's not his again. "Greg, no. Please don't."

His eyes flash with anger. "I don't like being told no, Ashley. You know that." His fingers reach out for me again as I back away.

"No, Greg. You will not touch me again." Courage

surges in my voice and I even believe the words coming out of my mouth.

He steps back with his eyebrows raised. "I haven't seen this side of you before. I like it." A smile forms on his twisted lips. "I like when you play hard to get, it turns me on and makes me want your pathetic ass even more." He circles me, slowly coming closer. I step away from him, hoping to escape. Another step backwards and my back hits a wall; he's maneuvered me into the position he wanted all along. He stalks forward and places his hands on either side of my face, trapping me in place. Pushing his knee between my legs, he forces them apart and settles between them. I reach up to try and push at his chest, but he only chuckles with my feeble attempts. I scratch and claw at his arms and wiggle my body under his to try and throw him off balance. His left arm rests on my chest as his right hand slides to the top of my pants. With the flick of his fingers he unbuttons them and lowers the zipper so he can slide his fingers under the tops of my underwear.

The tears stream freely as I plead with him, "Please…no. Get off of me." Squeezing my eyes closed, I try to picture Colton's face: anything to pull me out of reality.

The pressure on my chest lightens and his hand disappears from my underwear. Popping my eyes open, I see Greg go flying through the air and into the side of the bar. Colton's face appears before my eyes as his gentle hands lift up to the sides of my cheeks. "Ash, you're safe now. Are you okay?" His eyes roam my entire body looking for any injuries. "I promise he'll never touch you again." He brushes my hair out of my face and stares into my eyes. "Ash, I need you to listen to me. You need to go upstairs and call the police. Lock yourself in the office." He swipes the tears from my cheeks.

A quick movement catches my eye as Greg lunges for Colton's throat. "Colton!" I scream.

He turns and Greg's fist lands on his jaw. Colton's eyes flare as he circles Greg. "Ash, Go. Now," he demands as I head toward the stairs while buttoning my jeans. I hear a loud crack and glance over my shoulder to see Greg stumbling backwards. Colton continues to circle him; he looks like a predator playing with his prey. Another sharp right hook flies out and catches Greg straight in the jaw. He stumbles again, grasping onto the bar for support.

Colton's eyes flash to me as I stand frozen at the bottom of the stairs unable to take my eyes from the scene in front of me. "Go," he mouths. Greg scrambles to his feet and lunges toward me, bypassing Colton. I scream, but before Greg can reach me Colton tackles him to the ground. The shock of it all is enough for me to break out of my paralyzing fear and run up the stairs to Matt's office. Slamming the door shut behind me, I run over to his office phone to call the police.

What feels like hours later, but is only minutes, the sounds of sirens break the silence and pull me from my frantic thoughts. Rushing out of the office, I run to the front door. The officers standing there take one look at me and pull their guns from their holster.

"Ma'am, where is he?" The younger officer asks.

"They're in the basement. He's attacking Colton you have to help him." Panicked, I grab one of the other officer's arms.

"Ma'am, I'm going to ask you to wait out here with me, we'll have the paramedics look you over while they head inside. Let's head over here, okay?" he gently asks.

I must have nodded because he gently pats my hand that's still resting on his arm as he walks me away from the front door. The other two officers take off inside the bar with their guns drawn while a female paramedic comes over to my side. Her lips are moving and with the tilt of my head, I watch her. She waves a hand in front of my face and then turns to look over her shoulder. Another paramedic appears at my side, and he holds my elbow. Why is he holding my elbow? Why isn't she talking louder? I can't understand a word they are saying. I glance down at her small hand resting on my arm; she places a piece of gauze down dabbing the blood. I didn't even realize I was cut. Moving my hand, I test to see if there is any pain. The ringing in my ears grows louder, breaking through the fog in my brain. I glance up and watch the paramedic as she leads me away towards the ambulance. *No, I can't leave.* Colton's still not out. Stopping in my tracks, I pull my arm back from her grip. Her eyes widen as I turn and head back to the bar. A loud bang sounds from inside; the whole scene fast forwards in my vision.

"We need some paramedics in here now!" A voice shouts from inside.

Two more men appear from nowhere and rush into the bar carrying medical bags and a stretcher. My hand flies up, covering my mouth and a silent scream forms on my lips. Someone tugs on my arms to pull me away from the entrance, but I wiggle and swing trying to remove their hands. I have to get inside. I need to see Colton. Please let him be alive.

"Ma'am, come back here with us. We're just going to get you cleaned up a little while they're helping the others. It's going to be okay. Come on, honey," the sweet-faced female paramedic says. As she's talking, all I can picture is me pushing her out of my way to get inside.

"No, I have to see Colton. Get off of me." Panic rises in my throat. I try walking around her, but the officer from earlier blocks my path.

"Ma'am it's not safe in there right now, I can't let you

enter the building," he says, but I can see the pity in his eyes.

"Come on, dear; it's just for a few minutes. We can check on Colton shortly after we check you out. We have to make sure you're okay." The paramedic tries corralling me back again.

Tears stream down my cheeks as I stare her down. Anger sprawls down my spine and through each nerve ending. "I said no. Now back off," I seethe.

As she tries another tactic my attention is pulled to the front of the bar. The other paramedics pull a stretcher through the door and I run over to see who is being carried out. I skid to a halt as I near them. Colton is lying on the stretcher, blood covering the right side of his t-shirt. His skin a sickly white and his eyes glazed over.

"Colton?" I breathe. *No, he can't be hurt. He can't be!* "Colton! Please talk to me. I can't lose you! Please say something." I grab his clammy hand as the paramedics continue pushing him towards the ambulance.

His eyes slowly focus and they land on mine. With half a smirk, he gently squeezes my hand. "Ash." He winces in pain. "You're okay. I promised you..." He takes a deep breath. "I promised you I would keep you safe. I love you, Ash."

"Ma'am, we have to get him to the hospital. You can

talk to him there, but we need you to let go now." The male paramedic watches me with sympathy.

"What's wrong with him? Is he going to be okay?" I grip his hand tighter.

"He has a stab wound to his right side. He'll be fine if we can get him to the hospital. We'll take care of him, we promise, but you have to let us do our job." The paramedic lays a gentle hand on my shoulder.

The word stabbed swirls through my head. My hand falls from Colton's as the ambulance and stretcher spin in my view. Everything becomes blurry. He was stabbed. Stabbed and needs a hospital. Deep breaths. *Take deep breaths, Ash.*

"Can we get some help over here?" A voice calls from somewhere in the distance.

I wonder who else is hurt. I hope it's not one of the officers. This is all my fault. A hand catches me as I stumble backwards.

"Whoa, let's sit down. Take deep breaths." The person helps me sit. I watch Colton's eyes close as the door to the ambulance shuts. He has to live. He has to! Though I suck in breaths, I can't seem to get enough oxygen. Tiny black dots race towards me and block out my vision. People are talking in the background, but I ignore them, seeking solace in the darkness as they fade away.

CHAPTER 25

A FAINT BEEPING SOUND WEAVES ITS WAY THROUGH MY dreams. *I'm running—searching for Colton in a forest, surrounded by trees that block my path at each turn. I can feel the presence of evil just at my heels as the trees become farther away with each step.* Beep. Beep. *Stumbling, I grab at a branch to stop my fall.* Beep. Beep. *Colton is close; I can see his shadow just through the forest.* Beep. Beep. Beep.

The pounding in my head increases with each movement. I roll to my left side, but something pulls on my arm, which stops me from completely rolling over. Cracking open my eyelid, I peer around me; the bright white walls glare back at me and the smell of antiseptic floats through my nose, causing me to gag. Groaning, I throw an arm over my eyes to block out the light.

"Good morning, sunshine." His deep voice washes

over me breaking through the drug-induced fog in my mind.

Throwing my hand off of my face, I open my eyes to search for him. Colton sits in the chair next to the bed; his side has a bandage wrapped around it and he's cradling his arm. His deep blue eyes have deep circles under them from lack of sleep. "Colton…"

His smile doesn't reach his eyes as he assesses me with concern. "Ash, how are you feeling?" He shifts, scooting closer to my hospital bed and cringes in pain with each movement.

"Colton, why aren't you in a bed resting? You shouldn't be in here; you look like you're in pain." I sit up and the pounding in my head intensifies. Closing my eyes, I wait for the waves of nausea to pass.

His rough hand encompasses mine, his thumb rubbing small circles on my wrist. "Ash, try to stay still," he whispers. The headache eases with a few deep breaths and I slowly open my eyes. "You have a slight concussion and some bruising on your ribs. If you move it's going to make it more painful."

"How are you alive? I saw you, you were stabbed!" I panic, my voice shaking.

A slow smile curves on his lips. "Ash, it takes more than a stab wound to kill me. I wouldn't let anyone take me from this world until I knew you were safe."

"What about Greg? Is he…" My heart beats wildly

against my chest and the beeping of the monitor increases.

"Hey, hey. You're safe. Take a deep breath." Colton's hand brushes the sweat soaked hair from my forehead. "Ash, he can't hurt you anymore. He's been arrested." Closing his eyes, I watch as he battles for control. "When the officers showed up he tried attacking one and making threats. He won't hurt you anymore. I promise."

Sighing, I let out all of the pent-up fear I had been holding onto for the last ten years. All the unknowns and what if's have finally disappeared. I can live without being afraid every second of the day. "Thank you." I squeeze his hand while holding back the tears that have risen in my eyes. "I appreciate you coming for me even when you didn't want to. I don't know what would have happened if you hadn't." The words catch in my throat and I close my eyes as tears begin to fall freely down my cheeks

"What do you mean even when I didn't want to?" he asks. My eyes pop open to see him shifting closer in the chair with an intense look in his eyes. He leans over me and his right hand cups my cheek. "You listen here, Ashley Andrews. I would climb to the ends of the earth to be with you, to protect you. Don't ever say I don't want to because, Ashley, after losing you ten damn years ago, I'm not giving up that easily now that I have you in my life again. I will never let anyone hurt you again."

His voice hitches. "I'm sorry for leaving you last night, for not being there to protect you sooner. I should have been there to stop the bastard before he ever laid a hand on you. But I'm here now. I promise you I'm here to stay and you can't get rid of me that easily."

I place my hand on his arm to show my appreciation at his declaration. "Colton. It's not your responsibility to protect me. I don't want you around just to be my protector." I stare into his eyes and show him the truth behind my words. "I need you because my heart belongs to you. Can't you see that?" Squeezing his arm, I push myself closer to him just to make sure he truly hears what I'm saying. "After all these years, we still found each other again. What are the chances of that happening?" My body shakes as the realization hits me. "It's our fate, it always was."

He watches me intently, unmoving. His uninjured hand reaches out and wraps behind my head as he places his forehead to mine. The breath from his lips grazes over mine as he speaks. "Soul mates." He growls, "I should have been there sooner."

Reaching out I trace my finger over his jaw, "Colton. You can't always save me. I have to learn to save myself." His eyes harden and his mouth opens, ready to argue.

"Before you say anything, I need you to listen. I know you want to protect me and care for me. But this whole ordeal has made me realize there will be times when you won't be around and I'll have to know how to protect myself." His lips part but before he can speak I place my finger on them. "What I'm saying is, I want to keep going to your self-defense classes." I watch as confusion crosses his face. "Will you teach me how to defend myself still? You know, just in case."

A hint of a smile pulls at his lips. "You want me to teach you again?" He releases a shaky breath. "I thought you were going to tell me you needed space and you wanted to run again." A bubble of laughter escapes from his mouth. "Of course I'll teach you how. I'll teach you anything you want to know. You're stuck with me, sunshine, until the end of time if you'll keep me."

His hard lips press into mine softly, begging me to accept them. I part my lips with an exhale as his tongue enters, swirling with mine. Making me whole. I slide my hand through his hair and pull him closer, trying to meld our bodies together. Our tongues and lips pick up speed and my core heats with each lingering moment. He inhales a sharp breath, pulling his lips away and ending our connection. As he leans his forehead gently against mine his eyes close, masked with pain.

He lowers to the chair, but never lets go of my hand. As he eases into the backrest, he sighs. "Sorry, Ash. We'll have to pick up where we left off once my side is healed." He breathes out, trying to mask the pain he's in.

My breathing slows as I lay back against the bed.

The pressure behind my eyes is building again, but I don't want to say anything to make him worry. Something is still nagging at the back of my mind. "Colton, I was wondering…why did you leave the hotel room after you found out everything that happened? Did you not want me anymore after you saw how damaged I was?" I whisper my deepest fears to him. My fingers absently pick at the blanket and I try to brace myself for his answer.

He breathes out as he shifts in the chair. "Honestly? I left because I wanted to murder the son of bitch for doing that to you. I never wanted you to feel the way he made you feel again. What he did to you…" His eyes flare with anger and his hand clenches into a fist. "I left because I didn't want to scare you with my anger since you had already been through so much. I thought the best thing to do was to walk it off. I made a few calls to people I know, to see if I could locate Greg. When you called, I was heading back to the hotel to find you and apologize for leaving."

His hand finds mine as he rubs his thumb in circles on my palm. "I'm so sorry for making you think I didn't want you anymore. I will always want you. All of you, Ash. You have my heart and soul." His eyes plead with mine, begging for me to understand. "When your voice came through the line, the fear I felt was unbearable. I can't lose you, Ash. I wanted to murder him and had you not been there I probably would have. I love you."

Sucking in a breath, I watch as those three little words slip past his lips with ease. "I love you too, Colton." I try to find the words to let him know how much I truly have loved him over the years, and how much he's already saved me. Memories of the past flood through me. *I was lying on the cool tile floor in the bathroom after Greg had slapped me, I wanted to end the pain right there. I pictured Colton's blue eyes and the hope of seeing him again stopped me from wanting to end it all. The first time Greg lost his temper and he ransacked my closet pulling out all of the clothes he stated were whorish and he threw them in the fireplace burning them to a crisp. That night I laid in bed and thought of Colton taking me on a picnic lunch, his infectious laughter filling the air. But most of all I think of the night Greg raped me and the memories of Colton saved me from being shattered into a million tiny pieces.*

"I always have loved you and I always will. You saved me in more ways than you could even imagine. It's going to take time to for me to heal. I hope you'll still love me even on my bad days."

"I'll be there for the good and the bad. You won't have to fight this alone." He smiles and it takes my breath away.

"I just need to know, if we're going into this with full trust and starting over, I need to know..." I take a deep breath and hold his gaze, this one time I can't let my anxiety win. "Why did you leave me all those years ago?"

His jaw ticks, but the rest of him remains solid as a statue. Time passes by and I start to think he's never going to answer. He leans back and rubs his hand down his face. "Are you sure you want to know this Ash?" I nod, but don't say anything, fearful if I speak that the truth will shatter what's left of our hearts.

He stares at the ceiling for a moment and then turns back to me. "You have to know first, I honestly thought leaving you was what was best for you. My 17-year-old brain didn't think beyond the fact that I had to keep you safe and not burden you with my troubles." He blows out a sigh.

My hands start to feel clammy as my mind races with the possibilities of what troubles he's referring to.

CHAPTER 26

COLTON

10 YEARS BEFORE

I watch Ashley disappear from the rearview mirror as I pull out of the school parking lot. Her red pony tail sways in the breeze and my heart jumps in my chest as I put the distance between us. I wish I didn't have to lie to her, it chips away a piece of my soul every time those little lies slip past my lips.

My phone buzzes from the passenger seat and my grip tightens on the steering wheel as I hear a second buzz from another incoming text. I lift up my phone and click the read text button, cussing under my breath as soon as I see who it's from.

J: Meet up, 4:00, HLP, 40

"Shit," I chuck my phone onto the seat. Jay and his dumbass self apparently doesn't understand what the fuck "I'm done" means. When I spoke to him the other day I thought I made it pretty clear I was done with this shit. I mean I did have the weaselly little fucker pressed against the wall by the neck I don't know how much clearer I could have made it.

My fist connects with the dash, causing the radio screen to crack. Great, another shitty thing to add to my day. I snatch the phone off the seat and type out a quick reply.

Me: No. I'm out

Not even a moment after I hit send my phone vibrates in my hand.

J: No such thing. Be at Harper Lake Park or else A…

Red fills my vision as I read the meaning behind his cryptic ass texts. That little shit better not lay a hand on her. I flip on my blinker and swerve through the dead back roads of our little fucked up town towards the one place I swore I'd never step foot in again.

The ramshackle of a house comes into view from between the pine tree covered drive. The grass is growing thick beneath the well-worn path. No one's been out here in a bit, either that or they found a new way to get in without drawing attention to this place. I pull slowly down the drive looking for anything out of place, there are no cars to show someone has been here. I pull to a stop right in front of the side window.

Crossing my arms on the steering wheel, I lean forward and try to peer through the dust covered pain of glass. There doesn't seem to be any movement inside. What the hell am I doing? I lean back with my hands behind my head and stare at the roof of my car. There's a tiny heart sticker right above my seat. Ashley gave it to me when we were sophomores, before we even started dating and it's been here ever since. I wonder if she's ever noticed it before. I shake my head to try and dispel thoughts of Ashley. She doesn't deserve to be a part of my mess.

I know I should turn around, tell Jay to go screw himself, but whoever he's working for has changed hands. I don't like not knowing who has my life and potentially Ashley's in their hands. What started as a small side hustle dealing weed to kids in my class has turned into a full-blown operation with serious consequences if I get caught.

Rubbing my hand down my face, I struggle with my options. My phone buzzes across the floorboards, pulling me from my internal war. I lean across the seat and snatch it off the floor.

J: B4 you decide, go inside. You'll make the right choice after

Jay knows me too well, I suppose that's what happens when you go into business with an ex-best friend. I guess I'm doing this. The car door squeals as I push it open, encouraging me to stop and turn around. Ignoring it, I push my feet forward to keep moving and open the wooden door to the house.

The light shines through the cracks in the wood slats of the walls, specks of dust float in the air and look like golden flakes in the sunlight. All that sits in the now empty room is a single table with an object on top. The last time I was here the whole place was filled to each corner with a fully running operation: tables used to line the walls with the product being sorted by a few guys. The floorboards now have a light coating of dust across it and I wonder how Jay got this set up without disturbing the dust.

Cautiously, I move towards the table and my palms begin to shake as I eye what's on it. Lying in the middle of the table is a brown package sealed so you can't see what's inside, but that's not what's causing my lunch to make its way back up my throat. No what has my insides ready to come out my mouth are the pictures surrounding the mystery package. Pictures of Ashley are splayed out covering every inch of the table. Some of her laughing in the courtyard at school, a few of her in her yard gardening with her mom, others of her walking down random streets in town.

The one that catches my eye though, is the one circled in red with the word "collateral" written across the top. Ashley stands outside of the movie theater in her work uniform. Her arms are crossed as if she's chilled. I remember this night, it was only 4 days ago. I was running late to pick her up because I was having my little chat with Jay.

"Fucking asshole!" I scream and before I know what's happening I flip the table completely over, scattering the pictures across the room. They flurry down around me, reminders of the memories I won't get to keep after today because I won't pull her into whatever this shit is that Jay has me mixed up in. No, today is the day I take Jay and whoever his supplier is down.

I carefully grab the still intact package from the center of the floor and leave the ramshackle house one last time. My memories left scattered on the floor.

CHAPTER 27

I show up at the park a few minutes before 4 o'clock. I'm not letting Jay set me up into a trap. I slowly circle the entrance a few times looking for anything out of the ordinary, once I feel it's safe enough I pull into a parking spot across the street. I can't believe I'm doing this again. The last drop I went to, the shady jerks who showed up had me freaked out. They didn't look like the usual high school guys I usually meet. No, these were men in their late 40's, they had more hidden guns on them than an outdoor sports store has on their shelves. The bulge at both of their backs had me almost peeing in my pants when I shakily handed over the stash.

That's when I knew Jay had dragged me into something deeper than either of us were prepared for. Sitting back, I close my eyes while taking a few deep breaths. I started selling just to help out my parents when my dad was laid off from work. Of course they had no idea what the hell I was doing, and they would have beaten me into an inch of my life if they did. I lied, told them I picked up some shifts helping tutor kids after school.

In fact, I feel like that's when the lies and truths started becoming so blurred that I lost track of where reality was. Shaking my head, I pull myself from the past memories and try to focus on the present. You never want to get caught off guard, especially with this much illegal substance on you. Shit, I don't even know what's in the damn package. For all I know it could be something that could end up getting me killed.

Movement across the park catches my eye and I sit forward, trying to see what I'm about to walk into. A younger kid, if I had to guess he's about 16, sits on the park bench facing the parking lot I'm parked in. He's wearing regular clothes, but has a red wrist band wrapped around his right wrist. That's the signature our supplier wants us to use so we know who we're supposed to meet with.

This I can handle, a 16-year-old kid is probably picking up some weed for his school. That's all. I try to release my unease as I slip the red wristband around my wrist too. Opening my car door, I casually walk over to the park like I'm meeting an old friend. The kid seems a little jittery as he picks absentmindedly at his red band and looks around the park. It must be his first run.

Anger shoots through me as I think of all these kids these fuckers are dragging into this mess. This kid probably just needed the extra cash to help his family out. My grip tightens and I push it in my pocket before I freak the poor kid out more.

His eyes make contact with me as I get about ten feet away, they widen as they notice the red wristband. I force a smile on my face and fight off my irritation. "Hey, man! Long time no see," I smile and reach out to bump fists with him.

"He...hey man," he stutters.

Come on, get your shit together, kid. "Happy Birthday, dude. I can't believe you just turned 17. Man, we're getting old." I joke with him like we're long-lost brothers.

"Yeah, real old." He shoves his hand in his pockets and looks around nervously.

Shit, I'm losing him. I grab the package out of my jacket pocket and hand it to him while hugging him. "Hope you enjoy your gift, my mom picked it out."

He smiles. "Thanks, man." He puts it in his pocket. "I'm sure I'll love it."

"Well, I got to get going and pick up my little sister from dance." I hold out my hand to shake his.

His hand wraps around mine and gives a sweaty shake, and when he pulls away the money he was supposed to hide in my palm flutters to the ground. "Shit," he curses under his breath as he scrambles to grab it off the ground.

My pulse races as I see this entire drop falling off course with every passing second. "No worries, dude."

He snatches the money and shoves it into my hands as he turns and jogs away, mumbling under his breath. I stand there stunned and watch as the kid runs through the trees on the other side of the park. Shit, if Jay was here he'd be making heads roll.

"Freeze, this is the Arandale Police Department. Put your hands behind your head and turn around slowly." A loud voice booms from behind me.

I freeze and my stomach drops, my entire future flashes before my eyes. I put my hands behind my head and I turn around. I'm surrounded by half the town's police department and all of them have their guns drawn. I knew today was going to be shitty, but I had no idea it was going to be the end of my future.

I SIT IN MY CAR DOWN THE STREET AS I WATCH ASHLEY pull into her driveway. I swallow over the lump in my throat as I watch her through her window tucking her hair behind her ear. She must think I forgot about her when I didn't show up at her work tonight. My vision blurs as I turn and glance out my side window.

The shit deal the cops gave me may have saved me from a long time in prison, but it also tore Ashley right out of my life. When the cop told me I either could go to prison for selling heroin to a teen for ten years or I could become a confidential informant for them I was tempted to take the jail time. But I knew Jay and his boss would just find some other young kids life to ruin when they replaced me. I couldn't let them get away with that.

And heroin? The thought of Jay getting into that shit has me seeing red. My fist clenches around the steering wheel as I see everything I built for my life slipping through my fingers. I watch as Ashley exits her car, and my throat burns with unshed tears as I put the car into drive and pull up behind her. This is the moment that Colton Graves is officially declared dead and I don't have any say in the matter.

CHAPTER 28

ASHLEY

PRESENT DAY

Vomit weighs heavily in my throat with his confession. Drugs? I didn't see that coming at all. He never used any when we were together. "Are you serious?" I whisper.

His glossy eyes stare at me, begging me for forgiveness. "I'm so sorry, Ash."

My heart drops and my stomach does a flip at his words. He shakes his head like he's trying to rid the memory from his mind. He grimaces. "I couldn't drag you into my shit. You had your whole life ahead of you."

"Why didn't you just tell me then what happened? Why not give me the choice?" Anger surges in me with the thought of what could have been. "That wasn't your choice, it should have been mine."

He leans forward with his head in his hands. "I know. I was young and stupid. I thought I was protecting you from me."

"Colton, I would have stayed by your side. I loved you. I would have been pissed, yes. But I would have helped you get through it." I push myself up to a full sitting position and reach out for his hand. His good hand reaches out and encircles mine. "Promise me, no matter what happens between us in the future, you will always let me make my own choices. I deserve that right."

"I promise. I would never do that again. If I could go back and change it, I would." He lays a gentle kiss against my knuckles. "I love you, Ashley. I'll never leave you again."

As I sit here and watch this man before me, I see my Colton from years ago; the fun-loving, fiercely loyal, and kind-hearted boy. But I also see the man he's become: the fierce protector determined to take care of anyone he deems worthy. Smiling, I wonder what I did to deserve him by my side again. How did I ever become so lucky to have his love?

If someone would have asked me yesterday, I

wouldn't have known how to answer that question. Today, though, I realize that true love, the kind that buries deep inside your soul and stays with you through time, never leaves you. You can't outrun it and it only grows stronger each passing second. I would go through the trials and pain from the last seven years all over again if it brought me right to this very moment. I am right where I want to be and need to be, with the man I love by my side both of us fighting for each other.

THREE DAYS LATER AND WE ARE BOTH FINALLY RELEASED. Sitting in the hotel room, I watch as Colton packs his few belongings, stopping every few seconds to relax his side. He refuses any help I offer, saying I need my rest. So, since he's being a stubborn ass I'm sitting on the bed flipping through a magazine and pretending to read.

A soft knock sounds at the door and pulls me from the latest celebrity drama. Since Greg's been in jail I feel a little more at ease but I still become jumpy with any unexpected visitors, fearing the person on the other side of door. I peek through the peephole and see a mass of blonde and blue hair. Smiling, I swing open the door and watch as Mia fidgets with her sweatshirt sleeves. Her eyes dart from my face to the hallway behind her every few seconds.

"Hey, Mia. You okay?" My smile falters at her nervous behavior.

Turning, her tired, shadowed eyes stand out starkly against her sunken cheekbones. Biting her lip, she continues picking at her shirt sleeves. "Hey, I just thought I heard something that's all. I'm a little jumpier these days since…you know." She nods at my bruised face and starts peering over her shoulder again.

I step back and open the door more to allow her entrance to the room. She shuffles through the opening and glances around seemingly unable to focus on anything in particular. "Thanks. I just wanted to see you before you guys took off. I just didn't want you to leave without saying goodbye."

I gently close the door and watch her sit in the chair. She perches on the edge of the seat, ready to bolt any minute. "I wouldn't leave without saying goodbye, Mia. Trust me, you have been my saving grace these last few days." I try to reassure her. Colton stills with packing his bags and cocks his head towards Mia, a frown playing on his lips.

"Yeah, well I just wanted to let you know I'm going to miss you, especially at work." Staring off into space, she smirks. "Who's going to give Matt a run for his money with me? We all are going to miss you." She glances down at her hands clasped in her lap and her smile falters.

"Hey, you know I am coming back right? We're only leaving for a few weeks to visit Colton's family. Once things settle down and we find a place, we'll be back. I wouldn't leave you. You're my family now, there's no changing that." Sitting on the chair next to her, I place my hand over hers.

Her distant gaze lifts to mine and I see the hopelessness in her eyes. "I know, but sometimes people say they're coming back and they don't." Shrugging, she stands, causing my hand to fall to my side.

"You don't have to leave so soon, Mia. We can all go grab some lunch together." Standing myself, I rub my hands on my jeans: a nervous habit I can't seem to break.

Colton stands beside me, his hand gently lying against my back. "Not to intrude, but I think it would be a great idea if we all went out for lunch. I know I'm pretty hungry myself," he encourages.

Biting her lip, Mia's inner turmoil plays across her face. "It's okay, I have to get to the bar anyhow. I told Matt I would come in early and help get the schedules figured out for next week." She briskly walks over to me and wraps her arms around me in a desperate hug.

As I wrap my arms around her, I can feel her bones through the material of her shirt and my brain screams at me to question her. But my heart holds back, knowing that if I push her too fast she will run from me and I don't want to lose her. "Mia, I'm only a phone call away. Please promise me if you need me you will call." I squeeze her tightly, trying to let her know how much she means to me.

Her arms tighten as she nods her head into my shoulder in agreement. Whispering for only me to hear, "I don't want to lose you and I thought I had. Take care of yourself, Ash. I can't lose you." Pulling back, her haunted eyes turn toward the door.

A soft sob floats out of me as she opens the door. "Mia, I'll be back. I promise you that." She doesn't turn around, just nods while softly closing the door behind her. Tears slowly flow as my heart breaks with her exit.

Colton's hand rubs circles on my back, but even that can't ease the cold, hard stone of fear that has settled in my gut. "Baby, she's going to be okay. You know Mia; she's a tough girl. She's just shaken up a bit." Brushing a strand of hair behind my ear, he cups my cheek and raises my eyes to meet his. "If it makes you feel better I'll try to see what's going on with her. I have a few friends around here; I'll get the word out to keep an eye on her. I promise you, Ash, we'll come back as soon as we can. As soon as we find a house we'll be right back in this town. We won't be gone for long and you can be near Mia again."

The sincerity in his words calms my rapidly beating heart. Maybe he's right; maybe she is just shaken up. Since I met Mia she has always held her emotions at bay, never letting anyone see how she's truly feeling. It might have finally caught up to her and she just needs time to heal. That's what it is: she needs time to heal. But even as the words sound in my head, I know in my heart they couldn't be further from the truth.

EPILOGUE

1 YEAR LATER

I can't believe how much my life has changed in just the last few months; the nightmare is finally coming to an end and our lives are heading onto a better path. I watch Colton who is deep in conversation with his parents next to the barbeque in our backyard. His head falls back with a burst of laughter and his eyes twinkle from something his father said. A slight smile curves at my lips. I've noticed this has been happening more frequently, my lips curving upwards with something Colton does. I feel a part of me is finally falling back into place and is allowing me to feel happiness again.

His blue eyes meet mine from across the yard and my body stirs in reaction. The need for my husband's touch is insatiable, every waking moment I crave his body against mine. My husband. I'll never tire of hearing those two words. The day he left me he thought he was making the right decision. The need to protect me outweighed his better judgment. With the years that followed, there were many days I felt like my life had ended. Perhaps we both felt that way. Colton told me not long ago that every time he stepped into the ring he prayed someone would end his misery for him. A shudder courses down my spine at the thought of him playing Russian Roulette with his life. Then when we were both at rock bottom, he came spiraling back into my life. My eyes landed on his and I knew from that moment on nothing would ever be the same again.

Mia flops down in the chair on the porch next to me. "Thanks for inviting me, Ash."

"You're welcome. It's been a while since you've been around. Everything okay?" I watch her intently, waiting for her to finally open up to me. Tell me the truth.

Blowing out a deep sigh, she shifts in her chair. "Yeah, it's just been busy at the bar. Matt hired a new girl and she's completely ditzy. She can't get a single order right and is late almost every day. It's driving me nuts that he won't just fire her."

Ever since I left the bar, Matt has started hiring a few more women. He realized the girls had begun to bring in more of a younger crowd and that helped out his profits. "Why is he keeping her on?"

Mia rolls her eyes and stares at something across the yard. "You know Matt. He feels bad for them so he lets them stay. It's fucking annoying."

Colton's shoes come into view in front of us. "Jesus, Mia. Watch your language."

A deep voice chuckles beside him. I take in the man next to Colton. He's wearing jeans with a tight black t-shirt and motorcycle boots. His arms are straining against the shirt sleeves and are covered in tattoos. He has disheveled dark brown hair that looks messy, probably from wearing a helmet. His deep green eyes pop from his tan skin as he eyes Mia. Glancing over, I notice his good looks were not missed by Mia. She's staring at him with a slack jaw and is completely speechless for the first time. "Who's your friend, Colton?" I break the silence and try to give Mia time to wipe the drool from her mouth.

"Jackson, this is my wife, Ashley and her best friend Mia."

Jackson holds out his hand and I slip mine between his with a firm shake. "Nice to meet you, Jackson. I thought I'd met most of Colton's friends."

A bright smile spreads across his face, revealing perfectly straight teeth. "I've known Colton for quite a while, we just haven't seen each other in a few years. I happened to run into him a few weeks ago. It's nice to meet you." His eyes wander back to Mia who is now sitting up straight and glaring at him.

Mia eyes him up and down without saying a word.

"It's nice to meet you too, Mia. I've heard a lot about you both." Jackson holds his hand out to her.

I watch as she debates on how to react to him. Her face settles and her shoulders relax the moment she decides to let her guard down. "Nice to meet you too." She slips her hand into his and immediately pulls away. "Do you ride a bike?" She nods to his boots.

"You have an observant eye." He chuckles. "I ride a Harley." He runs his fingers through his hair, making it even more disheveled. "I came over right after work and forgot to bring a hat that would cover up my helmet hair. Is it that noticeable?"

A small smile tugs at the corner of her lips. "A Harley, huh? You mind showing me it? My dad used to own a 1980 Harley Davidson Sportster."

"That's a classic. I wouldn't mind, we can look at it now before dinner. It's parked out front." Jackson holds out his hand to help Mia from the chair.

She slips her hand into his and stands. Hesitating, she turns around and stares at me with wide eyes. A smile tugs at my lips and I nod at her, trying to encourage her to go. With a deep breath, she follows Jackson out front. In those few minutes with Jackson, I saw a little bit of the old Mia come back. My heart aches from missing that side of her for so long.

A warm hand brushes through my hair, pulling me out of my thoughts. Closing my eyes, I picture him underneath of me as I relieve the ache built up between my legs.

"Ash, baby. Dinner is almost ready." His warm breath caresses my ear. Shifting in my seat I try to ease the need before anyone notices. A low chuckle vibrates against my neck. "If you keep moving like that and moaning our guests are going to start to notice." His nose nuzzles under my ear.

My breathing speeds up as I try to regain control, but am quickly losing the battle. *Baseball, balloons, ankle biter dogs.* Shit, anything to get my mind off of him. "Colton." Another involuntary moan slips past my lips. I trail my eyes down his toned body, his t-shirt pulled tightly against his arms. His heated stare trails over my body in return. My tongue darts out to wet my lips and I swallow, trying to relieve the dryness in my mouth. *Is it hot out here?*

A low rumble flies past his lips. "Ash, we can't. If you keep this up, I'm going to carry you upstairs and everyone will notice. I don't think you want that."

My eyes widen with his threat and the thought makes me more excited. "I don't know, it could be kind of fun sneaking around like teens again." I watch him intently, begging him to challenge me. I slide my tongue slowly across my lips as I stand from the chair. I peer behind his shoulder and notice no one is paying a bit of attention to us. I'm not sure how they haven't noticed. I feel like I'm burning up with the heat we are projecting. Backing up towards the sliding glass doors to the house, I pull my bottom lip between my teeth. Colton's eyes harden and his chest rises and falls faster with each passing second.

He moves forward and a slow smile spreads across his lips. My heart thunders in my chest and my eyes widen, I know exactly what he's up to. Colton calls out over his shoulder, "Mom, can you keep an eye on dinner? I have some things I need to discuss with Ashley for a few minutes."

Redness flushes through my heated cheeks with his words; I walk into the house and my eyes never waver from his.

"Shit, you two. Get a damn room, the looks you two are giving each other are nauseating." Mia's sarcastic voice rings out as she enters the room.

Rolling his eyes, Colton follows me into the house and out of the view of others. As we turn the corner, he slips his arms around my waist and hauls me over his shoulder. I giggle as he takes the steps two at a time. He shuts the bedroom door behind us, flipping the lock. I can feel him slowly stalk towards the bed as he gently lays me down sprawled out in front of him.

EPILOGUE

Inching forward he steps between my legs and spreads them with his knees. My heart jumps in my chest, I can't believe he's finally mine. His broad chest ripples as he pulls his shirt over his head. His finger gently strokes over my t-shirt. I close my eyes and arch my back, pushing my chest against him.

"Colton…" I sigh.

Closing my eyes, I imagine his soft lips encompassing me and a shiver roams down my spine. Glancing at him under my lowered lids I slowly lift my shirt over my head and toss it on the bed next to us.

It took us six months after the confrontation with Greg for me to even let Colton touch me without jumping from fear. As time went on and a few therapy sessions later, Colton owns my whole heart and body. I curl my finger at him, letting him know I'm ready.

Many moments later, we both fall apart panting. With a deep sigh, I roll over and lay my head on his chest. My body is still lightly convulsing from the release moments before.

"Hmm." He places a kiss against my temple. His hand slips under my chin and pulls my eyes to his. "I can't seem to get enough of you, Mrs. Graves." I close my eyes with his words and he places a small kiss against each of my eyelids.

"Well, right now we need to get back to our guests.

We don't have time for round two, Mr. Graves." I nip at his earlobe.

"If you keep that up we'll be here all night and our guests can let themselves out." He rolls over in one swift movement and pulls me on top of him again.

His hands move my hips against him and a soft giggle escapes my lips. "Stop, Colton. We have to get back down there. Stop goofing off, you sex fiend." Slapping him playfully, I scoot off of him before he has time to convince me to stay in bed with him. I turn my back and pick up the clothes that are scattered around the room. I slip my arms into my bra and slide my panties up my legs. I can feel his eyes on me, so stooping down I grab his jeans off the floor and toss them at him.

With a smirk, Colton stands and slips his clothes on. I know we have to show our faces downstairs; even if we'd both rather stay up here for another few hours. "You win for now, but just wait until our guests leave." He lays a gentle kiss on my cheek, causing me to blush.

Shaking my head, I head down the staircase. "I like the sound of that."

"Well, well, well. Where did you two run off to?" Mia smirks while throwing her feet up on the coffee table. Her pale skin looks even lighter these days with the dark circles under her eyes more prominent. Her eyes have become lifeless over the last few months and instead of the optimistic Mia I once knew, all I see is vengeful and spiteful Mia. With her drastic changes, I had asked Colton to do so some digging and see what she's been getting into in her spare time. I left out the issue I stumbled upon before our lives were destroyed by Greg; I should have been a better friend and made her show me what was in that envelope that night. There's something going on with her and I'm waiting for Colton to get up the courage to tell me what it is. His eyes grow darker and angrier every time he sees her. If whatever he found out is causing that reaction with him, I can see why he hasn't told me yet. Colton walks over and pushes her feet off of the table and onto the floor with a thud. She sticks her tongue out at him as a smile creases his lips.

"Now, Mia, Colton and Ashley were apart so long it's only natural for them to want to make up for lost time. Even if it is during the most awkward times." Colton's mother stares him down from across the table.

"Jesus, Mom." Colton's face pales. He sits down across from Jackson and gives his mom a wide berth.

Heat rushes to my cheeks as all eyes land on me. My lip pulls into my mouth and I rub my hands on my shorts. "I'm going to check on dinner." I head into the kitchen and the door swings closed behind me. The closer Colton gets to his mom the more she nags on him about domestic life. I personally think Colton has the whole marriage thing down, but I guess moms always know more than us. She gives him advice on how to take care of me, paint colors for our new house, and worst of all, sex advice. I head back into the room, carrying a plate full of chicken.

"Do not take the Lord's name in vain, Colton. I raised you better than that. Ashley, you have my permission to slap my boy if he forgets his manners." Crossing her hands in her lap, his mom sits up a little straighter.

"Oh, I will, Mrs. G. I promise I'll keep him in line."

"Baby, let me help you with that." Jumping up, Colton rushes over and takes the plate from me. After I wink at him, I head back into the kitchen to grab the rest of the food.

I sweep back into the room carrying the last of the bowls and I place them on the table. "Come on, everyone, dinner's ready." My hands fidget with my apron and my pulse increases with each passing second.

Colton walks over and places a kiss to my forehead. "What's wrong, Ash? You look stressed." He whispers into my ear.

I glance up at him and a small smile curves my lips. "Nothing, I'm fine. Have a seat so we can all eat." I untie my apron and move from his arms, avoiding his gaze.

He cautiously watches me fidget with anything I can get my hands on. The rest of our family comes in from the patio and sits around the table. His mother and father take the seats next to me, my mom sits at the end of the table, Jackson sits next to my mom, Mia next to him, and next to Mia is Colton at the head of the table. I watch my family and friend's chatter amongst themselves and laughing with each other.

"Let's dig in." I grab the plate with the chicken on it and pass it down the table followed by the side dishes. Once we all have our food on our plates we make small talk and joke with each other. The dinner goes well; even Mia seems a little happier as she chuckles at something Jackson said. Colton's mom throws her head back in a deep laugh.

"What's so funny?" Colton eyes us all curiously.

"Oh, honey, remember when you were eight you thought you could actually fly? You used to run around the house with just a little pair of whitie tighties on and a blanket tied around your neck. You'd climb on top of the sofa and lunge off of it onto the cushions you placed on the floor as a barrier. You were so adorable and determined. I was just talking to your father about that and how it took almost a year for us to convince you that you couldn't fly." His mother gazes off into the distance, the memory no doubt playing vividly in her head.

"Hey, I really thought I could fly. And I never wore clothes because in my head the weight of them would hold me down. You never see birds wearing clothes while flying, do you?" Colton chuckles while stabbing a carrot with his fork. As he pops it into his mouth, my stomach somersaults with nervousness.

"I bet he kept you all on your toes when he was kid." I smile. I wrap my hand around Colton's on the table and absentmindedly stroke his palm with my thumb.

"I was a pretty big handful, but I enjoyed it." He squeezes my hand and smiles at his mother and father.

Scooting my chair back from the table, I place my napkin down and interrupt their moment. "Anyone want dessert? Let me go grab the cake." Colton starts to stand to help me, but Mia taps him on the shoulder, shaking her head. She follows me into the kitchen. Leaning against the door, I take a few deep breaths. Mia doesn't say a word while I try to get my emotions under control. I can hear the conversations in the other room still.

"What's going on with Ashley?" My mother chimes in with concern.

"I'm sure she's just nervous since it's the first time you've all been in the same room since the wedding a few months ago. You know how she gets with big things like this; she wants things to go smoothly." Colton tries to ease her concerns, but I can hear the nervousness in his voice.

My mother takes a deep breath. "You're probably right. And with the trial happening in a few weeks she's probably nervous about that too."

I clench my fist against my leg at the mention of Greg's trial. I know it's coming soon and I will have to testify, but I am trying to not think about it tonight. Each day I've been driving myself insane worrying about the outcome of the trial and what will happen if he goes free. Colton tries to console me, but no matter how hard he tries I still worry and cry myself to sleep in his arms.

"You're probably right, but let's not talk about that in front of her tonight though." Colton clears his throat.

I glance down and notice my clenched fingers turning red in my hands.

"You're right. I won't bring it up again," my mother murmurs.

Grabbing the cake, I head back into the room hoping to stop the conversation. "Bring what up?" Mia follows me without saying a word and carries clean plates for everyone.

"Nothing, honey, we were talking politics. You know how feisty my dad gets with all that." Colton smiles at me. Everyone else at the table nods in agreement.

If that's the out he wants to go with, it works for me. "Oh. Yeah, mom, politics and golf are good topics to avoid with Mr. Graves." I wink at his father and everyone laughs. He really does get quite heated with both topics. I've had to split up a few arguments between him and Colton a few times. My fingers shake as I cut the cake and hand each person a plate. When I hand Colton his he just stares at it for a moment. I usually make a yellow cake with Chocolate icing which is Colton's favorite, but this cake is pink inside with the chocolate icing on top. I glance up at everyone else and they are all staring at the cake the same as Colton.

"What flavor is this cake?" My mother asks as she takes a small bite.

I wring my hands around the spoon I'm holding. "It's yellow cake I just added a little dye to it."

"It tastes good." Colton's father gives his approval as he takes a gigantic bite.

Mia nudges me. Colton's eyes move between Mia and me. He places his plate down on the table and takes a small bite. "Why did you add food coloring to the cake mix?"

"Umm…because…" I shuffle my feet while biting my lip. Shit, I just had sex in my house while everyone else was downstairs and I can't get more than two words past my lips!

"Ash, what's wrong?" He starts to push his chair back.

I raise my hand and clear my throat while pulling my shoulders back. I brace myself for whatever reactions I'm about to get. "Everyone, I have an announcement to make. I'm expecting."

His mother squeals and my mother gasps. Colton watches me confused waiting for the rest of my sentence. "What are you expecting, baby? Did you get some news that we don't know about?" I watch as he tries to figure out what I said.

"Jesus, Colton. She's expecting means she's pregnant, you daft idiot." Mia snorts.

All the sound in the room fades out as Colton and I stare at each other. The moment Mia's words sink in, his eyes widen in surprise. "We're having a baby?" he whispers.

I nod while continuing to fidget with the spoon.

"Thank you, God! Yes, we're having a baby!" Colton yells and jumps out of his seat. He wraps his arms around me and twirls me around in excitement. All the nerves and fear of his reaction slip away. I don't know why I was so worried. He places his hand on my stomach, "We're really having a baby?" he whispers in shock.

I shake my head while happy tears trail down my cheeks. "Yes, we're really having a baby," I breathe. A baby that we made. I wonder if it will have my looks or his blue eyes.

"Is it a boy or girl? Do you know yet? Why didn't you tell me sooner?" His hands cradle my face as he plants kisses along my cheeks and nose.

"Colton, I only found out the other day. I would have told you sooner, but I wanted to tell everyone together. I couldn't get up the nerve to tell you. I was afraid you'd be upset." My grip tightens on his shirt.

"I would never be upset. I'm ecstatic. I've been wanting to start a family, I just wasn't sure if you were ready. How are you handling this?" He eyes me, the excitement shining through his worry.

"Me?" I look down at my stomach where his hand rests. A piece of both of us now sits inside of me. "I never thought I could be happier with my life, until I found out I was pregnant. This," I rub my hand over his. "This baby is something I can't imagine living without. I feel whole."

He lifts me in a gentle bear hug. "I do too."

I squeeze him and for the first time tonight I relax. There's no more running, no more crying over things I can't control, only the three of us exist in my world and we are going to defeat everything.

His mother's joy breaks the silence. "Oh my goodness, I'm going to be a Grandma! Oh, congratulations you two."

Colton sets me down and we turn to face our family.

"Congratulations, son. You've finally become the man I knew you could be." His father sits back with a proud smile.

"I guess the kid can call me Aunt Mia. I mean I don't do well with kids, but if it's yours, Ash, I'm sure we'll get along just fine." She shrugs while crossing her arms.

I pull out of Colton's arms and wrap mine around Mia. "The baby will love you, Mia. Whether it's a boy or girl, they will see the Mia I know and love. She's still in there you know, the happy Mia." She blushes while wrapping her arms around me in a return hug.

"Congrats, Bud. You're going to make a great dad," Jackson says.

I glance down at the end of the table where my mother sits. I worry about how she's going to react. We've only been back in each other's lives a few weeks and things have been rocky. She sits there with her hands in her lap a small tear trailing down her cheek. She pushes from the table and glides over to me as I pull back from Mia's hug. My hands start fiddling with my jeans pocket. We both stand there silently watching each other for a few seconds.

My mother sighs. "Ashley, I am so happy for you. I know you will make a better mother than I ever could." She slides her hand over her skirt, wiping away imaginary wrinkles. "If you'll let me I'd like to be a better grandmother and to make up for everything I did wrong for you."

I watch my mother silently, and memories of our estranged relationship float to the surface. I can say I honestly believe that she is telling the truth and she will try harder. Colton moves next to my side and slips his arm around my shoulder, giving me the strength I need. With his touch, I pull back my shoulders. "Mother, I would love for you to be in your grandchild's life. I think you will make a wonderful grandmother even if we did have our ups and downs. I believe we can all change if we want to."

Her lips pull up at the corners, the most I've ever seen her smile. "Yes, we can change if we want to. I truly do wish to change and I will prove it to you that I can."

Pulling my mother into a hug, I say with excitement, "I'm having a baby!"

"We're having a baby," Colton cheers.

As I watch our family and friends flock around us in excitement I am amazed at my own strength. Most people would have given up and let their tortured pasts tear them down, permanently shattering their souls. But I didn't. I fought with determination to claw my way out of the pits of hell only to emerge even stronger on the other side. This is the moment I realize I have to forgive someone who doesn't know what they did was wrong for me to be able to heal. I release my anger and hatred; only love and hope stay. And now, our family is growing by another precious life and I only hope that I can protect my new baby in the future: to shield them from any evil.

A person's life doesn't always go as planned, but as long as we keep fighting there is hope in this world for us to survive. I guess this really is kismet, our lives becoming one and creating a new family to love.

The End

NOTE FROM THE AUTHOR

If you or someone you know are a victim of domestic violence, please reach out for help. You are never alone. Below are the links for Domestic Violence resources and the Domestic Violence Hotline.

The National Domestic Violence Hotline
1-800-799-7233 (SAFE)
www.ndvh.org

Domestic violence resources:
https://ncadv.org/resources

ACKNOWLEDGMENTS

Writing a book is hard. Whoever thinks it is easy, please tell me your secrets. After 3 years of hard work, tears, and a dozen cups of coffee I have finally finished this story. But over the last three years, none of this would have been possible without the help of a lot of people and an amazing Indie community.

My family. Thank you for bearing with me on the late nights I sat huddled in a corner with headphones on, ignoring the messy rooms and dirty dishes around me. There were a lot of nights we ate leftovers or takeout just so I could finish a chapter that wouldn't stop talking to me. I love you both for dealing with me and my crazy writer life.

Jess C. Thank you for being there for me all these years. You are my other piece to my puzzle, two crazy peas in a pod. I'm so thankful for having a great friend like you and I hope to be two old ladies in a nursing home together raising hell with the young nurses.

Amanda Michelle. Thank you for always being there when I felt I couldn't go on with this book journey. There were times I wanted to throw in the towel and you pulled me out. You reminded me why I started writing in the first place. For my love of it. Thank you for being you!

Katrina Crane. Thank you for your patience with me as I asked tons of questions and advice from you throughout this entire process. Your editing suggestions and grammar fixes have made this book actually readable. Without you this book wouldn't be published today.

Lana Sky. What can I say that I haven't said to you already. You are amazing. Thank you for helping me build this plot up and make my characters go from likeable to loveable. The late night and panic-stricken messages I sent you never went unread. You always knew what to say to bring my ideas to paper without losing my voice in the process. Thank you for all your help and advice.

My beta readers. Without you all and the feedback you gave, this story wouldn't be the best I could make it. I appreciate all of you and the time you took out of your days to read this book before it was even close to being ready for publication.

And finally, my readers. Without you taking a chance on a new author, this book would be sitting on my computer hard drive still. Not ready to be shared with the world. The love of reading we all share is what encouraged me to take a chance on this story. I hope you all loved it as much as I enjoyed writing it.

FOLLOW T.L. ANDERSON

Mia's Story Coming Soon…
Follow T.L. Anderson
Facebook:
https://www.facebook.com/authorTLAnderson/
Instagram: @tl.andersonbooks
Twitter: https://twitter.com/TLAnderson6

Made in the USA
Monee, IL
09 December 2020